THE CLOCKS

AGATHA CHRISTIE is known throughout the world as the Queen of Crime. Her seventy-seven detective novels and books of stories have been translated into every major language, and her sales are calculated in tens of millions.

She began writing at the end of the First World War, when she created Hercule Poirot, the little Belgian detective with the egg-shaped head and the passion for order – the most popular sleuth in fiction since Sherlock Holmes. Poirot, fluffy Miss Marple and her other detectives have appeared in the films, radio programmes and stage plays based on her books.

Agatha Christie also wrote six romantic novels under the pseudonymn Mary Westmacott, several plays and a book of poems; as well, she assisted her archaeologist husband Sir Max Mallowan on many expeditions to the Near East.

Postern of Fate was the last book she wrote before her death in 1976, but since its publication William Collins has also published two books Agatha Christie wrote in the 1940s: *Curtain: Poirot's Last Case* in 1975 and *Sleeping Murder*, the last Miss Marple book, in 1976.

AGATHA CHRISTIE

The Clocks

FONTANA / Collins

First published 1963
First issued in Fontana Books 1966
Eighteenth Impression February 1978

Printed in Canada

To my old friend
MARIO
with happy memories of delicious food at the
CAPRICE

PROLOGUE

The afternoon of the 9th of September was exactly like any other afternoon. None of those who were to be concerned in the events of that day could lay claim to having had a premonition of disaster. (With the exception, that is, of Mrs. Packer of 47, Wilbraham Crescent, who specialised in premonitions, and who always described at great length afterwards the peculiar forebodings and tremors that had beset her. But Mrs. Packer at No. 47, was so far away from No. 19, and so little concerned with the happenings there, that it seemed unnecessary for her to have had a premonition at all.)

At the Cavendish Secretarial and Typewriting Bureau, Principal, Miss K. Martindale, September 9th had been a dull day, a day of routine. The telephone rang, typewriters clicked, the pressure of business was average, neither above nor below its usual volume. None of it was particularly interesting. Up till 2.35, September 9th might have been a day like any other day.

At 2.35 Miss Martindale's buzzer went, and Edna Brent in the outer office answered it in her usual breathy and slightly nasal voice, as she manœuvred a toffee along the line of her jaw.

" Yes, Miss Martindale?"

" Now, Edna—that is *not* the way I've told you to speak when answering the telephone. Enunciate *clearly*, and keep your breath *behind* your tone."

" Sorry, Miss Martindale."

" That's better, You can do it when you try. Send Sheila Webb in to me."

" She's not back from lunch yet, Miss Martindale."

" Ah." Miss Martindale's eye consulted the clock on her desk. 2.36. Exactly six minutes late. Sheila Webb had been getting slack lately. " Send her in when she comes."

" Yes, Miss Martindale."

Edna restored the toffee to the centre of her tongue and, sucking pleasurably, resumed her typing of *Naked Love* by Armand Levine. Its painstaking eroticism left her uninterested

5

—as indeed it did most of Mr. Levine's readers, in spite of his efforts. He was a notable example of the fact that nothing can be duller than dull pornography. In spite of lurid jackets and provocative titles, his sales went down every year, and his last typing bill had already been sent in three times.

The door opened and Sheila Webb came in, slightly out of breath.

" Sandy Cat's asking for you," said Edna.

Sheila Webb made a face.

" Just my luck—on the one day I'm late back ! "

She smoothed down her hair, picked up pad and pencil, and knocked at the Principal's door.

Miss Martindale looked up from her desk. She was a woman of forty-odd, bristling with efficiency. Her pompadour of pale reddish hair and her Christian name of Katherine had led to her nickname of Sandy Cat.

" You're late back, Miss Webb."

" Sorry, Miss Martindale. There was a terrific bus jam."

" There is always a terrific bus jam at this time of day. You should allow for it." She referred to a note on her pad. " A Miss Pebmarsh rang up. She wants a stenographer at three o'clock. She asked for you particularly. Have you worked for her before?"

" I can't remember doing so, Miss Martindale. Not lately, anyway."

" The address is 19, Wilbraham Crescent." She paused questioningly, but Sheila Webb shook her head.

" I can't remember going there."

Miss Martindale glanced at the clock.

" Three o'clock. You can manage that easily. Have you any other appointments this afternoon? Ah, yes," her eye ran down the appointment book at her elbow. " Professor Purdy at the Curlew Hotel. Five o'clock. You ought to be back before then. If not, I can send Janet."

She gave a nod of dismissal, and Sheila went back to the outer office.

" Anything interesting, Sheila?"

" Just another of those dull days. Some old pussy up at Wilbraham Crescent. And at five Professor Purdy—all those awful archaeological names ! How I wish something exciting could sometimes happen."

Miss Martindale's door opened.

"I see I have a memo here, Sheila. If Miss Pebmarsh is not back when you arrive, you are to go in, the door will not be latched. Go in and go into the room on the right of the hall and wait. Can you remember that or shall I write it down?"

"I can remember it, Miss Martindale."

Miss Martindale went back into her sanctum.

Edna Brent fished under her chair and brought up, secretly, a rather flashy shoe and a stiletto heel that had become detached from it.

"However am I going to get home?" she moaned.

"Oh, do stop fussing—we'll think of something," said one of the other girls, and resumed her typing.

Edna sighed and put in a fresh sheet of paper: '*Desire had him in its grasp. With frenzied fingers he tore the fragile chiffon from her breasts and forced her down on the soap.*' "Damn," said Edna and reached for the eraser.

Sheila picked up her handbag and went out.

Wilbraham Crescent was a fantasy executed by a Victorian builder in the 1880's. It was a half-moon of double houses and gardens set back to back. This conceit was a source of considerable difficulty to persons unacquainted with the locality. Those who arrived on the outer side were unable to find the lower numbers and those who hit the inner side first were baffled as to the whereabouts of the higher numbers. The houses were neat, prim, artistically balconied and eminently respectable. Modernisation had as yet barely touched them— on the outside, that is to say. Kitchens and bathrooms were the first to feel the wind of change.

There was nothing unusual about No. 19. It had neat curtains and a well-polished brass front-door handle. There were standard rose trees each side of the path leading to the front door.

Sheila Webb opened the front gate, walked up to the front door and rang the bell. There was no response and after waiting a minute or two, she did as she had been directed, and turned the handle. The door opened and she walked in. The door on the right of the small hall was ajar. She tapped on it, waited, and then walked in. It was an ordinary quite pleasant sitting-room, a little over-furnished for modern tastes.

The only thing at all remarkable about it was the profusion of clocks—a grandfather clock ticking in the corner, a Dresden china clock on the mantelpiece, a silver carriage clock on the desk, a small fancy gilt clock on a whatnot near the fireplace and on a table by the window, a faded leather travelling clock, with ROSEMARY in worn gilt letters across the corner.

Sheila Webb looked at the clock on the desk with some surprise. It showed the time to be a little after ten minutes past four. Her gaze shifted to the chimney piece. The clock there said the same.

Sheila started violently as there was a whir and a click above her head, and from a wooden carved clock on the wall a cuckoo sprang out through his little door and announced loudly and definitely: *Cuckoo, Cuckoo, Cuckoo!* The harsh note seemed almost menacing. The cuckoo disappeared again with a snap of his door.

Sheila Webb gave a half-smile and walked round the end of the sofa. Then she stopped short, pulling up with a jerk.

Sprawled on the floor was the body of a man. His eyes were half open and sightless. There was a dark moist patch on the front of his dark grey suit. Almost mechanically Sheila bent down. She touched his cheek—cold—his hand, the same . . . touched the wet patch and drew her hand away sharply, staring at it in horror.

At that moment she heard the click of a gate outside, her head turned mechanically to the window. Through it she saw a woman's figure hurrying up the path. Sheila swallowed mechanically—her throat was dry. She stood rooted to the spot, unable to move, to cry out . . . staring in front of her.

The door opened and a tall elderly woman entered, carrying a shopping bag. She had wavy grey hair pulled back from her forehead, and her eyes were a wide and beautiful blue. Their gaze passed unseeingly over Sheila.

Sheila uttered a faint sound, no more than a croak. The wide blue eyes came to her and the woman spoke sharply:

" Is somebody there?"

" I—it's——" The girl broke off as the woman came swiftly towards her round the back of the sofa.

And then she screamed.

" Don't—don't . . . you'll tread on it—him . . . *And he's dead. . . .*"

CHAPTER 1

To use police terms: at 2.59 p.m. on September 9th, I was proceeding along Wilbraham Crescent in a westerly direction. It was my first introduction to Wilbraham Crescent, and frankly Wilbraham Crescent had me baffled.

I had been following a hunch with a persistence becoming more dogged day by day as the hunch seemed less and less likely to pay off. I'm like that.

The number I wanted was 61, and could I find it? No, I could not. Having studiously followed the numbers from 1 to 35, Wilbraham Crescent then appeared to end. A thorough-fare uncompromisingly labelled Albany Road barred my way. I turned back. On the north side there were no houses, only a wall. Behind the wall, blocks of modern flats soared upwards, the entrance of them being obviously in another road. No help there.

I looked up at the numbers I was passing. 24, 23, 22, 21. Diana Lodge (presumably 20, with an orange cat on the gate post washing its face), 19——

The door of 19 opened and a girl came out of it and down the path with what seemed to be the speed of a bomb. The likeness to a bomb was intensified by the screaming that accompanied her progress. It was high and thin and singularly inhuman. Through the gate the girl came and collided with me with a force that nearly knocked me off the pavement. She did not only collide. She clutched—a frenzied desperate clutching.

"Steady," I said, as I recovered by balance. I shook her slightly. "Steady now."

The girl steadied. She still clutched, but she stopped screaming. Instead she gasped—deep sobbing gasps.

I can't say that I reacted to the situation with any brilliance. I asked her if anything was the matter. Recognising that my question was singularly feeble I amended it.

"What's the matter?"

9

The girl took a deep breath.

" In *there!*" she gestured behind her.

" Yes?"

" There's a man on the floor . . . dead. . . . She was going to step on him."

" Who was? Why?"

" I think—because she's blind. And there's blood on him." She looked down and loosened one of her clutching hands. " And on me. There's blood on *me*."

" So there is," I said. I looked at the stains on my coat sleeve. " And on me as well now," I pointed out. I sighed and considered the situation. " You'd better take me in and show me," I said.

But she began to shake violently.

" I can't—I *can't* . . . I won't go in there again."

" Perhaps you're right." I looked round. There seemed nowhere very suitable to deposit a half-fainting girl. I lowered her gently to the pavement and sat her with her back against the iron railings.

" You stay there," I said, " until I come back. I shan't be long. You'll be all right. Lean forward and put your head between your knees if you feel queer."

" I—I think I'm all right now."

She was a little doubtful about it, but I didn't want to parley. I gave her a reassuring pat on the shoulder and strode off briskly up the path. I went in through the door, hesitated a moment in the hallway, looked into the door on the left, found an empty dining-room, crossed the hall and entered the sitting-room opposite.

The first thing I saw was an elderly woman with grey hair sitting in a chair. She turned her head sharply as I entered and said:

" Who's that?"

I realised at once that the woman was blind. Her eyes which looked directly towards me were focused on a spot behind my left ear.

I spoke abruptly and to the point.

" A young woman rushed out into the street saying there was a dead man in here."

I felt a sense of absurdity as I said the words. It did not seem possible that there should be a dead man in this tidy room with this calm woman sitting in her chair with her hands folded.

But her answer came at once.

"Behind the sofa," she said.

I moved round the angle of the sofa. I saw it then—the outflung arms—the glazed eyes—the congealing patch of blood.

"How did this happen?" I asked abruptly.

"I don't know."

"But—surely. Who is he?"

"I have no idea."

"We must get the police." I looked round. "Where's the telephone?"

"I have not got a telephone."

I concentrated upon her more closely.

"You live here? This is your house?"

"Yes."

"Can you tell me what happened?"

"Certainly. I came in from shopping——" I noted the shopping bag flung on a chair near the door. "I came in here. I realised at once there was someone in the room. One does very easily when one is blind. I asked who was there. There was no answer—only the sound of someone breathing rather quickly. I went towards the sound—and then whoever it was cried out—something about someone being dead and that I was going to tread on him. And then whoever it was rushed past me out of the room screaming."

I nodded. Their stories clicked.

"And what did you do?"

"I felt my way very carefully until my foot touched an obstacle."

"And then?"

"I knelt down. I touched something—a man's hand. It was cold—there was no pulse . . . I got up and came over here and sat down—to wait. Someone was bound to come in due course. The young woman, whoever she was, would give the alarm. I thought I had better not leave the house."

I was impressed with the calm of this woman. She had not screamed, or stumbled panic-stricken from the house. She had sat down calmly to wait. It was the sensible thing to do, but it must have taken some doing.

Her voice inquired:

"Who exactly are you?"

"My name is Colin Lamb. I happened to be passing by."

"Where is the young woman?"

"I left her propped up by the gate. She's suffering from shock. Where is the nearest telephone?"

"There is a call-box about fifty yards down the road just before you come to the corner."

"Of course. I remember passing it. I'll go and ring the police. Will you——" I hesitated.

I didn't know whether to say "Will you remain here?" or to make it "Will you be all right?"

She relieved me from my choice.

"You had better bring the girl into the house," she said decisively.

"I don't know that she will come," I said doubtfully.

"Not into this room, naturally. Put her in the dining-room the other side of the hall. Tell her I am making some tea."

She rose and came towards me.

"But—can you manage——"

A faint grim smile showed for a moment on her face.

"My dear young man. I have made meals for myself in my own kitchen ever since I came to live in this house— fourteen years ago. To be blind is not necessarily to be helpless."

"I'm sorry. It was stupid of me. Perhaps I ought to know your name?"

"Millicent Pebmarsh—Miss."

I went out and down the path. The girl looked up at me and began to struggle to her feet.

"I—I think I'm more or less all right now."

I helped her up, saying cheerfully:

"Good."

"There—there was a dead man in there, wasn't there?"

I agreed promptly.

"Certainly there was. I'm just going down to the telephone box to report it to the police. I should wait in the house if I were you." I raised my voice to cover her quick protest. "Go into the dining-room—on the left as you go in. Miss Pebmarsh is making a cup of tea for you."

"So that was Miss Pebmarsh? And she's blind?"

" Yes. It's been a shock to her, too, of course, but she's being very sensible. Come on, I'll take you in. A cup of tea will do you good whilst you are waiting for the police to come."

I put an arm round her shoulders and urged her up the path. I settled her comfortably by the dining-room table, and hurried off again to telephone.

II

An unemotional voice said, " Crowdean Police Station."

" Can I speak to Detective Inspector Hardcastle?"

The voice said cautiously:

" I don't know whether he is here. Who is speaking?"

" Tell him it's Colin Lamb."

" Just a moment, please."

I waited. Then Dick Hardcastle's voice spoke.

" Colin? I didn't expect you yet awhile. Where are you?"

" Crowdean. I'm actually in Wilbraham Crescent. There's a man lying dead on the floor of Number 19, stabbed I should think. He's been dead approximately half an hour or so."

" Who found him. You?"

" No, I was an innocent passer-by. Suddenly a girl came flying out of the house like a bat out of hell. Nearly knocked me down. She said there was a dead man on the floor and a blind woman was trampling on him."

" You're not having me on, are you?" Dick's voice asked suspiciously.

" It does sound fantastic, I admit. But the facts seem to be as stated. The blind woman is Miss Millicent Pebmarsh who owns the house."

" And was she trampling on the dead man?"

" Not in the sense you mean it. It seems that being blind she just didn't know he was there."

" I'll set the machinery in motion. Wait for me there. What have you done with the girl?"

" Miss Pebmarsh is making her a cup of tea."

Dick's comment was that it all sounded very cosy.

CHAPTER 2

At 19, Wilbraham Crescent the machinery of the Law was in possession. There was a police surgeon, a police photographer, fingerprint men. They moved efficiently, each occupied with his own routine.

Finally came Detective Inspector Hardcastle, a tall, poker-faced man with expressive eyebrows, godlike, to see that all he had put in motion was being done, and done properly. He took a final look at the body, exchanged a few brief words with the police surgeon and then crossed to the dining-room where three people sat over empty tea-cups. Miss Pebmarsh, Colin Lamb and a tall girl with brown curling hair and wide, frightened eyes. "Quite pretty," the inspector noted, parenthetically as it were.

He introduced himself to Miss Pebmarsh.

"Detective Inspector Hardcastle."

He knew a little about Miss Pebmarsh, though their paths had never crossed professionally. But he had seen her about, and he was aware that she was an ex-school teacher, and that she had a job connected with the teaching of Braille at the Aaronberg Institute for handicapped children. It seemed wildly unlikely that a man should be found murdered in her neat, austere house—but the unlikely happened more often than one would be disposed to believe.

"This is a terrible thing to have happened, Miss Pebmarsh," he said. "I'm afraid it must have been a great shock to you. I'll need to get a clear statement of exactly what occurred from you all. I understand that it was Miss——" he glanced quickly at the note-book the constable had handed him, "Sheila Webb who actually discovered the body. If you'll allow me to use your kitchen, Miss Pebmarsh, I'll take Miss Webb in there where we can be quiet."

He opened the connecting door from the dining-room to the kitchen and waited until the girl had passed through. A young plain-clothes detective was already established in the kitchen, writing unobtrusively at a formica-topped small table.

" This chair looks comfortable," said Hardcastle, pulling forward a modernised version of a Windsor chair.

Sheila Webb sat down nervously, staring at him with large frightened eyes.

Hardcastle very nearly said: " I shan't eat you, my dear," but repressed himself, and said instead:

" There's nothing to worry about. We just want to get a clear picture. Now your name is Sheila Webb—and your address?"

" 14, Palmerston Road—beyond the gasworks."

" Yes, of course. And you are employed, I suppose?"

" Yes. I'm a shorthand typist—I work at Miss Martindale's Secretarial Bureau."

" The Cavendish Secretarial and Typewriting Bureau— that's its full name, isn't it?"

" That's right."

" And how long have you been working there?"

" About a year. Well, ten months actually."

" I see. Now just tell me in your own words how you came to be at 19, Wilbraham Crescent to-day."

" Well, it was this way." Sheila Webb was speaking now with more confidence. " This Miss Pebmarsh rang up the Bureau and asked for a stenographer to be here at three o'clock. So when I came back from lunch Miss Martindale told me to go."

" That was just routine, was it? I mean—you were the next on the list—or however you arrange these things."

" Not exactly. Miss Pebmarsh had asked for me specially."

" Miss Pebmarsh had asked for you specially." Hardcastle's eyebrows registered this point. " I see . . . Because you had worked for her before?"

" But I hadn't," said Sheila quickly.

" You hadn't? You're quite sure of that?"

" Oh, yes, I'm positive. I mean, she's not the sort of person one would forget. That's what seems so odd."

" Quite. Well, we won't go into that just now. You reached here when?"

" It must have been just before three o'clock, because the cuckoo clock——" She stopped abruptly. Her eyes widened. " How queer. How very queer. I never really noticed at the time."

" What didn't you notice, Miss Webb? "

" Why—the clocks. "

" What about the clocks? "

" The cuckoo clock struck three all right, but all the others were about an hour fast. How very odd! "

" Certainly very odd, " agreed the inspector. " Now when did you first notice the body? "

" Not till I went round behind the sofa. And there it—he—was. It was awful, yes awful . . . "

" Awful, I agree. Now did you recognise the man? Was it anyone you had seen before? "

" Oh *no.* "

" You're quite sure of that? He might have looked rather different from the way he usually looked, you know. Think carefully. You're quite sure he was someone you'd never seen before? "

" Quite sure. "

" Right. That's that. And what did you do? "

" What did I *do?* "

" Yes. "

" Why—nothing . . . nothing at all. I couldn't. "

" I see. You didn't touch him at all? "

" Yes—yes I did. To see if—I mean—just to see— But he was—quite cold—and—and I got blood on my hand. It was horrible—thick and sticky. "

She began to shake.

" There, there, " said Hardcastle in an avuncular fashion. " It's all over now, you know. Forget about the blood. Go on to the next thing. What happened next? "

" I don't know . . . Oh, yes, she came home. "

" Miss Pebmarsh, you mean? "

" Yes. Only I didn't think about her being Miss Pebmarsh then. She just came in with a *shopping* basket. " Her tone underlined the shopping basket as something incongruous and irrelevant.

" And what did you say? "

" I don't think I said anything . . . I tried to, but I couldn't. I felt all choked up *here.* " She indicated her throat.

The inspector nodded.

" And then—and then—she said: ' Who's there? ' and she came round the back of the sofa and I thought—I thought she was going to—to tread on *It*. And I screamed . . . And once I began I couldn't stop screaming, and somehow I got out of the room and through the front door——"

" Like a bat out of hell," the inspector remembered Colin's description.

Sheila Webb looked at him out of miserable frightened eyes and said rather unexpectedly:

" I'm sorry."

" Nothing to be sorry about. You've told your story very well. There's no need to think about it any more now. Oh, just one point, why were you in that room at all?"

" Why?" She looked puzzled.

" Yes. You'd arrived here, possibly a few minutes early, and you'd pushed the bell, I suppose. But if nobody answered, why did you come in?"

" Oh that. Because she told me to."

" Who told you to?"

" Miss Pebmarsh did."

" But I thought you hadn't spoken to her at all."

" No, I hadn't. It was Miss Martindale she said it to—that I was to come in and wait in the sitting-room on the right of the hall."

Hardcastle said: " Indeed " thoughtfully.

Sheila Webb asked timidly:

" Is—is that all?"

" I think so. I'd like you to wait here about ten minutes longer, perhaps, in case something arises I might want to ask you about. After that, I'll send you home in a police car. What about your family—you have a family?"

" My father and mother are dead. I live with an aunt."

" And her name is?"

" Mrs. Lawton."

The inspector rose and held out his hand.

" Thank you very much, Miss Webb," he said. " Try and get a good night's rest to-night. You'll need it after what you've been through."

She smiled at him timidly as she went through the door into the dining-room.

" Look after Miss Webb, Colin," the inspector said. " Now, Miss Pebmarsh, can I trouble you to come in here?"

Hardcastle had half held out a hand to guide Miss Pebmarsh, but she walked resolutely past him, verified a chair against the wall with a touch of her fingertips, drew it out a foot and sat down.

Hardcastle closed the door. Before he could speak, Millicent Pebmarsh said abruptly:

"Who's that young man?"

"His name is Colin Lamb."

"So he informed me. But who is he? Why did he come here?"

Hardcastle looked at her in faint surprise.

"He happened to be walking down the street when Miss Webb rushed out of this house screaming murder. After coming in and satisfying himself as to what had occurred he rang us up, and was asked to come back here and wait."

"You spoke to him as Colin."

"You are very observant, Miss Pebmarsh—(observant? hardly the word. And yet none other fitted)—Colin Lamb is a friend of mine, though it is some time since I have seen him." He added: "He's a marine biologist."

"Oh! I see."

"Now, Miss Pebmarsh, I shall be glad if you can tell me anything about this rather surprising affair."

"Willingly. But there is very little to tell."

"You have resided here for some time, I believe?"

"Since 1950. I am—was—a schoolmistress by profession. When I was told nothing could be done about my failing eyesight and that I should shortly go blind, I applied myself to become a specialist in Braille and various techniques for helping the blind. I have a job here at the Aaronberg Institute for Blind and Handicapped children."

"Thank you. Now as to the events of this afternoon. Were you expecting a visitor?"

"No."

"I will read you a description of the dead man to see if it suggests to you anyone in particular. Height five feet nine to ten, age approximately sixty, dark hair going grey, brown eyes, clean shaven, thin face, firm jaw. Well nourished but not fat. Dark grey suit, well-kept hands. Might be a bank clerk, an accountant, a lawyer, or a professional man of some kind. Does that suggest to you anyone that you know?"

Millicent Pebmarsh considered carefully before replying.

" I can't say that it does. Of course it's a very generalised description. It would fit quite a number of people. It might be someone I have seen or met on some occasion, but certainly not anyone I know well."

" You have not received any letter lately from anyone proposing to call upon you?"

" Definitely not."

" Very good. Now, you rang up the Cavendish Secretarial Bureau and asked for the services of a stenographer and——"

She interrupted him.

" Excuse me. I did nothing of the kind."

" You did *not* ring up the Cavendish Secretarial Bureau and ask——" Hardcastle stared.

" I don't have a telephone in the house."

" There is a call-box at the end of the street," Inspector Hardcastle pointed out.

" Yes, of course. But I can only assure you, Inspector Hardcastle, that I had no need for a stenographer and did not —repeat *not*—ring up this Cavendish place with any such request."

" You did not ask for Miss Sheila Webb particularly?"

" I have never heard that name before."

Hardcastle stared at her, astonished.

" You left the front door unlocked," he pointed out.

" I frequently do so in the daytime."

" Anybody might walk in."

" Anybody seems to have done so in this case," said Miss Pebmarsh dryly.

" Miss Pebmarsh, this man according to the medical evidence died roughly between 1.30 and 2.45. Where were you yourself then?"

Miss Pebmarsh reflected.

" At 1.30 I must either have left or been preparing to leave the house. I had some shopping to do."

" Can you tell me exactly where you went?"

" Let me see. I went to the post office, the one in Albany Road, posted a parcel, got some stamps, then I did some household shopping, yes and I got some patent fasteners and safety pins at the drapers, Field and Wren. Then I returned here. I can tell you exactly what the time was. My cuckoo clock cuckooed three times as I came to the gate. I can hear it from the road."

" And what about your other clocks?"

" I beg your pardon?"

" Your other clocks seem all to be just over an hour fast."

" Fast? You mean the grandfather clock in the corner?"

" Not that only—all the other clocks in the sitting-room are the same."

" I don't understand what you mean by the ' other clocks.' There are no other clocks in the sitting-room."

CHAPTER 3

Hardcastle stared.

" Oh come, Miss Pebmarsh. What about that beautiful Dresden china clock on the mantelpiece? And a small French clock—ormolu. And a silver carriage clock, and—oh yes, the clock with ' Rosemary ' across the corner."

It was Miss Pebmarsh's turn to stare.

" Either you or I must be mad, Inspector. I assure you I have no Dresden china clock, no—what did you say—clock with ' Rosemary ' across it—no French ormolu clock and—what was the other one?"

" Silver carriage clock," said Hardcastle mechanically.

" Nor that either. If you don't believe me, you can ask the woman who comes to clean for me. Her name is Mrs. Curtin."

Detective Inspector Hardcastle was taken aback. There was a positive assurance, a briskness in Miss Pebmarsh's tone that carried conviction. He took a moment or two turning over things in his mind. Then he rose to his feet.

" I wonder, Miss Pebmarsh, if you would mind accompanying me into the next room?"

" Certainly. Frankly, I would like to see those clocks myself."

" See?" Hardcastle was quick to query the word.

" Examine would be a better word," said Miss Pebmarsh,

" but even blind people, Inspector, use conventional modes of speech that do not exactly apply to their own powers. When I say I would like to *see* those clocks, I mean I would like to examine and *feel* them with my own fingers."

Followed by Miss Pebmarsh, Hardcastle went out of the kitchen, crossed the small hall and into the sitting-room. The fingerprint man looked up at him.

" I've about finished in here, sir," he said. " You can touch anything you like."

Hardcastle nodded and picked up the small travelling clock with " Rosemary " written across the corner. He put it into Miss Pebmarsh's hands. She felt it over carefully.

" It seems an ordinary travelling clock," she said, " the leather folding kind. It is not mine, Inspector Hardcastle, and it was not in this room, I am fairly sure I can say, when I left the house at half past one."

" Thank you."

The inspector took it back from her. Carefully he lifted the small Dresden clock from the mantelpiece.

" Be careful of this," he said, as he put it into her hands, " it's breakable."

Millicent Pebmarsh felt the small china clock with delicate probing fingertips. Then she shook her head. " It must be a charming clock," she said, " but it's not mine. Where was it, do you say?"

" On the right hand side of the mantelpiece."

" There should be one of a pair of china candlesticks there," said Miss Pebmarsh.

" Yes," said Hardcastle, " there is a candlestick there, but it's been pushed to the end."

" You say there was still another clock?"

" Two more."

Hardcastle took back the Dresden china clock and gave her the small French gilt ormolu one. She felt it over rapidly, then handed it back to him.

" No. That is not mine either."

He handed her the silver one and that, too, she returned.

" The only clocks ordinarily in this room are a grandfather clock there in that corner by the window——"

" Quite right."

"——and a cuckoo on the wall near the door."

Hardcastle found it difficult to know exactly what to say next. He looked searchingly at the woman in front of him with the additional security of knowing that she could not return his survey. There was a slight frown as of perplexity on her forehead. She said sharply,

" I can't understand it. I simply can't understand it."

She stretched out one hand, with the easy knowledge of where she was in the room, and sat down. Hardcastle looked at the fingerprint man who was standing by the door.

" You've been over these clocks?" he asked.

" I've been over everything, sir. No dabs on the gilt clock, but there wouldn't be. The surface wouldn't take it. The same goes for the china one. But there are no dabs on the leather travelling clock or the silver one and that is a bit unlikely if things were normal—there ought to be dabs. By the way, none of them are wound up and they are all set to the same time—thirteen minutes past four."

" What about the rest of the room?"

" There are about three or four different sets of prints in the room, all women's, I should say. The contents of the pockets are on the table."

By an indication of his head he drew attention to a small pile of things on a table. Hardcastle went over and looked at them. There was a notecase containing seven pounds ten, a little loose change, a silk pocket handkerchief, unmarked, a small box of digestive pills and a printed card. Hardcastle bent to look at it.

Mr. R. H. Curry,
Metropolis and Provincial Insurance Co. Ltd.
7, Denvers Street,
London, w.2.

Hardcastle came back to the sofa where Miss Pebmarsh sat.

" Were you by any chance expecting someone from an insurance company to call upon you?"

" Insurance company? No, certainly not."

" The Metropolis and Provincial Insurance Company," said Hardcastle.

Miss Pebmarsh shook her head. " I've never heard of it," she said.

"You were not contemplating taking out insurance of any kind?"

"No, I was not. I am insured against fire and burglary with the Jove Insurance Company which has a branch here. I carry no personal insurance. I have no family or near relations so I see no point in insuring my life."

"I see," said Hardcastle. "Does the name of Curry mean anything to you? Mr. R. H. Curry?" He was watching her closely. He saw no reaction in her face.

"Curry," she repeated the name, then shook her head. "It's not a very usual name, is it? No, I don't think I've heard the name or known anyone of that name. Is that the name of the man who is dead?"

"It would seem possible," said Hardcastle.

Miss Pebmarsh hesitated a moment. Then she said:

"Do you want me to—to—touch——"

He was quick to understand her.

"Would you, Miss Pebmarsh? If it's not asking too much of you, that is? I'm not very knowledgeable in these matters, but your fingers will probably tell you more accurately what a person looks like than you would know by description."

"Exactly," said Miss Pebmarsh. "I agree it is not a very pleasant thing to have to do but I am quite willing to do it if you think it might be a help to you."

"Thank you," said Hardcastle. "If you will let me guide you——"

He took her round the sofa, indicated to her to kneel down, then gently guided her hands to the dead man's face. She was very calm, displaying no emotion. Her fingers traced the hair, the ears, lingering a moment behind the left ear, the line of the nose, mouth and chin. Then she shook her head and got up.

"I have a clear idea what he would look like," she said, "but I am quite sure that it is no one I have seen or known."

The fingerprint man had packed up his kit and gone out of the room. He stuck his head back in.

"They've come for him," he said, indicating the body. "All right to take him away?"

"Right," said Inspector Hardcastle. "Just come and sit over here, will you, Miss Pebmarsh?"

He established her in a corner chair. Two men came into the room. The removal of the late Mr. Curry was rapid and professional. Hardcastle went out to the gate and then returned to the sitting-room. He sat down near Miss Pebmarsh.

" This is an extraordinary business, Miss Pebmarsh," he said. " I'd like to run over the main points with you and see if I've got it right. Correct me if I am wrong. You expected no visitors to-day, you've made no inquiries re insurance of any kind and you have received no letter from anyone stating that a representative of an insurance company was going to call upon you to-day. Is that correct? "

" Quite correct."

" You did *not* need the services of a shorthand typist or stenographer and you did *not* ring up the Cavendish Bureau or request that one should be here at three o'clock."

" That again is correct."

" When you left the house at approximately 1.30, there were in this room only two clocks, the cuckoo clock and the grandfather clock. No others."

About to reply, Miss Pebmarsh checked herself.

" If I am to be absolutely accurate, I could not swear to that statement. Not having my sight I would not notice the absence or presence of anything not usually in the room. That is to say, the last time I can be sure of the contents of this room was when I dusted it early this morning. Everything then was in its place. I usually do this room myself as cleaning women are apt to be careless with ornaments."

" Did you leave the house at all this morning? "

" Yes. I went at ten o'clock as usual to the Aaronberg Institute. I have classes there until twelve-fifteen. I returned here at about quarter to one, made myself some scrambled eggs in the kitchen and a cup of tea and went out again, as I have said, at half past one. I ate my meal in the kitchen, by the way, and did not come into this room."

" I see," said Hardcastle. " So while you can say definitely that at ten o'clock this morning there were no superfluous clocks here, they *could* possibly have been introduced some time during the morning."

" As to that you would have to ask my cleaning woman,

Mrs. Curtin. She comes here about ten and usually leaves about twelve o'clock. She lives at 17, Dipper Street."

"Thank you, Miss Pebmarsh. Now we are left with these following facts and this is where I want you to give me any ideas or suggestions that occur to you. At some time during to-day four clocks were brought here. The hands of these four clocks were set at thirteen minutes past four. Now does that time suggest anything to you?"

"Thirteen minutes past four." Miss Pebmarsh shook her head. "Nothing at all."

"Now we pass from the clocks to the dead man. It seems unlikely that he would have been let in by your cleaning woman and left in the house by her unless you had told her you were expecting him, but that we can learn from her. He came here presumably to see you for some reason, either a business one or a private one. Between one-thirty and two-forty-five he was stabbed and killed. If he came here by appointment, you say you know nothing of it. Presumably he was connected with insurance—but there again you cannot help us. The door was unlocked so he could have come in and sat down to wait for you—but why?"

"The whole thing's daft," said Miss Pebmarsh impatiently. "So you think that this—what's-his-name Curry—brought those clocks with him?"

"There's no sign of a container anywhere," said Hardcastle. "He could hardly have brought four clocks in his pockets. Now Miss Pebmarsh, think very carefully. Is there any association in your mind, any suggestion you could possibly make about anything to do with clocks, or if not with clocks, say with *time*. 4.13. Thirteen minutes past four?"

She shook her head.

"I've been trying to say to myself that it is the work of a lunatic or that somebody came to the wrong house. But even that doesn't really explain anything. No, Inspector, I can't help you."

A young constable looked in. Hardcastle went to join him in the hall and from there went down to the gate. He spoke for a few minutes to the men.

"You can take the young lady home now," he said, " 14, Palmerston Road is the address."

He went back and into the dining-room. Through the open door to the kitchen he could hear Miss Pebmarsh busy at the sink. He stood in the doorway.

"I shall want to take those clocks, Miss Pebmarsh. I'll leave you a receipt for them."

"That will be quite all right, Inspector—they don't belong to me——"

Hardcastle turned to Sheila Webb.

"You can go home now, Miss Webb. The police car will take you."

Sheila and Colin rose.

"Just see her into the car, will you, Colin?" said Hardcastle as he pulled a chair to the table and started to scribble a receipt.

Colin and Sheila went out and started down the path. Sheila paused suddenly.

"My gloves—I left them——"

"I'll get them."

"No—I know just where I put them. I don't mind *now*—now that they've taken *it* away."

She ran back and rejoined him a moment or two later.

"I'm sorry I was so silly—before."

"Anybody would have been," said Colin.

Hardcastle joined them as Sheila entered the car. Then, as it drove away, he turned to the young constable.

"I want those clocks in the sitting-room packed up carefully—all except the cuckoo clock on the wall and the big grandfather clock."

He gave a few more directions and then turned to his friend.

"I'm going places. Want to come?"

"Suits me," said Colin.

CHAPTER 4

COLIN'S NARRATIVE

"Where do we go?" I asked Dick Hardcastle.

He spoke to the driver.

" Cavendish Secretarial Bureau. It's on Palace Street, up towards the Esplanade on the right."

" Yes, sir."

The car drew away. There was quite a little crowd by now, staring with fascinated interest. The orange cat was still sitting on the gate post of Diana Lodge next door. He was no longer washing his face but was sitting up very straight, lashing his tail slightly, and gazing over the heads of the crowd with that complete disdain for the human race that is the special prerogative of cats and camels.

" The Secretarial Bureau, and then the cleaning woman, in that order," said Hardcastle, " because the time is getting on." He glanced at his watch. " After four o'clock." He paused before adding, " Rather an attractive girl?"

" Quite," I said.

He cast an amused look in my direction.

" But she told a very remarkable story. The sooner it's checked up on, the better."

" You don't think that she——"

He cut me short.

" I'm always interested in people who find bodies."

" But that girl was half mad with fright! If you had heard the way she was screaming . . ."

He gave me another of his quizzical looks and repeated that she was a very attractive girl.

" And how did you come to be wandering about in Wilbraham Crescent, Colin? Admiring our genteel Victorian architecture? Or had you a purpose?"

" I had a purpose. I was looking for Number 61—and I couldn't find it. Possibly it doesn't exist?"

" It exists all right. The numbers go up to—88, I think."

" But look here, Dick, when I came to Number 28, Wilbraham Crescent just petered out."

" It's always puzzling to strangers. If you'd turned to the right up Albany Road and then turned to the right again you'd have found yourself in the other half of Wilbraham Crescent. It's built back to back, you see. The gardens back on each other."

" I see," I said, when he had explained this peculiar geography at length. " Like those Squares and Gardens in London. Onslow Square, isn't it? Or Cadogan. You start

down one side of a square, and then it suddenly becomes a
Place or Gardens. Even taxis are frequently baffled. Anyway,
there *is* a 61. Any idea who lives there?"

"61? Let me see . . . Yes, that would be Bland the
builder."

"Oh dear," I said. "That's bad."

"You don't want a builder?"

"No. I don't fancy a builder at all. Unless—perhaps he's
only just come here recently—just started up?"

"Bland was born here, I think. He's certainly a local man
—been in business for years."

"Very disappointing."

"He's a very bad builder," said Hardcastle encouragingly.
"Uses pretty poor materials. Puts up the kind of houses that
looks more or less all right until you live in them, then everything falls down or goes wrong. Sails fairly near the wind
sometimes. Sharp practice—but just manages to get away
with it."

"It's no good tempting me, Dick. The man I want would
almost certainly be a pillar of rectitude."

"Bland came into a lot of money about a year ago—or
rather his wife did. She's a Canadian, came over here in the
war and met Bland. Her family didn't want her to marry
him, and more or less cut her off when she did. Then last
year a great-uncle died, his only son had been killed in an air
crash and what with war casualties and one thing and
another, Mrs. Bland was the only one left of the family. So
he left his money to her. Just saved Bland from going bank-
rupt, I believe."

"You seem to know a lot about Mr. Bland."

"Oh that—well, you see, the Inland Revenue are always
interested when a man suddenly gets rich overnight. They
wonder if he's been doing a little fiddling and salting away—
so they check up. They checked and it was all O.K."

"In any case," I said, "I'm not interested in a man who
has suddenly got rich. It's not the kind of set-up that I'm
looking for."

"No? You've had that, haven't you?"

I nodded.

"And finished with it? Or—not finished with it?"

"It's something of a story," I said evasively. "Are we

dining together to-night as planned—or will this business put paid to that?"

"No, that will be all right. At the moment the first thing to do is set the machinery in motion. We want to find out all about Mr. Curry. In all probability once we know just who he is and what he does, we'll have a pretty good idea as to who wanted him out of the way." He looked out of the window. "Here we are."

The Cavendish Secretarial and Typewriting Bureau was situated in the main shopping street, called rather grandly Palace Street. It had been adapted, like many other of the establishments there, from a Victorian house. To the right of it a similar house displayed the legend Edwin Glen, Artist Photographer. Specialist, Children's Photographs, Wedding Groups, etc. In support of this statement the window was filled with enlargements of all sizes and ages of children, from babies to six-year-olds. These presumably were to lure in fond mammas. A few couples were also represented. Bashful looking young men with smiling girls. On the other side of the Cavendish Secretarial Bureau were the offices of an old-established and old-fashioned coal merchant. Beyond that again the original old-fashioned houses had been pulled down and a glittering three-storey building proclaimed itself as the Orient Café and Restaurant.

Hardcastle and I walked up the four steps, passed through the open front door and obeying the legend on a door on the right which said "Please Enter," entered. It was a good-sized room, and three young women were typing with assiduity. Two of them continued to type, paying no attention to the entrance of strangers. The third one who was typing at a table with a telephone, directly opposite the door, stopped and looked at us inquiringly. She appeared to be sucking a sweet of some kind. Having arranged it in a convenient position in her mouth, she inquired in faintly adenoidal tones:

"Can I help you?"

"Miss Martindale?" said Hardcastle.

"I think she's engaged at the moment on the telephone——"
At that moment there was a click and the girl picked up the telephone receiver and fiddled with a switch, and said: "Two gentlemen to see you, Miss Martindale." She looked at us and asked, "Can I have your names, please?"

"Hardcastle," said Dick.

"A Mr. Hardcastle, Miss Martindale." She replaced the receiver and rose. "This way, please," she said, going to a door which bore the name MISS MARTINDALE on a brass plate. She opened the door, flattened herself against it to let us pass, said "Mr. Hardcastle," and shut the door behind us.

Miss Martindale looked up at us from a large desk behind which she was sitting. She was an efficient-looking woman of about fifty with a pompadour of pale red hair and an alert glance.

She looked from one to the other of us.

"Mr. Hardcastle?"

Dick took out one of his official cards and handed it to her. I effaced myself by taking an upright chair by the door.

Miss Martindale's sandy eyebrows rose in surprise and a certain amount of displeasure.

"Detective Inspector Hardcastle? What can I do for you, Inspector?"

"I have come to you to ask for a little information, Miss Martindale. I think you may be able to help me."

From his tone of voice, I judged that Dick was going to play it in a roundabout way, exerting charm. I was rather doubtful myself whether Miss Martindale would be amenable to charm. She was of the type that the French label so aptly a *femme formidable*.

I was studying the general layout. On the walls above Miss Martindale's desk was hung a collection of signed photographs. I recognised one as that of Mrs. Ariadne Oliver, detective writer, with whom I was slightly acquainted. *Sincerely yours, Ariadne Oliver*, was written across it in a bold black hand. *Yours gratefully, Garry Gregson* adorned another photograph of a thriller writer who had died about sixteen years ago. *Yours ever, Miriam* adorned the photograph of Miriam Hogg, a woman writer who specialised in romance. Sex was represented by a photograph of a timid-looking balding man, signed in tiny writing, *Gratefully, Armand Levine*. There was a sameness about these trophies. The men mostly held pipes and wore tweeds, the women looked earnest and tended to fade into furs.

Whilst I was using my eyes, Hardcastle was proceeding with his questions.

"I believe you employ a girl called Sheila Webb?"

"That is correct. I am afraid she is not here at present—at least——"

She touched a buzzer and spoke to the outer office.

"Edna, has Sheila Webb come back?"

"No, Miss Martindale, not yet."

Miss Martindale switched off.

"She went out on an assignment earlier this afternoon," she explained. "I thought she might have been back by now. It is possible she has gone on to the Curlew Hotel at the end of the Esplanade where she had an appointment at five o'clock."

"I see," said Hardcastle. "Can you tell me something about Miss Sheila Webb?"

"I can't tell you very much," said Miss Martindale. "She has been here for—let me see, yes, I should say close on a year now. Her work has proved quite satisfactory."

"Do you know where she worked before she came to you?"

"I dare say I could find out for you if you specially want the information, Inspector Hardcastle. Her references will be filed somewhere. As far as I can remember off-hand, she was formerly employed in London and had quite a good reference from her employers there. I think, but I am not sure, that it was some business firm—estate agents possibly, that she worked for."

"You say she is good at her job?"

"Fully adequate," said Miss Martindale, who was clearly not one to be lavish with praise.

"Not first-class?"

"No, I should not say that. She has good average speed and is tolerably well educated. She is a careful and accurate typist."

"Do you know her personally, apart from your official relations?"

"No. She lives, I believe, with an aunt." Here Miss Martindale got slightly restive. "May I ask, Inspector Hardcastle, *why* you are asking all these questions? Has the girl got herself into trouble in any way?"

"I would not quite say that, Miss Martindale. Do you know a Miss Millicent Pebmarsh?"

"Pebmarsh," said Miss Martindale, wrinkling her sandy brows. "Now when—oh, of course. It was to Miss Pebmarsh's house that Sheila went this afternoon. The appointment was for three o'clock."

"How was that appointment made, Miss Martindale?"

"By telephone. Miss Pebmarsh rang up and said she wanted the services of a shorthand typist and would I send her Miss Webb."

"She asked for Sheila Webb particularly?"

"Yes."

"What time was this call put through?"

Miss Martindale reflected for a moment.

"It came through to me direct. That would mean that it was in the lunch hour. As near as possible I would say that it was about ten minutes to two. Before two o'clock at all events. Ah yes, I see I made a note on my pad. It was 1.49 precisely."

"It was Miss Pebmarsh herself who spoke to you?"

Miss Martindale looked a little surprised.

"I presume so."

"But you didn't recognise her voice? You don't know her personally?"

"No. I don't know her. She said that she was Miss Millicent Pebmarsh, gave me her address, a number in Wilbraham Crescent. Then, as I say, she asked for Sheila Webb, if she was free, to come to her at three o'clock."

It was a clear, definite statement. I thought that Miss Martindale would make an excellent witness.

"If you would kindly tell me what all this is about?" said Miss Martindale with slight impatience.

"Well, you see, Miss Martindale, Miss Pebmarsh herself denies making any such call."

Miss Martindale stared.

"Indeed! How extraordinary."

"You, on the other hand, say such a call *was* made, but you cannot say definitely that it was Miss Pebmarsh who made that call."

"No, of course I can't say definitely. I don't know the

woman. But really, I can't see the point of doing such a thing. Was it a hoax of some kind?"

"Rather more than that," said Hardcastle. "Did this Miss Pebmarsh—or whoever it was—give any reason for wanting Miss Sheila Webb particularly?"

Miss Martindale reflected a moment.

"I think she said that Sheila Webb had done work for her before."

"And is that in fact so?"

"Sheila said she had no recollection of having done anything for Miss Pebmarsh. But that is not quite conclusive, Inspector. After all, the girls go out so often to different people at different places that they would be unlikely to remember if it had taken place some months ago. Sheila wasn't very definite on the point. She only said that she couldn't remember having been there. But really, Inspector, even if this was a hoax, I cannot see where your interest comes in?"

"I am just coming to that. When Miss Webb arrived at 19, Wilbraham Crescent she walked into the house and into the sitting-room. She has told me that those were the directions given her. You agree?"

"Quite right," said Miss Martindale. "Miss Pebmarsh said that she might be a little late in getting home and that Sheila was to go in and wait."

"When Miss Webb went into the sitting-room," continued Hardcastle, "she found a dead man lying on the floor."

Miss Martindale stared at him. For a moment she could hardly find her voice.

"Did you say a *dead man*, Inspector?"

"A murdered man," said Hardcastle. "Stabbed, actually."

"Dear, dear," said Miss Martindale. "The girl must have been very upset."

It seemed the kind of understatement characteristic of Miss Martindale.

"Does the name of Curry mean anything to you, Miss Martindale? Mr. R. H. Curry?"

"I don't think so, no."

"From the Metropolis and Provincial Insurance Company?"

B

Miss Martindale continued to shake her head.

"You see my dilemma," said the inspector. "You say Miss Pebmarsh telephoned to you and asked for Sheila Webb to go to her house at three o'clock. Miss Pebmarsh denies doing any such thing. Sheila Webb gets there. She finds a dead man there." He waited hopefully.

Miss Martindale looked at him blankly.

"It all seems to me wildly improbable," she said disapprovingly.

Dick Hardcastle sighed and got up.

"Nice place you've got here," he said politely. "You've been in business some time, haven't you?"

"Fifteen years. We have done extremely well. Starting in quite a small way, we have extended the business until we have almost more than we can cope with. I now employ eight girls, and they are kept busy all the time."

"You do a good deal of literary work, I see." Hardcastle was looking up at the photographs on the wall.

"Yes, to start with I specialised in authors. I had been secretary to the well-known thriller writer, Mr. Garry Gregson, for many years. In fact, it was with a legacy from him that I started this Bureau. I knew a good many of his fellow authors and they recommended me. My specialised knowledge of authors' requirements came in very useful. I offer a very helpful service in the way of necessary research—dates and quotations, inquiries as to legal points and police procedure, and details of poison schedules. All that sort of thing. Then foreign names and addresses and restaurants for people who set their novels in foreign places. In old days the public didn't really mind much about accuracy, but nowadays readers take it upon themselves to write to authors on every possible occasion, pointing out flaws."

Miss Martindale paused. Hardcastle said politely: "I'm sure you have every cause to congratulate yourself."

He moved towards the door. I opened it ahead of him.

In the outer office, the three girls were preparing to leave. Lids had been placed on typewriters. The receptionist, Edna, was standing forlornly, holding in one hand a stiletto heel and in the other a shoe from which it had been torn.

"I've only had them a month," she was wailing. "And they were quite expensive. It's that beastly grating—the one at the corner by the cake shop quite near here. I caught my heel in it and off it came. I couldn't walk, had to take both shoes off and come back here with a couple of buns, and how I'll ever get home or get on to the bus I really don't know——"

At that moment our presence was noted and Edna hastily concealed the offending shoe with an apprehensive glance towards Miss Martindale whom I appreciated was not the sort of woman to approve of stiletto heels. She herself was wearing sensible flat-heeled leather shoes.

"Thank you, Miss Martindale," said Hardcastle. "I'm sorry to have taken up so much of your time. If anything should occur to you——"

"Naturally," said Miss Martindale, cutting him short rather brusquely.

As we got into the car, I said:

"So Sheila Webb's story, in spite of your suspicions, turns out to have been quite true."

"All right, all right," said Dick. "You win."

CHAPTER 5

"Mom!" said Ernie Curtin, desisting for a moment from his occupation of running a small metal model up and down the window pane, accompanying it with a semi-zooming, semi-moaning noise intended to reproduce a rocket ship going through outer space on its way to Venus, "Mom, what d'you think?"

Mrs. Curtin, a stern-faced woman who was busy washing up crockery in the sink, made no response.

"Mom, there's a police car drawn up outside our house."

"Don't you tell no more of yer lies, Ernie," said Mrs. Curtin as she banged cups and saucers down on the draining-board. "You know what I've said to you about that before."

"I never," said Ernie virtuously. "And it's a police car right enough, and there's two men gettin' out."

Mrs. Curtin wheeled round on her offspring.

"What've you been doing *now*?" she demanded. "Bringing us into disgrace, that's what it is!"

"Course I ain't," said Ernie. "I 'aven't done nothin'."

"It's going with that Alf," said Mrs. Curtin. "Him and his gang. Gangs indeed! I've told you, and yer father's told you, that gangs isn't respectable. In the end there's trouble. First it'll be the juvenile court and then you'll be sent to a remand home as likely as not. And I won't have it, d'you hear?"

"They're comin' up to the front door," Ernie announced.

Mrs. Curtin abandoned the sink and joined her offspring at the window.

"Well," she muttered.

At that moment the knocker was sounded. Wiping her hands quickly on the tea-towel, Mrs. Curtin went out into the passage and opened the door. She looked with defiance and doubt at the two men on her doorstep.

"Mrs. Curtin?" said the taller of the two, pleasantly.

"That's right," said Mrs. Curtin.

"May I come in a moment? I'm Detective Inspector Hardcastle."

Mrs. Curtin drew back rather unwillingly. She threw open a door and motioned the inspector inside. It was a very neat, clean little room and gave the impression of seldom being entered, which impression was entirely correct.

Ernie, drawn by curiosity, came down the passage from the kitchen and sidled inside the door.

"Your son?" said Detective Inspector Hardcastle.

"Yes," said Mrs. Curtin, and added belligerently, "he's a good boy, no matter what you say."

"I'm sure he is," said Detective Inspector Hardcastle, politely.

Some of the defiance in Mrs. Curtin's face relaxed.

"I've come to ask you a few questions about 19, Wilbraham Crescent. You work there, I understand."

"Never said I didn't," said Mrs. Curtin, unable yet to shake off her previous mood.

"For a Miss Millicent Pebmarsh."

"Yes, I work for Miss Pebmarsh. A very nice lady."

"Blind," said Detective Inspector Hardcastle.

"Yes, poor soul. But you'd never know it. Wonderful the way she can put her hand on anything and find her way about. Goes out in the street, too, and over the crossings.

She's not one to make a fuss about things, not like some people I know."

"You work there in the mornings?"

"That's right. I come about half past nine to ten, and leave at twelve o'clock or when I'm finished." Then sharply, "You're not saying as anything 'as been *stolen*, are you?"

"Quite the reverse," said the inspector, thinking of four clocks.

Mrs. Curtin looked at him uncomprehendingly.

"What's the trouble?" she asked.

"A man was found dead in the sitting-room at 19, Wilbraham Crescent this afternoon."

Mrs. Curtin stared. Ernie Curtin wriggled in ecstasy, opened his mouth to say "Coo," thought it unwise to draw attention to his presence, and shut it again.

"Dead?" said Mrs. Curtin unbelievingly. And with even more unbelief, "In the *sitting-room*?"

"Yes. He'd been stabbed."

"You mean it's *murder*?"

"Yes, murder."

"'Oo murdered 'im?" demanded Mrs. Curtin.

"I'm afraid we haven't got quite so far as that yet," said Inspector Hardcastle. "We thought perhaps you may be able to help us."

"I don't know anything about murder," said Mrs. Curtin positively.

"No, but there are one or two points that have arisen. This morning, for instance, did any man call at the house?"

"Not that I can remember. Not to-day. What sort of man was he?"

"An elderly man about sixty, respectably dressed in a dark suit. He may have represented himself as an insurance agent."

"I wouldn't have let him in," said Mrs. Curtin. "No insurance agents and nobody selling vacuum cleaners or editions of the Encyclopaedia Britannica. Nothing of that sort. Miss Pebmarsh doesn't hold with selling at the door and neither do I."

"The man's name, according to a card that was on him, was Mr. Curry. Have you ever heard that name?"

"Curry? Curry?" Mrs. Curtin shook her head. "Sounds Indian to me," she said, suspiciously.

"Oh, no," said Inspector Hardcastle, " he wasn't an Indian."

"Who found him—Miss Pebmarsh?"

"A young lady, a shorthand typist, had arrived because, owing to a misunderstanding, she thought she'd been sent for to do some work for Miss Pebmarsh. It was she who discovered the body. Miss Pebmarsh returned almost at the same moment."

Mrs. Curtin uttered a deep sigh.

"What a to-do," she said, "what a to-do!"

"We may ask you at some time," said Inspector Hardcastle, " to look at this man's body and tell us if he is a man you have ever seen in Wilbraham Crescent or calling at the house before. Miss Pebmarsh is quite positive he has never been there. Now there are various small points I would like to know. Can you recall off-hand how many clocks there are in the sitting-room?"

Mrs. Curtin did not even pause.

"There's that big clock in the corner, grandfather they call it, and there's the cuckoo clock on the wall. It springs out and says ' cuckoo.' Doesn't half make you jump sometimes." She added hastily, "I didn't touch neither of them. I never do. Miss Pebmarsh likes to wind them herself."

"There's nothing wrong with them," the inspector assured her. " You're sure these were the only two clocks in the room this morning?"

"Of course. What others should there be?"

"There was not, for instance, a small square silver clock, what they call a carriage clock, or a little gilt clock—on the mantelpiece that was, or a china clock with flowers on it—or a leather clock with the name Rosemary written across the corner?"

"Of course there wasn't. No such thing."

"You would have noticed them if they had been there?"

"Of course I should."

"Each of these four clocks represented a time about an hour later than the cuckoo clock and the grandfather clock."

"Must have been foreign," said Mrs. Curtin. " Me and my old man went on a coach trip to Switzerland and Italy once and it was a whole hour further on there. Must be something to do with this Common Market. I don't hold with the Common Market and nor does Mr. Curtin. England's good enough for me."

Inspector Hardcastle declined to be drawn into politics.

" Can you tell me exactly when you left Miss Pebmarsh's house this morning?"

" Quarter past twelve, near as nothing," said Mrs. Curtin.

" Was Miss Pebmarsh in the house then?"

" No, she hadn't come back. She usually comes back some time between twelve and half past, but it varies."

" And she had left the house—when?"

" Before I got there. Ten o'clock's my time."

" Well, thank you, Mrs. Curtin."

" Seems queer about these clocks," said Mrs. Curtin. " Perhaps Miss Pebmarsh had been to a sale. Antiques, were they? They sound like it by what you say."

" Does Miss Pebmarsh often go to sales?"

" Got a roll of hair carpet about four months ago at a sale. Quite good condition. Very cheap, she told me. Got some velour curtains too. They needed cutting down, but they were really as good as new."

" But she doesn't usually buy bric-à-brac or things like pictures or china or that kind of thing at sales?"

Mrs. Curtin shook her head.

" Not that I've ever known her, but of course, there's no saying in sales, is there? I mean, you get carried away. When you get home you say to yourself ' whatever did I want with that?' Bought six pots of jam once. When I thought about it I could have made it cheaper myself. Cups and saucers, too. Them I could have got better in the market on a Wednesday."

She shook her head darkly. Feeling that he had no more to learn for the moment, Inspector Hardcastle departed. Ernie then made his contribution to the subject that had been under discussion.

" Murder! Coo!" said Ernie.

Momentarily the conquest of outer space was displaced in his mind by a present-day subject of really thrilling appeal.

" Miss Pebmarsh couldn't have done 'im in, could she?" he suggested yearningly.

"Don't talk so silly," said his mother. A thought crossed her mind. "I wonder if I ought to have told him——"

"Told him what, Mom?"

"Never you mind," said Mrs. Curtin. "It was nothing, really."

CHAPTER 6

COLIN'S NARRATIVE

When we had put ourselves outside two good underdone steaks, washed down with draught beer, Dick Hardcastle gave a sigh of comfortable repletion, announced that he felt better and said:

"To hell with dead insurance agents, fancy clocks and screaming girls! Let's hear about you, Colin. I thought you'd finished with this part of the world. And here you are wandering about the back streets of Crowdean. No scope for a marine biologist at Crowdean, I can assure you."

"Don't you sneer at marine biology, Dick. It's a very useful subject. The mere mention of it so bores people and they're so afraid you're going to talk about it, that you never have to explain yourself further."

"No chance of giving yourself away, eh?"

"You forget," I said coldly, "that I *am* a marine biologist. I took a degree in it at Cambridge. Not a very good degree, but a degree. It's a very interesting subject, and one day I'm going back to it."

"I know what you've been working on, of course," said Hardcastle. "And congratulations to you. Larkin's trial comes on next month, doesn't it?"

"Yes."

"Amazing the way he managed to carry on passing stuff out for so long. You'd think somebody would have suspected."

"They didn't, you know. When you've got it into your head that a fellow is a thoroughly good chap, it doesn't occur to you that he mightn't be."

"He must have been clever," Dick commented.

I shook my head.

" No, I don't think he was, really. I think he just did as he was told. He had access to very important documents. He walked out with them, they were photographed and returned to him, and they were back again where they belonged the same day. Good organisation there. He made a habit of lunching at different places every day. We think that he hung up his overcoat where there was always an overcoat exactly like it—though the man who wore the other overcoat wasn't always the same man. The overcoats were switched, but the man who switched them never spoke to Larkin, and Larkin never spoke to him. We'd like to know a good deal more about the mechanics of it. It was all very well planned with perfect timing. Somebody had brains."

" And that's why you're still hanging round the Naval Station at Portlebury?"

" Yes, we know the Naval end of it and we know the London end. We know just when and where Larkin got his pay and how. But there's a gap. In between the two there's a very pretty little bit of organisation. That's the part we'd like to know more about, because that's the part where the brains are. *Somewhere* there's a very good headquarters, with excellent planning, which leaves a trail that is confused not once but probably seven or eight times."

" What did Larkin do it for?" asked Hardcastle, curiously. " Political idealist? Boosting his ego? Or plain money?"

" He was no idealist," I said. " Just money, I'd say."

" Couldn't you have got on to him sooner that way? He spent the money, didn't he? He didn't salt it away."

" Oh, no, he splashed it about all right. Actually, we got on to him a little sooner than we're admitting."

Hardcastle nodded his head understandingly.

" I see. You tumbled and then you used him for a bit. Is that it?"

" More or less. He had passed out some quite valuable information before we got on to him, so we let him pass out more information, also apparently valuable. In the Service I belong to, we have to resign ourselves to looking fools now and again."

" I don't think I'd care for your job, Colin," said Hardcastle thoughtfully.

"It's not the exciting job that people think it is," I said. "As a matter of fact, it's usually remarkably tedious. But there's something beyond that. Nowadays one gets to feeling that nothing really *is* secret. We know Their secrets and They know our secrets. Our agents are often Their agents, too, and Their agents are very often our agents. And in the end who is double-crossing who becomes a kind of nightmare! Sometimes I think that everybody knows everybody else's secrets and that they enter into a kind of conspiracy to pretend that they don't."

"I see what you mean," Dick said thoughtfully.

Then he looked at me curiously.

"I can see why you should still be hanging around Portlebury. But Crowdean's a good ten miles from Portlebury."

"What I'm really after," I said, "are Crescents."

"Crescents?" Hardcastle looked puzzled.

"Yes. Or alternatively, moons. New moons, rising moons and so on. I started my quest in Portlebury itself. There's a pub there called The Crescent Moon. I wasted a long time over that. It sounded ideal. Then there's The Moon and Stars, The Rising Moon, The Jolly Sickle, The Cross and the Crescent—that was in a little place called Seamede. Nothing doing. Then I abandoned moons and started on Crescents. Several Crescents in Portlebury. Lansbury Crescent, Aldridge Crescent, Livermead Crescent, Victoria Crescent."

I caught sight of Dick's bewildered face and began to laugh.

"Don't look so much at sea, Dick. I had something tangible to start me off."

I took out my wallet, extracted a sheet of paper and passed it over to him. It was a single sheet of hotel writing paper on which a rough sketch had been drawn.

"A chap called Hanbury had this in his wallet. Hanbury did a lot of work in the Larkin case. He was good—very good. He was run over by a hit and run car in London. Nobody got its number. I don't know what this means, but it's something that Hanbury jotted down, or copied, because he thought it was important. Some idea that he had? Or something that he'd seen or heard? Something to do with a moon or crescent, the number 61 and the initial W. I took over after his death. I don't know what I'm looking for yet, but I'm pretty sure there's something to find. I don't know what

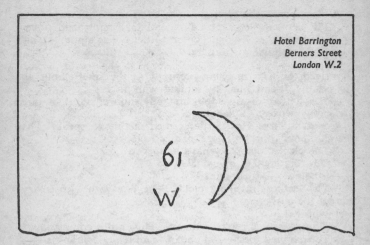

Hotel Barrington
Berners Street
London W.2

61 means. I don't know what **W** means. I've been working
in a radius from Portlebury outwards. Three weeks of unre-
mitting and unrewarding toil. Crowdean is on my route.
That's all there is to it. Frankly, Dick, I didn't expect very
much of Crowdean. There's only one Crescent here. That's
Wilbraham Crescent. Fits in rather nicely with **W**, doesn't
it? I was going to have a walk along Wilbraham Crescent
and see what I thought of Number 61 before asking you if
you'd got any dope that could help me. That's what I was
doing this afternoon—but I couldn't find Number 61."

"As I told you, 61 is occupied by a local builder."

"And that's not what I'm after. Have they got a foreign
help of any kind?"

"Could be. A good many people do nowadays. If so,
she'll be registered. I'll look it up for you by to-morrow."

"Thanks, Dick."

"I'll be making routine inquiries to-morrow at the two
houses on either side of 19. Whether they saw anyone come
to the house, et cetera. I might include the houses directly
behind 19, the ones whose gardens adjoin it. I rather think
that 61 is almost directly behind 19. I could take you along
with me if you liked."

I closed with the offer greedily.

"I'll be your Sergeant Lamb and take shorthand notes."

We agreed that I should come to the police station at nine thirty the following morning.

I arrived the next morning promptly at the agreed hour and found my friend literally fuming with rage.

When he had dismissed an unhappy subordinate, I inquired delicately what had happened.

For a moment Hardcastle seemed unable to speak. Then he spluttered out: "Those damned clocks!"

"The clocks again? What's happened now?"

"One of them is missing."

"Missing? Which one?"

"The leather travelling clock. The one with 'Rosemary' across the corner."

I whistled.

"That seems very extraordinary. How did it come about?"

"The damned fools—I'm one of them really, I suppose——" (Dick was a very honest man) "——One's got to remember to cross every t and dot every i or things go wrong. Well, the clocks were there all right yesterday in the sitting-room. I got Miss Pebmarsh to feel them all to see if they felt familiar. She couldn't help. Then they came to remove the body."

"Yes?"

"I went out to the gate to supervise, then I came back to the house, spoke to Miss Pebmarsh who was in the kitchen, and said I must take the clocks away and would give her a receipt for them."

"I remember. I heard you."

"Then I told the girl I'd send her home in one of our cars, and I asked you to see her into it."

"Yes."

"I gave Miss Pebmarsh the receipt though she said it wasn't necessary since the clocks weren't hers. Then I joined you. I told Edwards I wanted the clocks in the sitting-room packed up carefully and brought here. All of them except the cuckoo clock and, of course, the grandfather. And that's where I went wrong. I should have said, quite definitely, *four* clocks. Edwards says he went in at once and did as I told him. He insists there were only three clocks other than the two fixtures."

"That doesn't give much time," I said. "It means——"

"The Pebmarsh woman could have done it. She could have picked up the clock after I left the room and gone straight to the kitchen with it."

"True enough. But why?"

"We've got a lot to learn. Is there anybody else? Could the girl have done it?"

I reflected. "I don't think so. I——" I stopped, remembering something.

"So she did," said Hardcastle. "Go on. When was it?"

"We were just going out to the police car," I said unhappily. "She'd left her gloves behind. I said 'I'll get them for you' and she said, 'Oh, I know just where I must have dropped them. I don't mind going into that room now that the body's gone' and she ran back into the house. But she was only gone a minute——"

"Did she have her gloves on, or in her hand when she rejoined you?"

I hesitated. "Yes—yes, I think she did."

"Obviously she didn't," said Hardcastle, "or you wouldn't have hesitated."

"She probably stuffed them in her bag."

"The trouble is," said Hardcastle in an accusing manner, "you've fallen for that girl."

"Don't be idiotic," I defended myself vigorously. "I saw her for the first time yesterday afternoon, and it wasn't exactly what you'd call a romantic introduction."

"I'm not so sure of that," said Hardcastle. "It isn't every day that young men have girls falling into their arms screaming for help in the approved Victorian fashion. Makes a man feel a hero and a gallant protector. Only you've got to stop protecting her. That's all. So far as you know, that girl may be up to the neck in this murder business."

"Are you saying that this slip of a girl stuck a knife into a man, hid it somewhere so carefully that none of your sleuths could find it, then deliberately rushed out of the house and did a screaming act all over me?"

"You'd be surprised at what I've seen in my time," said Hardcastle darkly.

"Don't you realise," I demanded, indignantly, "that my life has been full of beautiful spies of every nationality? All of them with vital statistics that would make an American private eye forget all about the shot of rye in his collar drawer. I'm immune to all female allurements."

"Everybody meets his Waterloo in the end," said Hardcastle. "It all depends on the type. Sheila Webb seems to be your type."

"Anyway, I can't see why you're so set on fastening it on her."

Hardcastle sighed.

"I'm not fastening it on her—but I've got to start somewhere. The body was found in Pebmarsh's house. That involves her. The body was found by the Webb girl—I don't need to tell you how often the first person to find a dead body is the same as the person who last saw him alive. Until more facts turn up, those two remain in the picture."

"When I went into that room at just after three o'clock, the body had been dead at least half an hour, probably longer. How about that?"

"Sheila Webb had her lunch hour from 1.30 to 2.30."

I looked at him in exasperation.

"What have you found out about Curry?"

Hardcastle said with unexpected bitterness: "Nothing!"

"What do you mean—nothing?"

"Just that he doesn't exist—there's no such person."

"What do the Metropolis Insurance Company say?"

"They've nothing to say either, because there's no such thing. The Metropolis and Provincial Insurance Company doesn't exist. As far as Mr. Curry from Denvers Street goes, there's no Mr. Curry, no Denvers Street, Number 7 or any other number."

"Interesting," I said. "You mean he just had some bogus cards printed with a bogus name, address and insurance company?"

"Presumably."

"What is the big idea, do you think?"

Hardcastle shrugged his shoulders.

"At the moment it's guesswork. Perhaps he collected bogus premiums. Perhaps it was a way of introducing himself into houses and working some confidence trick. He may have been a swindler or a confidence trickster or a picker-up of un-considered trifles or a private inquiry agent. We just don't know."

"But you'll find out."

"Oh, yes, we'll know in the end. We sent up his finger-prints to see if he's got a record of any kind. If he has it'll be a big step on the way. If he hasn't, it'll be rather more difficult."

"A private dick," I said thoughtfully. "I rather like that. It opens up—possibilities."

"Possibilities are all we've got so far."

"When's the inquest?"

"Day after to-morrow. Purely formal and an adjourn-ment."

"What's the medical evidence?"

"Oh, stabbed with a sharp instrument. Something like a kitchen vegetable-knife."

"That rather lets out Miss Pebmarsh, doesn't it?" I said thoughtfully. "A blind woman would hardly be able to stab a man. She really *is* blind, I suppose?"

"Oh, yes, she's blind. We checked up. And she's exactly what she says she is. She was a teacher of mathematics in a North Country school—lost her sight about sixteen years ago —took up training in Braille, etc., and finally got a post with the Aaronberg Institute here."

"She could be mental, I suppose?"

"With a fixation on clocks and insurance agents?"

"It really is all too fantastic for words." I couldn't help speaking with some enthusiasm. "Like Ariadne Oliver in her worst moments, or the late Garry Gregson at the top of his form——"

"Go on—enjoy yourself. *You're* not the wretched D.D.I. in charge. *You* haven't got to satisfy a superintendent or a chief constable and all the rest of it."

"Oh well! Perhaps we'll get something useful out of the neighbours."

"I doubt it," said Hardcastle bitterly. "If that man was stabbed in the front garden and two masked men carried him into the house—nobody would have looked out of the window or seen anything. This isn't a village, worse luck. Wilbraham Crescent is a genteel residential road. By one o'clock, daily women who might have seen something have gone home. There's not even a pram being wheeled along——"

" No elderly invalid who sits all day by the window?"

"That's what we want—but that's not what we've got."

"What about numbers 18 and 20?"

" 18 is occupied by Mr. Waterhouse, Managing Clerk to Gainsford and Swettenham, Solicitors, and his sister who spends her spare time managing him. All I know about 20 is that the woman who lives there keeps about twenty cats. I don't like cats——"

I told him that a policeman's life was a hard one, and we started off.

CHAPTER 7

Mr. Waterhouse, hovering uncertainly on the steps of 18, Wilbraham Crescent, looked back nervously at his sister.

" You're quite sure you'll be all right?" said Mr. Waterhouse.

Miss Waterhouse snorted with some indignation.

" I really don't know what you mean, James."

Mr. Waterhouse looked apologetic. He had to look apologetic so often that it was practically his prevailing cast of countenance.

"Well, I just meant, my dear, considering what happened next door yesterday . . ."

Mr. Waterhouse was prepared for departure to the solicitors' office where he worked. He was a neat, grey-haired man with slightly stooping shoulders and a face that was also grey rather than pink, though not in the least unhealthy looking.

Miss Waterhouse was tall, angular, and the kind of woman with no nonsense about her who is extremely intolerant of nonsense in others.

" Is there any reason, James, because someone was murdered in the next door house that I shall be murdered to-day?"

"Well, Edith," said Mr. Waterhouse, " it depends so much, does it not, by whom the murder was committed?"

" You think, in fact, that there's someone going up and

down Wilbraham Crescent selecting a victim from every house? Really, James, that is almost blasphemous."

"Blasphemous, Edith?" said Mr. Waterhouse in lively surprise. Such an aspect of his remark would never have occurred to him.

"Reminiscent of the Passover," said Miss Waterhouse. "Which, let me remind you, is Holy Writ."

"That is a little far-fetched I think, Edith," said Mr. Waterhouse.

"I should like to see anyone coming here, trying to murder *me*," said Miss Waterhouse with spirit.

Her brother reflected to himself that it did seem highly unlikely. If he himself had been choosing a victim he would not have chosen his sister. If anyone were to attempt such a thing it was far more likely that the attacker would be knocked out by a poker or a lead doorstop and delivered over to the police in a bleeding and humiliated condition.

"I just meant," he said, the apologetic air deepening, "that there are—well—clearly undesirable characters about."

"We don't know very much about what did happen yet," said Miss Waterhouse. "All sorts of rumours are going about. Mrs. Head had some extraordinary stories this morning."

"I expect so, I expect so," said Mr. Waterhouse. He looked at his watch. He had no real desire to hear the stories brought in by their loquacious daily help. His sister never lost time in debunking these lurid flights of fancy, but nevertheless enjoyed them.

"Some people are saying," said Miss Waterhouse, "that this man was the treasurer or a trustee of the Aaronberg Institute and that there is something wrong in the accounts, and that he came to Miss Pebmarsh to inquire about it."

"And that Miss Pebmarsh murdered him?" Mr. Waterhouse looked mildly amused. "A blind woman? Surely——"

"Slipped a piece of wire round his neck and strangled him," said Miss Waterhouse. "He wouldn't be on his guard, you see. Who would be with anyone blind? Not that I believe it myself," she added. "I'm sure Miss Pebmarsh is a person of excellent character. If I do not see eye to eye with her on various subjects, that is not because I impute anything of a criminal nature to her. I merely think that her views are bigoted and extravagant. After all, there *are* other things besides education. All these new peculiar looking grammar schools, practically built of glass. You might think they were meant to grow cucumbers in, or tomatoes. I'm sure very prejudicial to children in the summer months. Mrs. Head herself told me that her Susan didn't like their new class-rooms. Said it was impossible to attend to your lessons because with all those windows you couldn't help looking out of them all the time."

"Dear, dear," said Mr. Waterhouse, looking at his watch again. "Well, well, I'm going to be very late, I'm afraid. Good-bye, my dear. Look after yourself. Better keep the door on the chain perhaps?"

Miss Waterhouse snorted again. Having shut the door behind her brother she was about to retire upstairs when she paused thoughtfully, went to her golf bag, removed a niblick, and placed it in a strategic position near the front door. "There," said Miss Waterhouse, with some satisfaction. Of course James talked nonsense. Still it was always as well to be prepared. The way they let mental cases out of nursing homes nowadays, urging them to lead a normal life, was in her view fraught with danger to all sorts of innocent people.

Miss Waterhouse was in her bedroom when Mrs. Head came bustling up the stairs. Mrs. Head was small and round and very like a rubber ball—she enjoyed practically every-thing that happened.

"A couple of gentlemen want to see you," said Mrs. Head with avidity. "Leastways," she added, "they aren't really gentlemen—it's the police."

She shoved forward a card. Miss Waterhouse took it.

"Detective Inspector Hardcastle," she read. "Did you show them into the drawing-room?"

"No. I put 'em in the dinin'-room. I'd cleared away breakfast and I thought that that would be more proper a place. I mean, they're only the police after all."

Miss Waterhouse did not quite follow this reasoning. However she said, "I'll come down."

"I expect they'll want to ask you about Miss Pebmarsh," said Mrs. Head. "Want to know whether you've noticed anything funny in her manner. They say these manias come on very sudden sometimes and there's very little to show beforehand. But there's usually *something*, some way of speaking, you know. You can tell by their eyes, they say. But then that wouldn't hold with a blind woman, would it? Ah——" she shook her head.

Miss Waterhouse marched downstairs and entered the dining-room with a certain amount of pleasurable curiosity masked by her usual air of belligerence.

" Detective Inspector Hardcastle?"

" Good morning, Miss Waterhouse." Hardcastle had risen. He had with him a tall, dark young man whom Miss Waterhouse did not bother to greet. She paid no attention to a faint murmur of " Sergeant Lamb."

" I hope I have not called at too early an hour," said Hardcastle, " but I imagine you know what it is about. You've heard what happened next door yesterday."

" Murder in one's next door neighbour's house does not usually go unnoticed," said Miss Waterhouse. " I even had to turn away one or two reporters who came here asking if I had observed anything."

" You turned them away?"

" Naturally."

" You were quite right," said Hardcastle. " Of course they like to worm their way in anywhere but I'm sure you are quite capable of dealing with anything of *that* kind."

Miss Waterhouse allowed herself to show a faintly pleasurable reaction to this compliment.

" I hope you won't mind us asking you the same kind of questions," said Hardcastle, " but if you did see anything at all that could be of interest to us, I can assure you we should be only too grateful. You were here in your house at the time, I gather?"

" I don't know when the murder was committed," said Miss Waterhouse.

" We think between half past one and half past two."

" I was here then, yes, certainly."

" And your brother?"

" He does not come home to lunch. Who exactly was murdered? It doesn't seem to say in the short account there was in the local morning paper."

" We don't yet know who he was," said Hardcastle.

" A stranger?"

" So it seems."

"You don't mean he was a stranger to Miss Pebmarsh also?"

"Miss Pebmarsh assures us that she was not expecting this particular guest and that she has no idea who he was."

"She can't be sure of that," said Miss Waterhouse. "She can't see."

"We gave her a very careful description."

"What kind of man was he?"

Hardcastle took a rough print from an envelope and handed it to her.

"This is the man," he said. "Have you any idea who he can be?"

Miss Waterhouse looked at the print. "No. No . . . I'm certain I've never seen him before. Dear me. He looks quite a respectable man."

"He was a most respectable-looking man," said the inspector. "He looks like a lawyer or a business man of some kind."

"Indeed. This photograph is not at all distressing. He just looks as though he might be asleep."

Hardcastle did not tell her that of the various police photographs of the corpse this one had been selected as the least disturbing to the eye.

"Death can be a peaceful business," he said. "I don't think this particular man had any idea that it was coming to him when it did."

"What does Miss Pebmarsh say about it all?" demanded Miss Waterhouse.

"She is quite at a loss."

"Extraordinary," commented Miss Waterhouse.

"Now, can you help us in any way, Miss Waterhouse? If you cast your mind back to yesterday, were you looking out of the window at all, or did you happen to be in your garden, say any time between half past twelve and three o'clock?"

Miss Waterhouse reflected.

"Yes, I *was* in the garden . . . Now let me see. It must have been before one o'clock. I came in about ten to one from the garden, washed my hands and sat down to lunch."

"Did you see Miss Pebmarsh enter or leave the house?"

"I think she came in—I heard the gate squeak—yes, some time after half past twelve."

" You didn't speak to her?"

" Oh no. It was just the squeak of the gate made me look up. It is her usual time for returning. She finishes her classes then, I believe. She teaches at the Disabled Children as probably you know."

" According to her own statement, Miss Pebmarsh went out again about half past one. Would you agree to that?"

" Well, I couldn't tell you the exact time but—yes, I do remember her passing the gate."

" I beg your pardon, Miss Waterhouse, you said ' passing the gate '."

" Certainly. It was in my sitting-room. That gives on the street, whereas the dining-room, where we are sitting now, gives as you can see, on the back garden. But I took my coffee into the sitting-room after lunch and I was sitting with it in a chair near the window. I was reading *The Times*, and I think it was when I was turning the sheet that I noticed Miss Pebmarsh passing the front gate. Is there anything extraordinary about that, Inspector?"

" Not extraordinary, no," said the inspector, smiling. " Only I understood that Miss Pebmarsh was going out to do a little shopping and to the post office, and I had an idea that the nearest way to the shops and the post office would be to go the other way along the crescent."

" Depends on which shops you are going to," said Miss Waterhouse. " Of course the shops *are* nearer that way, and there's a post office in Albany Road——"

" But perhaps Miss Pebmarsh usually passed your gate about that time?"

" Well, really, I don't know what time Miss Pebmarsh usually went out, or in which direction. I'm not really given to watching my neighbours in any way, Inspector. I'm a busy woman and have far too much to do with my own affairs. Some people I know spend their entire time looking out of the window and noticing who passes and who calls on whom. That is more a habit of invalids or for people who've nothing better to do than to speculate and gossip about their neighbours' affairs."

Miss Waterhouse spoke with such acerbity that the inspector felt sure that she had some one particular person in mind. He said hastily, " Quite so. Quite so." He added, " Since

Miss Pebmarsh passed your front gate, she might have been going to telephone, might she not? That is where the public telephone box is situated?"

"Yes. It's opposite Number 15."

"The important question I have to ask you, Miss Water-house, is if you saw the arrival of this man—the mystery man as I'm afraid the morning papers have called him."

Miss Waterhouse shook her head. "No, I didn't see him or any other caller."

"What were you doing between half past one and three o'clock?"

"I spent about half an hour doing the crossword in *The Times*, or as much of it as I could, then I went out to the kitchen and washed up the lunch. Let me see. I wrote a couple of letters, made some cheques out for bills, then I went upstairs and sorted out some things I wanted to take to the cleaners. I think it was from my bedroom that I noticed a certain amount of commotion next door. I distinctly heard someone screaming, so naturally I went to the window. There was a young man and a girl at the gate. He seemed to be embracing her."

Sergeant Lamb shifted his feet but Miss Waterhouse was not looking at him and clearly had no idea that he had been that particular young man in question.

"I could only see the back of the young man's head. He seemed to be arguing with the girl. Finally he sat her down against the gate post. An extraordinary thing to do. And he strode off and went into the house."

"You had not seen Miss Pebmarsh return to the house a short time before?"

Miss Waterhouse shook her head. "No. I don't really think I had looked out the window at all until I heard this extraordinary screaming. However, I didn't pay much attention to all this. Young girls and men are always doing such extraordinary things—screaming, pushing each other, giggling or making some kind of noise—that I had no idea it was anything serious. Not until some cars drove up with policemen did I realise anything out of the ordinary had occurred."

"What did you do then?"

"Well, naturally I went out of the house, stood on the steps and then I walked round to the back garden. I wondered what had happened but there didn't seem to be anything much to see from that side. When I got back again there was quite a little crowd gathering. Somebody told me there'd been a murder in the house. It seemed to me most extraordinary. *Most* extraordinary!" said Miss Waterhouse with a great deal of disapproval.

"There is nothing else you can think of? That you can tell us?"

"Really, I'm afraid not."

"Has anybody recently written to you suggesting insurance, or has anybody called upon you or proposed calling upon you?"

"No. Nothing of the kind. Both James and I have taken out insurance policies with the Mutual Help Assurance Society. Of course one is alway; getting letters which are really circulars or advertisements of some kind but I don't recall anything of that kind recently."

"No letters signed by anybody called Curry?"

"Curry? No, certainly not."

"And the name of Curry means nothing to you in any way?"

"No. Should it?"

Hardcastle smiled. "No. I really don't think it should," he said. "It just happens to be the name that the man who was murdered was calling himself by."

"It wasn't his real name?"

"We have some reason to think that it was not his real name."

"A swindler of some kind, eh?" said Miss Waterhouse.

"We can't say that till we have evidence to prove it."

"Of course not, of course not. You've got to be careful. I know that," said Miss Waterhouse. "Not like some of the people around here. They'd say anything. I wonder some aren't had up for libel all the time."

"Slander," corrected Sergeant Lamb, speaking for the first time.

Miss Waterhouse looked at him in some surprise, as though not aware before that he had an entity of his own and was anything other than a necessary appendage to Inspector Hardcastle.

"I'm sorry I can't help you, I really am," said Miss Waterhouse.

"I'm sorry too," said Hardcastle. "A person of your intelligence and judgment with a faculty of observation would have been a very useful witness to have."

"I wish I *had* seen something," said Miss Waterhouse.

For a moment her tone was as wistful as a young girl's.

"Your brother, Mr. James Waterhouse?"

"James wouldn't know anything," said Miss Waterhouse scornfully. "He never does. And anyway he was at Gainsford and Swettenhams in the High Street. Oh no, James wouldn't be able to help you. As I say, he doesn't come back to lunch."

"Where does he lunch usually?"

"He usually has sandwiches and coffee at the Three Feathers. A very nice respectable house. They specialise in quick lunches for professional people."

"Thank you, Miss Waterhouse. Well, we mustn't keep you any longer."

He rose and went out into the hall. Miss Waterhouse accompanied them. Colin Lamb picked up the golf club by the door.

"Nice club, this," he said. "Plenty of weight in the head." He weighed it up and down in his hand. "I see you are prepared, Miss Waterhouse, for any eventualities."

Miss Waterhouse was slightly taken aback.

"Really," she said, "I can't imagine how that club came to be there."

She snatched it from him and replaced it in the golf bag.

"A very wise precaution to take," said Hardcastle.

Miss Waterhouse opened the door and let them out.

"Well," said Colin Lamb, with a sigh, "we didn't get much out of her, in spite of you buttering her up so nicely all the time. Is that your invariable method?"

"It gets good results sometimes with a person of her type. The tough kind always respond to flattery."

"She was purring like a cat that has been offered a saucer of cream in the end," said Colin. "Unfortunately, it didn't disclose anything of interest."

"No?" said Hardcastle.

Colin looked at him quickly. "What's on your mind?"

"A very slight and possibly unimportant point. Miss Pebmarsh went out to the post office and the shops but she turned *left* instead of *right*, and that telephone call, according to Miss Martindale, was put through about ten minutes to two."

Colin looked at him curiously.

"You still think that in spite of her denial she might have made it? She was very positive."

"Yes," said Hardcastle. "She was very positive."

His tone was non-committal.

"But if she did make it, why?"

"Oh, it's all *why*," said Hardcastle impatiently. "Why, why? *Why* all this rigmarole? If Miss Pebmarsh made that call, why did she want to get the girl there? If it was someone else, why did they want to involve Miss Pebmarsh? We don't know anything yet. If that Martindale woman had known Miss Pebmarsh personally, she'd have known whether it was her voice or not, or at any rate whether is was reasonably like Miss Pebmarsh's. Oh well, we haven't got much from Number 18. Let's see whether Number 20 will do us any better."

CHAPTER 8

In addition to its number, 20, Wilbraham Crescent had a name. It was called Diana Lodge. The gates had obstacles against intruders by being heavily wired on the inside. Rather melancholy speckled laurels, imperfectly trimmed, also interfered with the efforts of anyone to enter through the gate.

"If ever a house could have been called The Laurels, this one could," remarked Colin Lamb. "Why call it Diana Lodge, I wonder?"

He looked round him appraisingly. Diana Lodge did not run to neatness or to flower-beds. Tangled and overgrown shrubbery was its most salient point together with a strong catty smell of ammonia. The house seemed in a rather tumble-down condition with gutters that could do with repairing. The only sign of any recent kind of attention being paid to it was a freshly painted front door whose colour of bright azure blue made the general unkempt appearance of the rest of the

house and garden even more noticeable. There was no electric
bell but a kind of handle that was clearly meant to be pulled.
The inspector pulled it and a faint sound of remote jangling
was heard inside.

"It sounds," said Colin, "like the Moated Grange."

They waited for a moment or two, then sounds were heard
from inside. Rather curious sounds. A kind of high crooning,
half singing, half speaking.

"What the devil——" began Hardcastle.

The singer or crooner appeared to be approaching the front
door and words began to be discernible.

"No, sweet-sweetie. In there, my love. Mindems tailems
Shah-Shah-Mimi. Cleo—Cleopatra. Ah de dcodlums. Ah
lou-lou."

Doors were heard to shut. Finally the front door opened.
Facing them was a lady in a pale moss-green, rather rubbed,
velvet tea gown. Her hair, in flaxen grey wisps, was twirled
elaborately in a kind of coiffure of some thirty years back.
Round her neck she was wearing a necklet of orange fur.
Inspector Hardcastle said dubiously:

"Mrs. Hemming?"

"I am Mrs. Hemming. Gently, Sunbeam, gently dood-
leums."

It was then that the inspector perceived that the orange fur
was really a cat. It was not the only cat. Three other cats
appeared along the hall, two of them miaowing. They took
up their place, gazing at the visitors, twirling gently round
their mistress's skirts. At the same time a pervading smell of
cat afflicted the nostrils of both men.

"I am Detective Inspector Hardcastle."

"I hope you've come about that dreadful man who came to
see me from the Prevention of Cruelty to Animals," said Mrs.
Hemming. "Disgraceful! I wrote and reported him. Saying
my cats were kept in a condition prejudicial to their health
and happiness! Quite disgraceful! I *live* for my cats, Inspector. They are my only joy and pleasure in life. Everything is
done for them. Shah-Shah-Mimi. Not *there*, sweetie."

Shah-Shah-Mimi paid no attention to a restraining hand
and jumped on the hall table. He sat down and washed his
face, staring at the strangers.

"Come in," said Mrs. Hemming. "Oh no, not that room. I'd forgotten."

She pushed open a door on the left. The atmosphere here was even more pungent.

"Come on, my pretties, come on."

In the room various brushes and combs with cat hairs in them lay about on chairs and tables. There were faded and soiled cushions, and there were at least six more cats.

"I live for my darlings," said Mrs. Hemming. "They understand every word I say to them."

Inspector Hardcastle walked in manfully. Unfortunately for him he was one of those men who have cat allergy. As usually happens on these occasions all the cats immediately made for him. One jumped on his knee, another rubbed affectionately against his trousers. Detective Inspector Hardcastle, who was a brave man, set his lips and endured.

"I wonder if I could ask you a few questions, Mrs. Hemming, about——"

"Anything you please," said Mrs Hemming, interrupting him. "I have nothing to hide. I can show you the cats' food, their beds where they sleep, five in my room, the other seven down here. They have only the very best fish cooked by myself."

"This is nothing to do with *cats*," said Hardcastle, raising his voice. "I came to talk to you about the unfortuate affair which happened next door. You have probably heard about it."

"Next door? You mean Mr. Joshua's dog?"

"No," said Hardcastle, "I do not. I mean at Number 19 where a man was found murdered yesterday."

"Indeed?" said Mrs. Hemming, with polite interest but no more. Her eyes were still straying over her pets.

"Were you at home yesterday afternoon, may I ask? That is to say between half past one and half past three?"

"Oh yes, indeed. I usually do my shopping quite early in the day and then get back so that I can do the darlings' lunch, and then comb and groom them."

"And you didn't notice any activity next door? Police cars—ambulance—anything like that?"

"Well, I'm afraid I didn't look out of the front windows.

I went out of the back of the house into the garden because dear Arabella was missing. She is quite a young cat and she had climbed up one of the trees and I was afraid she might not be able to get down. I tried to tempt her with a saucer of fish but she was frightened, poor little thing. I had to give up in the end and come back into the house. And would you believe it, just as I went through the door, down she came and followed me in." She looked from one man to the other as though testing their powers of belief.

"Matter of fact, I would believe it," said Colin, unable to keep silence any more.

"I beg your pardon?" Mrs. Hemming looked at him, slightly startled.

"I am much attached to cats," said Colin, "and I have therefore made a study of cat nature. What you have told me illustrates perfectly the pattern of cat behaviour and the rules they have made for themselves. In the same way your cats are all congregating round my friend who frankly does not care for cats, they will pay no attention to me in spite of all my blandishments."

If it occurred to Mrs. Hemming that Colin was hardly speaking in the proper role of sergeant of police, no trace of it appeared in her face. She merely murmured vaguely.

"They always know, the dear things, don't they?"

A handsome grey Persian put two paws on Inspector Hardcastle's knees, looked at him in an ecstasy of pleasure and dug his claws in hard with a kneading action as though the inspector was a pincushion. Goaded beyond endurance, Inspector Hardcastle rose to his feet.

"I wonder, madam," he said, "if I could see this back garden of yours."

Colin grinned slightly.

"Oh, of course, of course. Anything you please." Mrs. Hemming rose.

The orange cat unwound itself from her neck. She replaced it in an absent-minded way with the grey Persian. She led the way out of the room. Hardcastle and Colin followed.

"We've met before," said Colin to the orange cat and added, "And *you're* a beauty, aren't you," addressing another grey Persian who was sitting on a table by a Chinese lamp, swishing his tail slightly. Colin stroked him, tickled him behind the ears and the grey cat condescended to purr.

"Shut the door, please, as you come out, Mr.—er—er," said Mrs. Hemming from the hall. "There's a sharp wind to-day and I don't want my dears to get cold. Besides, there are those terrible boys—it's really not safe to let the dear things wander about in the garden by themselves."

She walked towards the back of the hall and opened a side door.

"What terrible boys?" asked Hardcastle.

"Mrs. Ramsay's two boys. They live in the south part of the crescent. Our gardens more or less back on each other. Absolute young hooligans, that's what they are. They have a catapult, you know, or they had. I insisted on its being confiscated but I have my suspicions. They make ambushes and hide. In the summer they throw apples."

"Disgraceful," said Colin.

The back garden was like the front only more so. It had some unkempt grass, some unpruned and crowded shrubs and a great many more laurels of the speckled variety, and some rather gloomy macrocarpas. In Colin's opinion, both he and Hardcastle were wasting their time. There was a solid barrage of laurels, trees and shrubs through which nothing of Miss Pebmarsh's garden could possibly be seen. Diana Lodge could be described as a fully detached house. From the point of view of its inhabitants, it might have had no neighbours.

"Number 19, did you say?" said Mrs. Hemming, pausing irresolutely in the middle of her back garden. "But I thought there was only one person living in the house, a blind woman."

"The murdered man was not an occupant of the house," said the inspector.

"Oh, I see," said Mrs. Hemming, still vaguely, "he came there to be murdered. How odd."

"Now that," said Colin thoughtfully to himself, "is a damned good description."

CHAPTER 9

They drove along Wilbraham Crescent, turned to the right up Albany Road and then to the right again along the second instalment of Wilbraham Crescent.

" Simple really," said Hardcastle.

" Once you know," said Colin.

" 61 really backs on Mrs. Hemming's house—but a corner of it touches on 19, so that's good enough. It will give you a chance to look at your Mr. Bland. No foreign help, by the way."

" So there goes a beautiful theory." The car drew up and the two men got out.

" Well, well," said Colin. " Some front garden!"

It was indeed a model of suburban perfection in a small way. There were beds of geraniums with lobelia edging. There were large fleshy-looking begonias, and there was a fine display of garden ornaments—frogs, toadstools, comic gnomes and pixies.

" I'm sure Mr. Bland *must* be a nice worthy man," said Colin, with a shudder. " He couldn't have these terrible ideas if he wasn't." He added as Hardcastle pushed the bell, " Do you expect him to be in at this time of the morning?"

" I rang up," explained Hardcastle. " Asked him if it would be convenient."

At that moment a smart little traveller van drew up and turned into the garage, which had obviously been a late addition to the house. Mr. Josiah Bland got out, slammed the door and advanced towards them. He was a man of medium height with a bald head and rather small blue eyes. He had a hearty manner.

" Inspector Hardcastle? Come right in."

He led the way into the sitting-room. It evinced several proofs of prosperity. There were expensive and rather ornate lamps, an Empire writing desk, a coruscated ormolu set of mantelpiece ornaments, a marquetry cabinet, and a *jardinière* full of flowers in the window. The chairs were modern and richly upholstered.

" Sit down," said Mr. Bland heartily. " Smoke? Or can't you when you're on the job?"

" No, thanks," said Hardcastle.

" Don't drink either, I suppose?" said Mr. Bland. " Ah well, better for both of us, I dare say. Now what's it all about? This business at Number 19 I suppose? The corners of our gardens adjoin, but we've not much real view of it except from the upper floor windows. Extraordinary business altogether it seems to be—at least from what I read in our local paper this morning. I was delighted when I got your message. A chance of getting some of the real dope. You've no idea the rumours that are flying about! It's made my wife quite nervous—feeling there's a killer on the loose, you know. The trouble is they let all these barmy people out of lunatic asylums nowadays. Send them home on parole or whatever they call it. Then they do in someone else and they clap them back again. And as I say, the rumours! I mean, what with our daily woman and the milk and paper boy, you'd be surprised. One says he was strangled with picture wire, and the other says he was stabbed. Someone else that he was coshed. At any rate it was a he, wasn't it? I mean, it wasn't the old girl who was done in? An unknown man, the papers said."

Mr. Bland came to a full stop at last.

Hardcastle smiled and said in a deprecating voice:

" Well, as to unknown, he *had* a card and an address in his pocket."

" So much for that story then," said Bland. " But you know what people are. *I* don't know who thinks up all these things."

" While we're on the subject of the victim," said Hardcastle, " perhaps you'll have a look at *this*."

Once more he brought out the police photograph.

" So that's him, is it?" said Bland. " He looks a perfectly ordinary chap, doesn't he? Ordinary as you and me. I suppose I mustn't ask if he had any particular reason to be murdered?"

" It's early days to talk about that," said Hardcastle. " What I want to know, Mr. Bland, is if you've ever seen this man before."

Bland shook his head.

"I'm sure I haven't. I'm quite good at remembering faces."

"He hasn't called upon you for any particular purpose—selling insurance or—vacuum cleaners or washing machines, or anything of that kind?"

"No, no. Certainly not."

"We ought perhaps to ask your wife," said Hardcastle. "After all, if he called at the house, it's your wife he would see."

"Yes, that's perfectly true. I don't know, though . . . Valerie's not got very good health, you know. I wouldn't like to upset her. What I mean is, well, I suppose that's a picture of him when he's dead, isn't it?"

"Yes," said Hardcastle, "that is quite true. But it is not a painful photograph in any way."

"No, no. Very well done. The chap might be asleep, really."

"Are you talking about me, Josaiah?"

An adjoining door from the other room was pushed open and a middle-aged woman entered the room. She had, Hardcastle decided, been listening with close attention on the other side of the door.

"Ah, there you are, my dear," said Bland, "I thought you were having your morning nap. This is my wife, Detective Inspector Hardcastle."

"That terrible murder," murmured Mrs. Bland. "It really makes me shiver to think of it."

She sat down on the sofa with a little gasping sigh.

"Put your feet up, dear," said Bland.

Mrs. Bland obeyed. She was a sandy-haired woman, with a faint whining voice. She looked anaemic, and had all the airs of an invalid who accepts her invalidism with a certain amount of enjoyment. For a moment or two, she reminded Inspector Hardcastle of somebody. He tried to think who it was, but failed. The faint, rather plaintive voice continued.

"My health isn't very good, Inspector Hardcastle, so my husband naturally tries to spare me any shocks or worry. I'm very sensitive. You were speaking about a photograph, I think, of the—of the murdered man. Oh dear, how terrible that sounds. I don't know that I can bear to look!"

'Dying to see it, really,' thought Hardcastle to himself.

With faint malice in his voice, he said:

" Perhaps I'd better not ask you to look at it, then, Mrs. Bland. I just thought you might be able to help us, in case the man has called at this house at any time."

" I must do my duty, mustn't I," said Mrs. Bland, with a sweet brave smile. She held out her hand.

" Do you think you'd better upset yourself, Val?"

" Don't be foolish, Josaiah. Of course I must see."

She looked at the photograph with much interest and, or so the inspector thought, a certain amount of disappointment.

" He looks—really, he doesn't look dead at all," she said. " Not at all as though he'd been *murdered*. Was he—he can't have been strangled?"

" He was stabbed," said the inspector.

Mrs. Bland closed her eyes and shivered.

" Oh dear," she said, " how terrible."

" You don't feel you've ever seen him, Mrs. Bland?"

" No," said Mrs. Bland with obvious reluctance, " no, no, I'm afraid not. Was he the sort of man who—who calls at houses selling things?"

" He seems to have been an insurance agent," said the inspector carefully.

" Oh, I see. No, there's been nobody of that kind, I'm sure. You never remember my mentioning anything of that kind, do you, Josaiah?"

" Can't say I do," said Mr. Bland.

" Was he any relation to Miss Pebmarsh?" asked Mrs. Bland.

" No," said the inspector, " he was quite unknown to her."

" Very peculiar," said Mrs. Bland.

" You know Miss Pebmarsh?"

" Oh yes, I mean, we know her as neighbours, of course. She asks my husband for advice sometimes about the garden."

" You're a very keen gardener, I gather?" said the inspector.

" Not really, not really," said Bland deprecatingly. " Haven't the time, you know. Of course, I know what's what. But I've got an excellent fellow—comes twice a week. He sees the garden's kept well stocked, and well tidied up.

C

I'd say you couldn't beat our garden round here, but I'm not one of those real gardeners like my neighbour."

"Mrs. Ramsay?" said Hardcastle in some surprise.

"No, no, farther along. 63. Mr. McNaughton. He just lives for his garden. In it all day long, and mad on compost. Really, he's quite a bore on the subject of compost—but I don't suppose that's what you want to talk about."

"Not exactly," said the inspector. "I only wondered if anyone—you or your wife, for instance—were out in your garden yesterday. After all, as you say, it does touch on the border of 19 and there's just a chance that you might have seen something interesting yesterday—or heard something, perhaps?"

"Midday, wasn't it? When the murder happened I mean?"

"The relevant times are between one o'clock and three o'clock."

Bland shook his head. "I wouldn't have seen much then. I was here. So was Valerie, but we'd be having lunch, you know, and our dining-room looks out on the roadside. We shouldn't see anything that was going on in the garden."

"What time do you have your meal?"

"One o'clock or thereabouts. Sometimes it's one-thirty."

"And you didn't go out in the garden at all afterwards?"

Bland shook his head.

"Matter of fact," he said, "my wife always goes up to rest after lunch and, if things aren't too busy, I take a bit of shut-eye myself in that chair there. I must have left the house about—oh, I suppose a quarter to three, but unfortunately I didn't go out in the garden at all."

"Oh, well," said Hardcastle with a sigh, "we have to ask everyone."

"Of course, of course. Wish I could be more helpful."

"Nice place you have here," said the inspector. "No money spared, if I may say so."

Bland laughed jovially.

"Ah well, we like things that are nice. My wife's got a lot of taste. We had a bit of a windfall a year ago. My wife came into some money from an uncle of hers. She hadn't seen him for twenty-five years. Quite a surprise it was! It made a bit of difference to us, I can tell you. We've been able to do ourselves well and we're thinking of going on one of these cruises later in the year. Very educational they are, I believe. Greece and all that. A lot of professors on them lecturing. Well, of course, I'm a self-made man and I haven't had much time for that sort of thing but I'd be interested. That chap who went and dug up Troy, he was a grocer, I believe. Very romantic. I must say I like going to foreign parts—not that I've done much of that—an occasional week-end in gay Paree, that's all. I've toyed with the idea of selling up here and going to live in Spain or Portugal or even the West Indies. A lot of people are doing it. Saves income tax and all that. But my wife doesn't fancy the idea."

"I'm fond of travel, but I wouldn't care to live out of England," said Mrs. Bland. "We've got all our friends here —and my sister lives here, and everybody knows *us*. If we went abroad we'd be strangers. And then we've got a very good doctor here. He really understands my health. I shouldn't care *at all* for a foreign doctor. I wouldn't have any confidence in him."

"We'll see," said Mr. Bland cheerfully. "We'll go on a cruise and you may fall in love with a Greek island."

Mrs. Bland looked as though that were very unlikely.

"There'd be a proper English doctor aboard, I suppose," she said doubtfully.

"Sure to be," said her husband.

He accompanied Hardcastle and Colin to the front door, repeating once more how sorry he was that he couldn't help them.

"Well," said Hardcastle. "What do you think of him?"

"I wouldn't care to let him build a house for me," said Colin. "But a crooked little builder isn't what I'm after. I'm looking for a man who is dedicated. And as regards your murder case, you've got the wrong kind of murder. Now if Bland was to feed his wife arsenic or push her into the Aegean in order to inherit her money and marry a slap-up blonde——"

"We'll see about that when it happens," said Inspector Hardcastle. "In the meantime we've got to get on with *this* murder."

CHAPTER 10

At No. 62, Wilbraham Crescent, Mrs. Ramsay was saying to herself encouragingly, "Only two days now. Only two days."

She pushed back some dank hair from her forehead. An almighty crash came from the kitchen. Mrs. Ramsay felt very disinclined even to go and see what the crash portended. If only she could pretend that there *hadn't* been a crash. Oh well—*only two days*. She stepped across the hall, flung the kitchen door open and said in a voice of far less belligerence than it would have held three weeks ago:

"*Now* what have you done?"

"Sorry, Mum," said her son Bill. "We were just having a bit of a bowling match with these tins and somehow or other they rolled into the bottom of the china cupboard."

"We didn't mean them to go into the bottom of the china cupboard," said his younger brother Ted agreeably.

"Well, pick up those things and put them back in the cupboard and sweep up that broken china and put it in the bin."

"Oh, Mum, not *now*."

"Yes, now."

"Ted can do it," said Bill.

"I like that," said Ted. "Always putting on me. I won't do it if you won't."

"Bet you will."

"Bet I won't."

"I'll make you."

"Yahh!"

The boys closed in a fierce wrestling match. Ted was forced back against the kitchen table and a bowl of eggs rocked ominously.

"Oh, get out of the kitchen!" cried Mrs. Ramsay. She pushed the two boys out of the kitchen door and shut it, and began to pick up tins and sweep up china.

'Two days,' she thought, 'and they'll be back at school! What a lovely, what a heavenly thought for a mother.'

She remembered vaguely some wicked remark by a woman columnist. *Only six happy days in the year for a woman.* The first and the last days of the holidays. How true that was, thought Mrs. Ramsay, sweeping up portions of her best dinner-service. With what pleasure, what joy, had she contemplated the return of her offspring a bare five weeks before! And now? "To-morrow," she repeated to herself, "to-morrow Bill and Ted will be back at school. I can hardly believe it. I can't wait!"

How heavenly it had been five weeks ago when she met them at the station. Their tempestuous and affectionate welcome! The way they had rushed all over the house and garden. A special cake baked for tea. And now—what was she looking forward to now? A day of complete peace. No enormous meals to prepare, no incessant clearing up. She loved the boys—they were fine boys, no doubt of that. She was proud of them. But they were also exhausting. Their appetite, their vitality, the *noise* they made.

At that moment, raucous cries arose. She turned her head in sharp alarm. It was all right. They had only gone out in the garden. That was better, there was far more room for them in the garden. They would probably annoy the neighbours. She hoped to goodness they would leave Mrs. Hemming's cats alone. Not, it must be confessed, for the sake of the cats, but because the wired enclosure surrounding Mrs. Hemming's garden was apt to tear their shorts. She cast a fleeting eye over the first-aid box which lay handy on the dresser. Not that she fussed unduly over the natural accidents of vigorous boyhood. In fact her first inevitable remark was: "Now haven't I told you a hundred times, you are *not* to bleed in the drawing-room! Come straight into the kitchen and bleed there, where I can wipe over the linoleum."

A terrific yell from outside seemed to be cut off mid-way and was followed by a silence so profound that Mrs. Ramsay felt a real feeling of alarm spring up in her breast. Really, that silence was most unnatural. She stood uncertainly, the dust-pan with broken china in her hand. The kitchen door opened and Bill stood there. He had an awed, ecstatic expression most unusual on his eleven-year-old face.

"Mum," he said, "*There's a detective inspector here and another man with him.*"

"Oh," said Mrs. Ramsay, relieved. "What does he want, dear?"

"He asked for you," said Bill, "but I think it must be about the murder. You know, the one at Miss Pebmarsh's yesterday."

"I don't see why he should come and wish to see me," said Mrs. Ramsay, in a slightly vexed voice.

Life was just one thing after another, she thought. How was she to get the potatoes on for the Irish stew if detective inspectors came along at this awkward hour?

"Oh well," she said with a sigh. "I suppose I'd better come."

She shot the broken china into the bin under the sink, rinsed her hands under the tap, smoothed her hair and prepared to follow Bill, who was saying impatiently,

"Oh, come *on*, Mum."

Mrs. Ramsay, closely flanked by Bill, entered the sitting-room. Two men were standing there. Her younger son, Ted, was in attendance upon them, staring at them with wide appreciative eyes.

"Mrs. Ramsay?"

"Good morning."

"I expect these young men have told you that I am Detective Inspector Hardcastle?"

"It's very awkward," said Mrs. Ramsay. "Very awkward this morning. I'm very busy. Will it take very long?"

"Hardly any time at all," said Detective Inspector Hardcastle reassuringly. "May we sit down?"

"Oh, yes, do, do."

Mrs. Ramsay took an upright chair and looked at them impatiently. She had suspicions that it was *not* going to take hardly any time at all.

"No need for you two to remain," said Hardcastle to the boys pleasantly.

"Aw, we're not going," said Bill.

"We're not going," echoed Ted.

"We want to hear all about it," said Bill.

"Sure we do," said Ted.

"Was there a lot of blood?" asked Bill.

"Was it a burglar?" said Ted.

"Be quiet, boys," said Mrs. Ramsay. "Didn't you hear the—Mr. Hardcastle say he didn't want you in here?"

"We're not going," said Bill. "We want to hear."

Hardcastle moved across to the door and opened it. He looked at the boys.

"Out," he said.

It was only one word, quietly uttered, but it had behind it the quality of authority. Without more ado both boys got up, shuffled their feet and shuffled out of the room.

"How wonderful," thought Mrs. Ramsay appreciatively. "Now why can't *I* be like that?"

But then, she reflected, she was the boys' mother. She knew by hearsay that the boys, when they went out, behaved in a manner entirely different from at home. It was always mothers who got the worst of things. But perhaps, she reflected, one would rather have it like that. To have nice quiet attentive polite boys at home and to have little hooligans going out, creating unfavourable opinions of themselves, would be worse—yes, that would be worse. She recalled herself to what was required of her, as Inspector Hardcastle came back and sat down again.

"If it's about what happened at Number 19 yesterday," she said nervously, "I really don't see that I can tell you anything, Inspector. I don't know anything about it. I don't even know the people who live there."

"The house is lived in by a Miss Pebmarsh. She's blind and works at the Aaronberg Institute."

"Oh, I see," said Mrs. Ramsay. "I'm afraid I know hardly anybody in the lower Crescent."

"Were you yourself here yesterday between half past twelve and three o'clock?"

"Oh, yes," said Mrs. Ramsay. "There was dinner to cook and all that. I went out before three, though. I took the boys to the cinema."

The inspector took the photograph from his pocket and handed it to her.

"I'd like you to tell me if you've ever seen this man before."

Mrs. Ramsay looked at it with a slight awakening of interest.

" No," she said, " no, I don't think so. I'm not sure if I
would remember if I had seen him."

" He did not come to this house on any occasion—trying to
sell you insurance or anything of that kind?"

Mrs. Ramsay shook her head more positively.

" No. No, I'm sure he didn't."

" His name, we have some reason to believe, is Curry.
Mr. R. Curry."

He looked inquiringly at her. Mrs. Ramsay shook her
head again.

" I'm afraid," she said apologetically, " I really haven't
time to see or notice *anything* during the holidays."

" That's always a busy time, isn't it," said the inspector.
" Fine boys you've got. Full of life and spirits. Rather too
many spirits sometimes, I expect?"

Mrs. Ramsay positively smiled.

" Yes," she said, " it gets a little tiring, but they're very
good boys really."

" I'm sure they are," said the inspector. " Fine fellows,
both of them. Very intelligent, I should say. I'll have a word
with them before I go, if you don't mind. Boys notice things
sometimes that nobody else in the house does."

" I don't really see how they can have noticed anything,"
said Mrs. Ramsay. " It's not as though we were next door or
anything."

" But your gardens back on each other."

" Yes, they do," agreed Mrs. Ramsay. " But they're quite
separate."

" Do you know Mrs. Hemming at Number 20?"

" Well, in a way I do," said Mrs. Ramsay, " because of the
cats and one thing and another."

" You are fond of cats?"

" Oh, no," said Mrs. Ramsay, " it's not that. I mean it's
usually complaints."

" Oh, I see. Complaints. What about?"

Mrs. Ramsay flushed.

" The trouble is," she said, " when people keep cats in that
way—fourteen, she's got—they get absolutely besotted about
them. And it's all a lot of nonsense. I like cats. We used to
have a cat ourselves, a tabby. Very good mouser, too. But all

the fuss that woman makes, cooking special food—hardly ever letting the poor things out to have a life of their own. Of course the cats are always trying to escape. I would, if I was one of those cats. And the boys are very good really, they wouldn't torment a cat in any way. What I say is cats can always take care of themselves very well. They're very sensible animals, cats, that is if they are treated sensibly."

" I'm sure you're quite right," said the inspector. " You must have a busy life," he went on, " keeping those boys of yours amused and fed during the holidays. When are they going back to school?"

" The day after to-morrow," said Mrs. Ramsay.

" I hope you'll have a good rest then."

" I mean to treat myself to a real lazy time," she said.

The other young man who had been silently taking down notes, startled her a little by speaking.

" You ought to have one of those foreign girls," he said. " *Au pair*, don't they call it, come and do chores here in return for learning English."

" I suppose I might try something of that kind," said Mrs. Ramsay, considering, " though I always feel that foreigners may be difficult. My husband laughs at me. But then of course he knows more about it than I do. I haven't travelled abroad as much as he has."

" He's away now, isn't he?" said Hardcastle.

" Yes—he had to go to Sweden at the beginning of August. He's a constructional engineer. A pity he had to go just then —at the beginning of the holidays, too. He's so good with the children. He really likes playing with electric trains more than the boys do. Sometimes the lines and the marshalling yards and everything go right across the hall and into the other room. It's very difficult not to fall over them." She shook her head. " Men are such children," she said indulgently.

" When do you expect him back, Mrs. Ramsay?"

" I never know." She sighed. " It makes it rather— difficult." There was a tremor in her voice. Colin looked at her keenly.

" We mustn't take up more of your time, Mrs. Ramsay." Hardcastle rose to his feet.

"Perhaps your boys will show us the garden?"

Bill and Ted were waiting in the hall and fell in with the suggestion immediately.

"Of course," said Bill apologetically, "it isn't a very *big* garden."

There had been some slight effort made to keep the garden of No. 62, Wilbraham Crescent in reasonable order. On one side there was a border of dahlias and Michaelmas daisies. Then a small lawn somewhat unevenly mown. The paths badly needed hoeing, models of aeroplanes, space guns and other representations of modern science lay about, looking slightly the worse for wear. At the end of the garden was an apple tree with pleasant-looking red apples on it. Next to it was a pear tree.

"That's *it*," said Ted, pointing at the space between the apple and the pear, through which the back of Miss Pebmarsh's house showed clearly. "That's Number 19 where the murder was."

"Got quite a good view of the house, haven't you," said the inspector. "Better still, I expect, from the upstairs windows."

"That's right," said Bill. "If only we'd been up there yesterday looking out, we might have seen something. But we didn't."

"We were at the cinema," said Ted.

"Were there fingerprints?" asked Bill.

"Not very helpful ones. Were you out in the garden at all yesterday?"

"Oh, yes, off and on," said Bill. "All the morning, that is. We didn't hear anything, though, or see anything."

"If we'd been there in the afternoon we might have heard screams," said Ted, wistfully. "Awful screams there were."

"Do you know Miss Pebmarsh, the lady who owns that house, by sight?"

The boys looked at each other, then nodded.

"She's blind," said Ted, "but she can walk around the garden all right. Doesn't have to walk with a stick or anything like that. She threw a ball back to us once. Quite nice about it she was."

"You didn't see her at all yesterday?"

The boys shook their heads.

"We wouldn't see her in the morning. She's always out," Bill explained. "She usually comes out in the garden after tea."

Colin was exploring a line of hosepipe which was attached to a tap in the house. It ran along the garden path and was laid down in the corner near the pear tree.

"Never knew that pear trees needed watering," he remarked.

"Oh, that," said Bill. He looked slightly embarrassed.

"On the other hand," said Colin, "if you climbed up in this tree." He looked at both boys and grinned suddenly. "You could get a very nice little line of water to play on a cat, couldn't you?"

Both boys scuffled the gravel with their feet and looked in every other direction but at Colin.

"That's what you do, isn't it?" said Colin.

"Aw, well," said Bill, "it doesn't hurt 'em. It's not," he said with an air of virtue, "like a catapult."

"I suppose you used to use a catapult at one time."

"Not properly," said Ted. "We never seemed to hit anything."

"Anyway, you do have a bit of fun with that hose sometimes," said Colin, "and then Mrs. Hemming comes along and complains?"

"She's always complaining," said Bill.

"You ever get through her fence?"

"Not through that wire here," said Ted, unguardedly.

"But you do get into her garden sometimes, is that right? How do you do it?"

"Well, you can get through the fence—into Miss Pebmarsh's garden. Then a little way down to the right you can push through the hedge into Mrs. Hemming's garden. There's a hole there in the wire."

"Can't you shut up, you fool?" said Bill.

"I suppose you've done a bit of hunting about for clues since the murder?" said Hardcastle.

The boys looked at each other.

"When you came back from the cinema and heard what had happened, I bet you went through the fence into the garden of 19 and had a jolly good look round."

"Well——" Bill paused cautiously.

" It's always possible," said Hardcastle seriously, " that you may have found something that we missed. If you have—er—a collection I should be much obliged if you would show it to me."

Bill made up his mind.

" Get 'em, Ted," he said.

Ted departed obediently at a run.

" I'm afraid we haven't got anything really good," admitted Bill. " We only—sort of pretended."

He looked at Hardcastle anxiously.

" I quite understand," said the inspector. " Most of police work is like that. A lot of disappointments."

Bill looked relieved.

Ted returned at a run. He passed over a grubby knotted handkerchief which chinked. Hardcastle unknotted it, with a boy on either side of him, and spread out the contents.

There was the handle off a cup, a fragment of willow pattern china, a broken trowel, a rusty fork, a coin, a clothespeg, a bit of iridescent glass and half a pair of scissors.

" An interesting lot," said the inspector solemnly.

He took pity on the eager faces of the boys and picked up the piece of glass.

" I'll take this. It may just possibly tie up with something."

Colin had picked up the coin and was examining it.

" It's not English," said Ted.

" No," said Colin, " It's not English." He looked across at Hardcastle. " We might perhaps take this, too," he suggested.

" Don't say a word about this to anyone," said Hardcastle in a conspiratorial fashion.

The boys promised delightedly that they wouldn't.

CHAPTER 11

" Ramsay," said Colin, thoughtfully.

" What about him?"

" I like the sound of him, that's all. He travels abroad—at a moment's notice. His wife say's he's a construction engineer, but that's all she seems to know about him."

" She's a nice woman," said Hardcastle.

" Yes—and not a very happy one."

" Tired, that's all. Kids *are* tiring."

" I think it's more than that."

" Surely the sort of person you want wouldn't be burdened with a wife and two sons," Hardcastle said sceptically.

" You never know," said Colin. " You'd be surprised what some of the boys do for camouflage. A hard-up widow with a couple of kids might be willing to come to an arrangement."

" I shouldn't have thought she was that kind," said Hardcastle primly.

" I don't mean living in sin, my dear fellow. I mean that she'd agree to be Mrs. Ramsay and supply a background. Naturally, he'd spin her a yarn of the right kind. He'd be doing a spot of espionage, say, on our side. All highly patriotic."

Hardcastle shook his head.

" You live in a strange world, Colin," he said.

" Yes we do. I think, you know, I'll have to get out of it one day . . . One begins to forget what is what and who is who. Half of these people work for both sides and in the end they don't know themselves which side they are really on. Standards get gummed up—Oh, well—let's get on with things."

" We'd better do the McNaughtons," said Hardcastle, pausing at the gates of 63. " A bit of his garden touches 19— same as Bland."

" What do you know about the McNaughtons?"

" Not much—they came here about a year ago. Elderly couple—retired professor, I believe. He gardens."

The front garden had rose bushes in it and a thick bed of autumn crocus under the windows.

A cheerful young woman in a brightly flowered overall opened the door to them and said:

" You want?—Yes?"

Hardcastle murmured, " The foreign help at last," and handed her his card.

" Police," said the young woman. She took a step or two back and looked at Hardcastle as though he were the Fiend in person.

" Mrs. McNaughton," said Hardcastle.

" Mrs. McNaughton is here."

She led them into the sitting-room, which overlooked the back garden. It was empty.

"She up the stairs is," said the no-longer-cheerful young woman. She went out into the hall and called, "Mrs. McNaughton—Mrs. McNaughton."

A voice far away said, "Yes. What is it, Gretel?"

"It is the police—two police. I put them in sitting-room."

There was a faint scurrying noise upstairs and the words "Oh, dear. Oh, dear, what next," floated down. Then there was a patter of feet and presently Mrs. McNaughton entered the room with a worried expression on her face. There was, Hardcastle decided quite soon, usually a worried expression on Mrs. McNaughton's face.

"Oh, dear," she said again, "oh, dear. Inspector—what is it—Hardcastle—oh, yes." She looked at the card. "But why do you want to see us? We don't know anything about it. I mean I suppose it is this murder, isn't it? I mean, it wouldn't be the television licence?"

Hardcastle reassured her on that point.

"It all seems so extraordinary, doesn't it," said Mrs. McNaughton, brightening up. "And more or less midday, too. Such an odd time to come and burgle a house. Just the time when people are usually at home. But then one does read of such terrible things nowadays. All happening in broad daylight. Why, some friends of ours—they were out for lunch and a furniture van drove up and the men broke in and carried out every stick of furniture. The whole street saw it happen but of course they never thought there was anything wrong. You know, I did think I heard someone screaming yesterday, but Angus said it was those dreadful boys of Mrs. Ramsay's. They rush about the garden making noises like space-ships, you know, or rockets, or atom bombs. It really is quite frightening sometimes."

Once again Hardcastle produced his photograph.

"Have you ever seen this man, Mrs. McNaughton?"

Mrs. McNaughton stared at it with avidity.

"I'm almost sure I've seen him. Yes. Yes, I'm practically certain. Now, where was it? Was it the man who came and asked me if I wanted to buy a new encyclopaedia in fourteen volumes? Or was it the man who came with a new model of vacuum cleaner. I wouldn't have anything to do with *him*, and he went out and worried my husband in the front garden. Angus was planting some bulbs, you know, and he didn't want to be interrupted and the man went on and on saying what the thing would do. You know, how it would run up and down curtains, and would clean doorsteps and do the stairs and cushions and spring-clean things. Everything, he said, absolutely everything. And then Angus just looked up at him and said, ' Can it plant bulbs?' and I must say I had to laugh because it took the man quite aback and he went away."

" And you really think that was the man in this photograph?"

" Well, no, I don't really," said Mrs. McNaughton, " because that was a much younger man, now I come to think of it. But all the same I think I *have* seen this face before. Yes. The more I look at it the more sure I am that he came here and asked me to buy something."

" Insurance perhaps?"

" No, no, not insurance. My husband attends to all that kind of thing. We are fully insured in every way. No. But all the same—yes, the more I look at that photograph——"

Hardcastle was less encouraged by this than he might have been. He put down Mrs. McNaughton, from the fund of his experience, as a woman who would be anxious for the excitement of having seen someone connected with murder. The longer she looked at the picture, the more sure she would be that she could remember someone just like it.

He sighed.

" He was driving a van, I believe," said Mrs. McNaughton. " But just when I saw him I can't remember. A baker's van, I think."

" You didn't see him yesterday, did you, Mrs. McNaughton?"

Mrs. McNaughton's face fell slightly. She pushed back her rather untidy grey waved hair from her forehead.

" No. No, not *yesterday*," she said. " At least——" she paused. " I don't *think* so." Then she brightened a little. " Perhaps my husband will remember."

" Is he at home?"

"Oh, he's out in the garden." She pointed through the window where at this moment an elderly man was pushing a wheelbarrow along the path.

"Perhaps we might go out and speak to him."

"Of course. Come this way."

She led the way out through a side door and into the garden. Mr. McNaughton was in a fine state of perspiration.

"These gentlemen are from the police, Angus," said his wife breathlessly. "Come about the murder at Miss Pebmarsh's. There's a photograph they've got of the dead man. Do you know, I'm sure I've seen him somewhere. It wasn't the man, was it, who came last week and asked us if we had any antiques to dispose of?"

"Let's see," said Mr. McNaughton. "Just hold it for me, will you," he said to Hardcastle. "My hands are too earthy to touch anything."

He took a brief look and remarked, "Never seen that fellow in my life."

"Your neighbour tells me you're very fond of gardening," said Hardcastle.

"Who told you that—not Mrs. Ramsay?"

"No. Mr. Bland."

Angus McNaughton snorted.

"Bland doesn't know what gardening means," he said. "Bedding out, that's all *he* does. Shoves in begonias and geraniums and lobelia edging. That's not what I call *gardening*. Might as well live in a public park. Are you interested in shrubs at all, Inspector? Of course, it's the wrong time of year now, but I've one or two shrubs here that you'd be surprised at my being able to grow. Shrubs that they say only do well in Devon and Cornwall."

"I'm afraid I can't lay claim to be a practical gardener," said Hardcastle.

McNaughton looked at him much as an artist looks at someone who says they know nothing of art but they know what they like.

"I'm afraid I've called about a much less pleasant subject," Hardcastle said.

"Of course. This business yesterday. I was out in the garden, you know, when it happened."

" Indeed?"

" Well, I mean I was here when the girl screamed."

" What did you do?"

" Well," said Mr. McNaughton rather sheepishly, " I didn't do anything. As a matter of fact I thought it was those blasted Ramsay boys. Always yelling and screaming and making a noise."

" But surely this scream didn't come from quite the same direction?"

" Not if those blasted boys ever stayed in their own garden. But they don't, you know. They get through people's fences and hedges. They chase those wretched cats of Mrs. Hemming's all over the place. There's nobody to keep a firm hand on them, that's the trouble. Their mother's weak as water. Of course, when there's no man in the house, boys do get out of hand."

" Mr. Ramsay is abroad a good deal I understand."

" Construction engineer, I believe," said Mr. McNaughton vaguely. " Always going off somewhere. Dams, you know. I'm not swearing, my dear," he assured his wife. " I mean jobs to do with the building of dams, or else it's oil or pipelines or something like that. I don't really know. He had to go off to Sweden a month ago at a moment's notice. That left the boys' mother with a lot to do—cooking and housework and that—and, well—of course they were bound to run wild. They're not bad boys, mind you, but they need discipline."

" You yourself didn't see anything—apart I mean from hearing the scream? When was that, by the way?"

" No idea," said Mr. McNaughton. " I take my watch off always before I come out here. Ran the hose over it the other day and had quite a job getting it repaired afterwards. What time was it, my dear? You heard it, didn't you?"

" It must have been half past two perhaps—it was at least half an hour after we finished lunch."

" I see. What time do you lunch?"

" Half past one," said Mr. McNaughton, " if we're lucky. Our Danish girl has got no sense of time."

" And afterwards—do you have a nap?"

" Sometimes. I didn't to-day. I wanted to get on with what I was doing. I was clearing away a lot of stuff, adding to the compost heap, and all that."

" Wonderful thing, a compost heap," said Hardcastle, solemnly.

Mr. McNaughton brightened immediately.

" Absolutely. Nothing like it. Ah! The number of people I've converted. Using all these chemical manures! Suicide! Let me show you."

He drew Hardcastle eagerly by the arm and trundling his barrow, went along the path to the edge of the fence that divided his garden from that of No. 19. Screened by lilac bushes, the compost heap was displayed in its glory. Mr. McNaughton wheeled the wheelbarrow to a small shed beside it. Inside the shed were several nicely arranged tools.

" Very tidy you keep everything," remarked Hardcastle.

" Got to take care of your tools," said McNaughton.

Hardcastle was looking thoughtfully towards No. 19. On the other side of the fence was a rose pergola which led up to the side of the house.

" You didn't see anyone in the garden at Number 19 or looking out of the window in the house, or anything like that while you were at your compost heap?"

McNaughton shook his head.

" Didn't see anything at all," he said. " Sorry I can't help you, Inspector."

" You know, Angus," said his wife, " I believe I did see a figure skulking in the garden of 19."

" I don't think you did, my dear," said her husband firmly. " I didn't, either."

" That woman would say she'd seen *anything*," Hardcastle growled when they were back in the car.

" You don't think she recognised the photograph?"

Hardcastle shook his head. " I doubt it. She just *wants* to think she's seen him. I know that type of witness only too well. When I pinned her down to it, she couldn't give chapter or verse, could she?"

" No."

" Of course she *may* have sat opposite him in a bus or something. I'll allow you that. But if you ask me, it's wishful thinking. What do you think?"

" I think the same."

" We didn't get much," Hardcastle sighed. " Of course there are things that seem queer. For instance, it seems almost impossible that Mrs. Hemming—no matter how wrapped up in her cats she is—should know so little about her neighbour, Miss Pebmarsh, as she does. And also that she should be so extremely vague and uninterested in the murder."

" She is a vague kind of woman."

" Scatty!" said Hardcastle. " When you meet a scatty woman—well, fires, burglaries, murders can go on all round them and they wouldn't notice it."

" She's very well fenced in with all that wire netting, and that Victorian shrubbery doesn't leave you much of a view."

They had arrived back at the police station. Hardcastle grinned at his friend and said,

" Well, Sergeant Lamb, I can let you go off duty now."

" No more visits to pay?"

" Not just now. I must pay one more later, but I'm not taking you with me."

" Well, thanks for this morning. Can you get these notes of mine typed up?" He handed them over.

" Inquest is the day after to-morrow you said? What time?"

" Eleven."

" Right. I'll be back for it."

" Are you going away?"

" I've got to go up to London to-morrow—make my report up to date."

" I can guess who to."

" You're not allowed to do that."

Hardcastle grinned.

" Give the old boy my love."

" Also, I may be going to see a specialist," said Colin.

" A specialist? What for? What's wrong with you?"

" Nothing—bar thick-headedness. I don't mean that kind of a specialist. One in your line."

" Scotland Yard?"

" No. A private detective—a friend of my Dad's—and a friend of mine. This fantastic business of yours will be just down his street. He'll love it—it will cheer him up. I've an idea he needs cheering up."

" What's his name?"

" Hercule Poirot."

" I've heard of him. I thought he was dead."

"He's not dead. But I have a feeling he's bored. That's worse."

Hardcastle looked at him curiously.

"You're an odd fellow, Colin. You make such unlikely friends."

"Including you," Colin said, and grinned.

CHAPTER 12

Having dismissed Colin, Inspector Hardcastle looked at the address neatly written in his note-book and nodded his head. Then he slipped the book back in his pocket and started to deal with the routine matters that had piled up on his desk.

It was a busy day for him. He sent out for coffee and sandwiches, and received reports from Sergeant Cray—no helpful lead had come up. Nobody at the railway station or buses had recognised the photograph of Mr. Curry. The laboratory reports on clothing added up to nil. The suit had been made by a good tailor, but the tailor's name had been removed. Desire for anonymity on the part of Mr. Curry? Or on the part of his killer. Details of dentistry had been circulated to the proper quarters and were probably the most helpful leads—it took a little time—but it got results in the end. Unless, of course, Mr. Curry had been a foreigner? Hardcastle considered the idea. There might be a possibility that the dead man was French—on the other hand his clothes were definitely not French. No laundry marks had helped yet.

Hardcastle was not impatient. Identification was quite often a slow job. But in the end, someone always came forward. A laundry, a dentist, a doctor, a landlady. The picture of the dead man would be circulated to police stations, would be reproduced in newspapers. Sooner or later, Mr. Curry would be known in his rightful identity.

In the meantime there was work to be done, and not only on the Curry case. Hardcastle worked without a break until half past five. He looked at his wrist-watch again and decided the time was ripe for the call he wanted to make.

Sergeant Cray had reported that Sheila Webb had resumed work at the Cavendish Bureau, and that at five o'clock she would be working with Professor Purdy at the Curlew Hotel and that she was very unlikely to leave there until well after six.

What was the aunt's name again? Lawton—Mrs. Lawton. 14, Palmerston Road. He did not take a police car but chose to walk the short distance.

Palmerston Road was a gloomy street that had known, as is said, better days. The houses, Hardcastle noted, had been mainly converted into flats or maisonettes. As he turned the corner, a girl who was approaching him along the sidewalk hesitated for a moment. His mind occupied, the inspector had some momentary idea that she was going to ask him the way to somewhere. However, if that was so, the girl thought better of it and resumed her walk past him. He wondered why the idea of shoes came into his mind so suddenly. Shoes . . . No, one shoe. The girl's face was faintly familiar to him. Who was it now—someone he had seen just lately . . . Perhaps she had recognised him and was about to speak to him?

He paused for a moment, looking back after her. She was walking quite fast now. The trouble was, he thought, she had one of those indeterminate faces that are very hard to recognise unless there is some special reason for doing so. Blue eyes, fair complexion, slightly open mouth. Mouth. That recalled something also. Something that she'd been doing with her mouth? Talking? Putting on lipstick? No. He felt slightly annoyed with himself. Hardcastle prided himself on his recognition of faces. He never forgot, he'd been apt to say, a face he had seen in the dock or in the witness-box, but there were after all other places of contact. He would not be likely to remember, for instance, every waitress who had ever served him. He would not remember every bus conductress. He dismissed the matter from his mind.

He had arrived now at No. 14. The door stood ajar and there were four bells with names underneath. Mrs. Lawton, he saw, had a flat on the ground floor. He went in and pressed the bell on the door on the left of the hall. It was a few moments before it was answered. Finally he heard steps inside and the door was opened by a tall, thin woman with straggling dark hair who had on an overall and seemed a little short of breath. The smell of onions wafted along from the direction of what was obviously the kitchen.

" Mrs. Lawton?"

" Yes?" She looked at him doubtfully, with slight annoyance.

She was, he thought, about forty-five. Something faintly gipsyish about her appearance.

" What is it?"

" I should be glad if you could spare me a moment or two."

" Well, what about? I'm really rather busy just now." She added sharply, " You're not a reporter, are you?"

" Of course," said Hardcastle, adopting a sympathetic tone, " I expect you've been a good deal worried by reporters."

" Indeed we have. Knocking at the door and ringing the bell and asking all sorts of foolish questions."

" Very annoying I know," said the inspector. " I wish we could spare you all that, Mrs. Lawton. I am Detective Inspector Hardcastle, by the way, in charge of the case about which the reporters have been annoying you. We'd put a stop to a good deal of that if we could, but we're powerless in the matter, you know. The Press has its rights."

" It's a shame to worry private people as they do," said Mrs. Lawton, " saying they have to have news for the public. The only thing I've ever noticed about the news that they print is that it's a tissue of lies from beginning to end. They'll cook up *anything* so far as I can see. But come in."

She stepped back and the inspector passed over the doorstep and she shut the door. There were a couple of letters which had fallen on the mat. Mrs. Lawton bent forward to pick them up, but the inspector politely forestalled her. His eyes swept over them for half a second as he handed them to her, addresses uppermost.

" Thank you."

She laid them down on the hall table.

" Come into the sitting-room, won't you? At least—if you go in this door and give me just a moment. I think something's boiling over."

She beat a speedy retreat to the kitchen. Inspector Hardcastle took a last deliberate look at the letters on the hall table. One was addressed to Mrs. Lawton and the two others to Miss R. S. Webb. He went into the room indicated. It was a small room, rather untidy, shabbily furnished but here and there it displayed some bright spot of colour or some unusual object. An attractive, probably expensive piece of Venetian glass of moulded colours and an abstract shape, two brightly coloured velvet cushions and an earthenware platter of foreign shells. Either the aunt or the niece, he thought, had an original streak in her make-up.

Mrs. Lawton returned, slightly more breathless than before.

"I think that'll be all right now," she said, rather uncertainly.

The inspector apologised again.

"I'm sorry if I've called at an inconvenient time," he said, "but I happened to be in this neighbourhood and I wanted to check over a few further points about this affair in which your niece was so unfortunately concerned. I hope she's none the worse for her experience? It must have been a great shock to any girl."

"Yes, indeed," said Mrs. Lawton. "Sheila came back in a terrible state. But she was all right by this morning and she's gone back to work again."

"Oh, yes, I know that," said the inspector. "But I was told she was out doing work for a client somewhere and I didn't want to interrupt anything of that kind so I thought it would be better if I came round here and talked to her in her own home. But she's not back yet, is that it?"

"She'll probably be rather late this evening," said Mrs. Lawton. "She's working for a Professor Purdy and from what Sheila says, he's a man with no idea of time at all. Always says 'this won't take more than another ten minutes so I think we might as well get it finished,' and then of course it takes nearer to three-quarters of an hour. He's a very nice man and most apologetic. Once or twice he's urged her to stay and have dinner and seemed quite concerned because he's kept her so much longer than he realised. Still, it is rather annoying sometimes. Is there something I can tell you, Inspector? In case Sheila is delayed a long time."

"Well, not really," said the inspector smiling. "Of course, we only took down the bare details the other day and I'm not sure really whether I've even got those right." He made a show of consulting his note-book once more. "Let me see. Miss Sheila Webb—is that her full name or has she another Christian name? We have to have these things very exact, you know, for the records at the inquest."

"The inquest is the day after to-morrow, isn't it? She got a notice to attend."

"Yes, but she needn't let that worry her," said Hardcastle. "She'll just have to tell her story of how she found the body."

"You don't know who the man was yet?"

"No. I'm afraid it's early days for that. There was a card in his pocket and we thought at first he was some kind of insurance agent. But it seems more likely now that it was a card he'd been given by someone. Perhaps he was contemplating insurance himself."

"Oh, I see." Mrs. Lawton looked vaguely interested.

"Now I'll just get these names right," said the inspector. "I think I've got it down as Miss Sheila Webb or Miss Sheila R. Webb. I just couldn't remember what the other name was. Was it Rosalie?"

"Rosemary," said Mrs. Lawton, "she was christened Rosemary Sheila but Sheila always thought Rosemary was rather fanciful so she's never called anything but Sheila."

"I see." There was nothing in Hardcastle's tone to show that he was pleased that one of his hunches had come out right. He noted another point. The name Rosemary occasioned no distress in Mrs. Lawton. To her Rosemary was simply a Christian name that her niece did not use.

"I've got it straight now all right," said the inspector smiling. "I gather that your niece came from London and has been working for the Cavendish Bureau for the last ten months or so. You don't know the exact date, I suppose?"

"Well, really, I couldn't say now. It was last November some time. I think more towards the end of November."

"Quite so. It doesn't really matter. She was not living with you here previously to taking the job at the Cavendish Bureau?"

"No. She was living in London before that."

"Have you got her address in London?"

"Well, I've got it somewhere," Mrs. Lawton looked round her with the vague expression of the habitually untidy. "I've got such a short memory," she said. "Something like Allington Grove, I think it was—out Fulham way. She shared a flat with two other girls. Terribly expensive rooms are in London for girls."

" Do you remember the name of the firm she worked at there?"

" Oh, yes. Hopgood and Trent. They were estate agents in the Fulham Road."

" Thank you. Well all that seems very clear. Miss Webb is an orphan, I understand?"

" Yes," said Mrs. Lawton. She moved uneasily. Her eyes strayed to the door. " Do you mind if I just go into the kitchen again?"

" Of course."

He opened the door for her. She went out. He wondered if he had been right or wrong in thinking that his last question had in some way perturbed Mrs. Lawton. Her replies had come quite readily and easily up to then. He thought about it until Mrs. Lawton returned.

" I'm so sorry," she said, apologetically, " but you know what it is—cooking things. Everything's quite all right now. Was there anything else you want to ask me? I've remembered, by the way, it wasn't Allington Grove. It was Carrington Grove and the number was 17."

" Thank you," said the inspector. " I think I was asking you whether Miss Webb was an orphan."

" Yes, she's an orphan. Her parents are dead."

" Long ago?"

" They died when she was a child."

There was something like defiance just perceptible in her tone.

" Was she your sister's child or your brother's?"

" My sister's."

" Ah, yes. And what was Mr. Webb's profession?"

Mrs. Lawton paused a moment before answering. She was biting her lips. Then she said, " I don't know."

" You don't know?"

" I mean I don't remember, it's so long ago."

Hardcastle waited, knowing that she would speak again. She did.

" May I ask what all this has got to do with it—I mean what does it matter who her father and mother were and what her father did and where he came from or anything like that?"

"I suppose it doesn't matter really, Mrs. Lawton, not from your point of view, that is. But you see, the circumstances are rather unusual."

"What do you mean—the circumstances are unusual?"

"Well, we have reason to believe that Miss Webb went to that house yesterday because she had been specially asked for at the Cavendish Bureau by name. It looks therefore as though someone had deliberately arranged for her to be there. Someone perhaps——" he hesitated "——with a grudge against her."

"I can't imagine that anyone could have a grudge against Sheila. She's a very sweet girl. A nice friendly girl."

"Yes," said Hardcastle mildly. "That's what I should have thought myself."

"And I don't like to hear anybody suggesting the contrary," said Mrs. Lawton belligerently.

"Exactly." Hardcastle continued to smile appeasingly. "But you must realise, Mrs. Lawton, that it looks as though your niece has been deliberately made a victim. She was being, as they say on the films, put on the spot. *Somebody* was arranging for her to go into a house where there was a dead man, and that dead man had died very recently. It seems on the face of it a malicious thing to do."

"You mean—you mean someone was trying to make it appear that Sheila killed him? Oh, no, I can't believe it."

"It is rather difficult to believe," agreed the inspector, "but we've got to make quite sure and clear up the matter. Could there be, for instance, some young man, someone perhaps who had fallen in love with your niece, and whom she, perhaps, did not care for? Young men sometimes do some very bitter and revengeful things, especially if they're rather ill-balanced."

"I don't think it could be anything of that kind," said Mrs. Lawton, puckering her eyes in thought and frowning. "Sheila has had one or two boys she's been friendly with, but there's been nothing serious. Nobody steady of any kind."

"It might have been while she was living in London?" the inspector suggested. "After all, I don't suppose you know very much about what friends she had there."

" No, no, perhaps not . . . Well, you'll have to ask her about that yourself, Inspector Hardcastle. But I never heard of any trouble of any kind."

" Or it might have been another girl," suggested Hardcastle. " Perhaps one of the girls she shared rooms with there was jealous of her?"

" I suppose," said Mrs. Lawton doubtfully, " that there might be a girl who'd want to do her a bad turn. But not involving murder, surely."

It was a shrewd appreciation and Hardcastle noted that Mrs. Lawton was by no means a fool. He said quickly:

" I know it all sounds most unlikely, but then this whole business *is* unlikely."

" It must have been someone mad," said Mrs. Lawton.

" Even in madness," said Hardcastle, " there's a definite idea behind the madness, you know. Something that's given rise to it. And that really," he went on, " is why I was asking you about Sheila Webb's father and mother. You'd be surprised how often motives arise that have their roots in the past. Since Miss Webb's father and mother died when she was a young child, naturally she can't tell me anything about them. That's why I'm applying to you."

" Yes, I see, but—well . . ."

He noted that the trouble and uncertainty were back in her voice.

" Were they killed at the same time, in an accident, anything like that?"

" No, there was no accident."

" They both died from natural causes?"

" I—well, yes, I mean—I don't really know."

" I think you must know a little more than you are telling me, Mrs. Lawton." He hazarded a guess. " Were they, perhaps, divorced—something of that kind?"

" No, they weren't divorced."

" Come now, Mrs. Lawton. You know—you must know of what your sister died?"

" I don't see what—I mean, I can't say—it's all very difficult. Raking up things. It's much better not raking them up." There was a kind of desperate perplexity in her glance.

Hardcastle looked at her keenly. Then he said gently, " Was Sheila Webb perhaps—an illegitimate child?"

He saw immediately a mixture of consternation and relief in her face.

" She's not *my* child," she said.

" She is your sister's illegitimate child?"

" Yes. But she doesn't know it herself. I've never told her. I told her her parents died young. So that's why—well, you see . . ."

" Oh, yes, I see," said the inspector, " and I assure you that unless something comes of this particular line of inquiry there is no need for me to question Miss Webb on this subject."

" You mean you needn't tell her?"

" Not unless there is some relevance to the case, which, I may say, seems unlikely. But I do want all the facts that you know, Mrs. Lawton, and I assure you that I'll do my best to keep what you tell me entirely between ourselves."

" It's not a nice thing to happen," said Mrs. Lawton, " and I was very distressed about it, I can tell you. My sister, you see, had always been the clever one of the family. She was a school teacher and doing very well. Highly respected and everything else. The last person you'd ever think would——"

" Well," said the inspector, tactfully, " it often happens that way. She got to know this man—this Webb——"

" I never even knew what his name was," said Mrs. Lawton. " I never met him. But she came to me and told me what had happened. That she was expecting a child and that the man couldn't, or wouldn't—I never knew which—marry her. She was ambitious and it would have meant giving up her job if the whole thing came out. So naturally I—I said I'd help."

" Where is your sister now, Mrs. Lawton?"

" I've no idea. Absolutely no idea at all." She was emphatic.

" She's alive, though."

" I suppose so."

" But you haven't kept in touch with her?"

" That's the way she wanted it. She thought it was best for the child and best for her that there should be a clean break. So it was fixed that way. We both had a little income of our own that our mother left us. Ann turned her half-share over to me to be used for the child's bringing up and keep.

She was going to continue with her profession, she said, but she would change schools. There was some idea, I believe, of a year's exchange with a teacher abroad. Australia or somewhere. That's all I know, Inspector Hardcastle, and that's all I can tell you."

He looked at her thoughtfully. Was that really all she knew? It was a difficult question to answer with any certainty. It was certainly all that she meant to tell him. It might very well be all she knew. Slight as the references to the sister had been, Hardcastle got an impression of a forceful, bitter, angry personality. The sort of woman who was determined not to have her life blasted by one mistake. In a cold hard-headed way she had provided for the upkeep and presumable happiness of her child. From that moment on she had cut herself adrift to start life again on her own.

It was conceivable, he thought, that she might feel like that about the child. But what about her sister? He said mildly:

"It seems odd that she did not at least keep in touch with you by letter, did not want to know how the child was progressing?"

Mrs. Lawton shook her head.

"Not if you knew Ann," she said. "She was always very clear-cut in her decisions. And then she and I weren't very close. I was younger than she was by a good deal—twelve years. As I say, we were never very close."

"And what did your husband feel about this adoption?"

"I was a widow then," said Mrs. Lawton. "I married young and my huband was killed in the war. I kept a small sweetshop at the time."

"Where was all this? Not here in Crowdean."

"No. We were living in Lincolnshire at the time. I came here in the holidays once, and I liked it so much that I sold the shop and came here to live. Later, when Sheila was old enough to go to school I took a job in Roscoe and West, the big drapers here, you know. I still work there. They're very pleasant people."

"Well," said Hardcastle, rising to his feet, "thank you very much, Mrs. Lawton, for your frankness in what you have told me."

"And you won't say a word of it to Sheila?"

"Not unless it should become necessary, and that would

only happen if some circumstances out of the past proved to have been connected with this murder at 19, Wilbraham Crescent. And that, I think, is unlikely." He took the photograph from his pocket which he had been showing to so many people, and showed it to Mrs. Lawton. "You've no idea who this man could be?"

"They've shown it me already," said Mrs. Lawton.

She took it and scrutinised it earnestly.

"No. I'm sure, quite sure I've never seen this man before. I don't think he belonged round here or I might have remembered seeing him about. Of course——" she looked closely. She paused a moment before adding, rather unexpectedly, "He looks a nice man I think. A gentleman, I'd say, wouldn't you?"

It was a slightly outmoded term in the inspector's experience, yet it fell very naturally from Mrs. Lawton's lips. "Brought up in the country," he thought. "They still think of things that way." He looked at the photograph again himself reflecting, with faint surprise, that he had not thought of the dead man in quite that way. Was he a nice man? He had been assuming just the contrary. Assuming it unconsciously perhaps, or influenced perhaps by the fact that the man had a card in his pocket which bore a name and an address which were obviously false. But the explanation he had given to Mrs. Lawton just now might have been the true one. It might have been that the card did represent some bogus insurance agent who had pressed the card upon the dead man. And that, he though wryly, would really make the whole thing even more difficult. He glanced at his watch again.

"I mustn't keep you from your cooking any longer," he said, "since your niece is not home yet——"

Mrs. Lawton in turn looked at the clock on the mantelpiece. "Only one clock in this room, thank heaven," thought the inspector to himself.

"Yes, she is late," she remarked. "Surprising really. It's a good thing Edna didn't wait."

Seeing a slightly puzzled expression on Hardcastle's face, she explained.

"It's just one of the girls from the office. She came here to see Sheila this evening and she waited a bit but after a while she said she couldn't wait any longer. She'd got a date with someone. She said it would do to-morrow, or some other time."

Enlightenment came to the inspector. The girl he had passed in the street! He knew now why she'd made him think of shoes. Of course. It was the girl who had received him in the Cavendish Bureau and the girl who, when he left, had been holding up a shoe with a stiletto heel torn off it, and had been discussing in unhappy puzzlement how on earth she was going to get home like that. A nondescript kind of girl, he remembered, not very attractive, sucking some kind of sweet as she talked. She had recognised him when she passed him in the street, although he had not recognised her. She had hesitated, too, as though she thought of speaking to him. He wondered rather idly what she had wanted to say. Had she wanted to explain why she was calling on Sheila Webb or had she thought he would expect her to say something? He asked:

" Is she a great friend of your niece's? "

" Well, not particularly," said Mrs. Lawton. " I mean they work in the same office and all that, but she's rather a dull girl. Not very bright and she and Sheila aren't particular friends. In fact, I wondered why she was so keen to see Sheila to-night. She said it was something she couldn't understand and that she wanted to ask Sheila about it."

" She didn't tell you what it was? "

" No, she said it would keep and it didn't matter."

" I see. Well, I must be going."

" It's odd," said Mrs. Lawton, " that Sheila hasn't telephoned. She usually does if she's late, because the professor sometimes asks her to stay to dinner. Ah, well, I expect she'll be here any moment now. There are a lot of bus queues sometimes and the Curlew Hotel is quite a good way along the Esplanade. There's nothing—no message—you want to leave for Sheila?"

" I think not," said the inspector.

As he went out he asked, " By the way, who chose your niece's Christian names, Rosemary and Sheila? Your sister or yourself?"

" Sheila was our mother's name. Rosemary was my sister's

choice. Funny name to choose really. Fanciful. And yet my sister wasn't fanciful or sentimental in any way."

" Well, good night, Mrs. Lawton."

As the inspector turned the corner from the gateway into the street he thought, " Rosemary—hm . . . Rosemary for remembrance. Romantic remembrance? Or—something quite different?"

CHAPTER 13

COLIN LAMB'S NARRATIVE

I walked up Charing Cross Road and turned into the maze of streets that twist their way between New Oxford Street and Covent Garden. All sorts of unsuspected shops did business there, antique shops, a dolls' hospital, ballet shoes, foreign delicatessen shops.

I resisted the lure of the dolls' hospital with its various pairs of blue or brown glass eyes, and came at last to my objective. It was a small dingy bookshop in a side street not far from the British Museum. It had the usual trays of books outside. Ancient novels, old text books, odds and ends of all kinds, labelled 3d., 6d., 1s., even some aristocrats which had nearly all their pages, and occasionally even their binding intact.

I sidled through the doorway. It was necessary to sidle since precariously arranged books impinged more and more every day on the passageway from the street. Inside, it was clear that the books owned the shop rather than the other way about. Everywhere they had run wild and taken possession of their habitat, breeding and multiplying and clearly lacking any strong hand to keep them down. The distance between bookshelves was so narrow that you could only get along with great difficulty. There were piles of books perched on every shelf or table. On a stool in a corner, hemmed in by books, was an old man in a pork-pie hat with a large flat face like a stuffed fish. He had the air of one who has given up an unequal struggle. He had attempted to master the books, but the books had obviously succeeded in mastering him. He was a kind of King Canute of the book world, retreating before the advancing book tide. If he ordered it to retreat it would have been with the sure and hopeless certainty that it would not do so. This was Mr. Soloman, proprietor of the shop. He recognised me, his fishlike stare softened for a moment and he nodded.

"Got anything in my line?" I asked.

"You'll have to go up and see, Mr. Lamb. Still on sea-weeds and that stuff?"

"That's right."

"Well, you know where they are. Marine biology, fossils—Antarctica second floor. I had a new parcel in day before yesterday. I started to unpack 'em but I haven't got round to it properly yet. You'll find them in a corner up there."

I nodded and sidled my way onwards to where a small rather rickety and very dirty staircase led up from the back of the shop. On the first floor were Orientalia, art books, medicine, and French classics. In this room was a rather interesting little curtained corner not known to the general public, but accessible to experts, where what is called "odd" or "curious" volumes reposed. I passed them and went on up to the second floor.

Here archaeological, natural history, and other respectable volumes were rather inadequately sorted into categories. I steered my way through students and elderly colonels and clergymen, passed round the angle of a bookcase, stepped over various gaping parcels of books on the floor and found my further progress barred by two students of opposite sexes lost to the world in a closely knit embrace. They stood there swaying to and fro. I said:

"Excuse me," pushed them firmly aside, raised a curtain which masked a door, and slipping a key from my pocket, turned it in the lock and passed through. I found myself incongruously in a kind of vestibule with cleanly distempered walls hung with prints of Highland cattle, and a door with a highly polished knocker on it. I manipulated the knocker discreetly and the door was opened by an elderly woman with grey hair, spectacles of a particularly old-fashioned kind, a black skirt and a rather unexpected peppermint-striped jumper.

"It's you, is it?" she said without any other form of greeting. "He was asking about you only yesterday. He

D

wasn't pleased." She shook her head at me, rather as an elderly governess might do at a disappointing child. "You'll have to try and do better," she said.

"Oh, come off it, Nanny," I said.

"And don't call me Nanny," said the lady. "It's a cheek. I've told you so before."

"It's your fault," I said. "You mustn't talk to me as if I were a small boy."

"Time you grew up. You'd better go in and get it over." She pressed a buzzer, picked up a telephone from the desk, and said,

"Mr. Colin . . . Yes, I'm sending him in." She put it down and nodded to me.

I went through a door at the end of the room into another room which was so full of cigar smoke that it was difficult to see anything at all. After my smarting eyes had cleared, I beheld the ample proportions of my chief sitting back in an aged, derelict grandfather chair, by the arm of which was an old-fashioned reading- or writing-desk on a swivel.

Colonel Beck took off his spectacles, pushed aside the reading-desk on which was a vast tome and looked disapprovingly at me.

"So it's you at last?" he said.

"Yes, sir," I said.

"Got anything?"

"No, sir."

"Ah! Well, it won't do, Colin, d'you hear? Won't do. Crescents indeed!"

"I still think," I began.

"All right. You still think. But we can't wait for ever while you're thinking."

"I'll admit it was only a hunch," I said.

"No harm in that," said Colonel Beck.

He was a contradictory man.

"Best jobs I've ever done have been hunches. Only this hunch of yours doesn't seem to be working out. Finished with the pubs?"

"Yes, sir. As I told you I've started on Crescents. Houses in crescents is what I mean."

"I didn't suppose you meant bakers' shops with French rolls in them, though, come to think of it, it's no reason why not. Some of these places make an absolute fetish of producing French croissants that aren't really French. Keep 'em in a deep freeze nowadays like everything else. That's why nothing tastes of anything nowadays."

I waited to see whether the old boy would enlarge upon this topic. It was a favourite one of his. But seeing that I was expecting him to do so, Colonel Beck refrained.

" Wash out all round?" he demanded.

" Almost. I've still got a little way to go."

" You want more time, is that it?"

" I want more time, yes," I said. " But I don't want to move on to another place this minute. There's been a kind of coincidence and it might—only *might*—mean something."

" Don't waffle. Give me facts."

" Subject of investigation, Wilbraham Crescent."

" And you drew a blank! Or didn't you?"

" I'm not sure."

" Define yourself, define yourself, boy."

" The coincidence is that a man was murdered in Wilbraham Crescent."

" Who was murdered?"

" As yet he's unknown. Had a card with a name and address in his pocket, but that was bogus."

" Hm. Yes. Suggestive. Tie up in any way?"

" I can't see that it does, sir, but all the same . . ."

" I know, I know. All the same . . . Well, what have you come for? Come for permission to go on nosing about Wilbraham Crescent—wherever that absurd-sounding place is?"

" It's at a place called Crowdean. Ten miles from Portlebury."

" Yes, yes. Very good locality. But what are you here for? You don't usually ask permission. You go your own pig-headed way, don't you?"

" That's right, sir, I'm afraid I do."

" Well, then, what is it?"

" There are a couple of people I want vetted."

With a sigh Colonel Beck drew his reading-desk back into position, took a ball-pen from his pocket, blew on it and looked at me.

" Well?"

"House called Diana Lodge. Actually, 20, Wilbraham Crescent. Woman called Mrs. Hemming and about eighteen cats live there."

"Diana? Hm," said Colonel Beck. "Moon goddess! Diana Lodge. Right. What does she do, this Mrs. Hemming?"

"Nothing," I said, "she's absorbed in her cats."

"Damned good cover, I dare say," said Beck appreciatively. "Certainly could be. Is that all?"

"No," I said. "There's a man called Ramsay. Lives at 62, Wilbraham Crescent. Said to be a construction engineer, whatever that is. Goes abroad a good deal."

"I like the sound of that," said Colonel Beck. "I like the sound of that very much. You want to know about him, do you? All right."

"He's got a wife," I said. "Quite a nice wife, and two obstreperous children—boys."

"Well, he might have," said Colonel Beck. "It has been known. You remember Pendleton? He had a wife and children. Very nice wife. Stupidest woman I've ever come across. No idea in her head that her husband wasn't a pillar of respectability in oriental book dealing. Come to think of it, now I remember, Pendleton had a German wife as well, and a couple of daughters. And he also had a wife in Switzerland. I don't know what the wives were—his private excesses or just camouflage. He'd *say* of course that they were camouflage. Well, anyway, you want to know about Mr. Ramsay. Anything else?"

"I'm not sure. There's a couple at 63. Retired professor. McNaughton by name. Scottish. Elderly. Spends his time gardening. No reason to think he and his wife are not all right—but——"

"All right. We'll check. We'll put 'em through the machine to make sure. What *are* all these people, by the way?"

"They're people whose gardens verge on or touch the garden of the house where the murder was committed."

"Sounds like a French exercise," said Beck. "Where is the dead body of my uncle? In the garden of the cousin of my aunt. What about Number 19 itself?"

"A blind woman, a former school teacher, lives there. She works in an institute for the blind and she's been thoroughly investigated by the local police."

"Live by herself?"

"Yes."

"And what is your idea about all these other people?"

"My idea is," I said, "that if a murder was committed by any of these other people in any of these other houses that I have mentioned to you, it would be perfectly easy, though risky, to convey the dead body into Number 19 at a suitable time of day. It's a mere possibility, that's all. And there's something I'd like to show you. *This.*"

Beck took the earthstained coin I held out to him.

"A Czech Haller? Where did you find it?"

"I didn't. But it was found in the back garden of Number 19."

"Interesting. You may have something after all in your persistent fixation on crescents and rising moons." He added thoughtfully, "There's a pub called The Rising Moon in the next street to this. Why don't you go and try your luck there?"

"I've been there already," I said.

"You've always got an answer, haven't you?" said Colonel Beck. "Have a cigar?"

I shook my head. "Thank you—no time to-day."

"Going back to Crowdean?"

"Yes. There's the inquest to attend."

"It will only be adjourned. Sure it's not some girl you're running after in Crowdean?"

"Certainly not," I said sharply.

Colonel Beck began to chuckle unexpectedly.

"You mind your step, my boy! Sex rearing its ugly head as usual. How long have you known her?"

"There isn't any—I mean—well—there *was* a girl who discovered the body."

"What did she do when she discovered it?"

"Screamed."

"Very nice too," said the colonel. "She rushed to you, cried on your shoulder and told you about it. Is that it?"

"I don't know what you're talking about," I said coldly. "Have a look at these."

I gave him a selection of the police photographs.

"Who's this?" demanded Colonel Beck.

"The dead man."

" Ten to one this girl you're so keen about killed him. The whole story sounds very fishy to me."

" You haven't even heard it yet," I said. " I haven't told it to you."

" I don't need telling," Colonel Beck waved his cigar. " Go away to your inquest, my boy, and look out for that girl. Is her name Diana, or Artemis, or anything crescenty or moon-like?"

" No, it isn't."

" Well, remember that it might be!"

CHAPTER 14

COLIN LAMB'S NARRATIVE

It had been quite a long time since I had visited Whitehaven Mansions. Some years ago it had been an outstanding build-ing of modern flats. Now there were many other more im-posing and even more modern blocks of buildings flanking it on either side. Inside, I noted, it had recently had a face lift. It had been repainted in pale shades of yellow and green.

I went up in the lift and pressed the bell of Number 203. It was opened to me by that impeccable man-servant, George. A smile of welcome came to his face.

" Mr. Colin! It's a long time since we've seen you here."

" Yes, I know. How are you, George?"

" I am in good health, I am thankful to say, sir."

I lowered my voice. " And how's he?"

George lowered his own voice, though that was hardly necessary since it had been pitched in a most discreet key from the beginning of our conversation.

" I think, sir, that sometimes he gets a little depressed."

I nodded sympathetically.

" If you will come this way, sir——" He relieved me of my hat.

" Announce me, please, as Mr. Colin Lamb."

" Very good, sir." He opened a door and spoke in a clear voice. " Mr. Colin Lamb to see you sir."

He drew back to allow me to pass him and I went into the room.

My friend, Hercule Poirot, was sitting in his usual large, square armchair in front of the fireplace. I noted that one bar of the rectangular electric fire glowed red. It was early September, the weather was warm, but Poirot was one of the first men to recognise the autumn chill, and to take precautions against it. On either side of him on the floor was a neat pile of books. More books stood on the table at his left side. At his right hand was a cup from which steam rose. A tisane, I suspected. He was fond of tisanes and often urged them on me. They were nauseating to taste and pungent to smell.

"Don't get up," I said, but Poirot was already on his feet. He came towards me on twinkling, patent-leather shod feet with outstretched hands.

"Aha, so it is *you*, it is *you*, my friend! My young friend Colin. But why do you call yourself by the name of Lamb? Let me think now. There is a proverb or a saying. Something about mutton dressed as lamb. No. That is what is said of elderly ladies who are trying to appear younger than they are. That does not apply to you. Aha, I have it. You are a wolf in sheep's clothing. Is that it?"

"Not even that," I said. "It's just that in my line of business I thought my own name might be rather a mistake, that it might be connected too much with my old man. Hence, Lamb. Short, simple, easily remembered. Suiting, I flatter myself, my personality."

"Of that I cannot be sure," said Poirot, "and how is my good friend, your father?"

"The old man's fine," I said. "Very busy with his hollyhocks—or is it chrysanthemums? The seasons go by so fast I can never remember what it is at the moment."

"He busies himself then, with the horticulture?"

"Everyone seems to come to that in the end," I said.

"Not me," said Hercule Poirot. "Once the vegetable marrows, yes—but never again. If you want the best flowers, why not go to the florist's shop? I thought the good Superintendent was going to write his memoirs?"

"He started," I said, "but he found that so much would have to be left out that he finally came to the conclusion that what was left in would be so unbearably tame as not to be worth writing."

"One has to have the discretion, yes. It is unfortunate," said Poirot, "because your father could tell some very interesting things. I have much admiration for him. I always had. You know, his methods were to me very interesting. He was so straightforward. He used the obvious as no man has used it before. He would set the trap, the very obvious trap and the people he wished to catch would say ' it is too obvious, that. It cannot be true' and so they fell into it!"

I laughed. "Well," I said, "it's not the fashion nowadays for sons to admire their fathers. Most of them seem to sit down, venom in their pens, and remember all the dirty things they can and put them down with obvious satisfaction. But personally, I've got enormous respect for my old man. I hope I'll even be as good as he was. Not that I'm exactly in his line of business, of course."

"But related to it," said Poirot. "Closely related to it, though you have to work behind the scenes in a way that he did not." He coughed delicately. "I think I am to congratulate you on having had a rather spectacular success lately. Is it not so? The *affaire Larkin*."

"It's all right so far as it goes," I said. "But there's a good deal more that I'd like to have, just to round it off properly. Still, that isn't really what I came here to talk to you about."

"Of course not, of course not," said Poirot. He waved me to a chair and offered me some tisane, which I instantly refused.

George entered at the apposite moment with a whisky decanter, a glass and a siphon which he placed at my elbow.

"And what are you doing with yourself these days?" I asked Poirot.

Casting a look at the various books around him I said: "It looks as though you are doing a little research?"

Poirot sighed. "You may call it that. Yes, perhaps in a way it is true. Lately I have felt very badly the need for a problem. It does not matter, I said to myself, what the problem is. It can be like the good Sherlock Holmes, the depth at which the parsley has sunk in the butter. All that matters is that there should *be* a problem. It is not the muscles I need to exercise, you see, it is the cells of the brain."

" Just a question of keeping fit. I understand."

" As you say." He sighed. " But problems, *mon cher*, are not so easy to come by. It is true that last Thursday one presented itself to me. The unwarranted appearance of three pieces of dried orange peel in my umbrella stand. How did they come there? How *could* they have come there? I do not eat oranges myself. George would never put old pieces of orange peel in the umbrella stand. Nor is a visitor likely to bring with him three pieces of orange peel. Yes, it was quite a problem."

" And you solved it?"

" I solved it," said Poirot.

He spoke with more melancholy than pride.

" It was not in the end very interesting. A question of a *remplacement* of the usual cleaning woman and the new one brought with her, strictly against orders, one of her children. Although it does not sound interesting, nevertheless it needed a steady penetration of lies, camouflage and all the rest of it. It was satisfactory, shall we say, but not important."

" Disappointing," I suggested.

" *Enfin*," said Poirot, " I am modest. But one should not need to use a rapier to cut the string of a parcel."

I shook my head in a solemn manner. Poirot continued,

" I have occupied myself of late in reading various real life unsolved mysteries. I apply to them my own solutions."

" You mean cases like the Bravo case, Adelaide Bartlett and all the rest of them?"

" Exactly. But it was in a way too easy. There is no doubt whatever in my own mind as to who murdered Charles Bravo. The companion may have been involved, but she was certainly not the moving spirit in the matter. Then there was that unfortunate adolescent, Constance Kent. The true motive that lay behind her strangling of the small brother whom she undoubtedly loved has always been a puzzle. But not to me. It was clear as soon as I read about the case. As for Lizzie Borden, one wishes only that one could put a few necessary questions to various people concerned. I am fairly sure in my own mind of what the answers would be. Alas, they are all by now dead, I fear."

I thought to myself, as so often before, that modesty was certainly not Hercule Poirot's strong point.

" And what did I do next?" continued Poirot.

I guessed that for some time now he had no one much to talk to and was enjoying the sound of his own voice.

" From real life I turned to fiction. You see me here with various examples of criminal fiction at my right hand and my left. I have been working backwards. Here——" he picked up the volume that he had laid on the arm of his chair when I entered, "——here, my dear Colin, is *The Leavenworth Case*." He handed the book to me.

" That's going back quite a long time," I said. " I believe my father mentioned that he read it as a boy. I believe I once read it myself. It must seem rather old-fashioned now."

" It is admirable," said Poirot. " One savours its period atmosphere, its studied and deliberate melodrama. Those rich and lavish descriptions of the golden beauty of Eleanor, the moonlight beauty of Mary!"

" I must read it again," I said. " I'd forgotten the parts about the beautiful girls."

" And there is the maid-servant, Hannah, so true to type, and the murderer, an excellent psychological study."

I perceived that I had let myself in for a lecture. I composed myself to listen.

" Then we will take the *Adventures of Arsene Lupin*," Poirot went on. " How fantastic, how unreal. And yet what vitality there is in them, what vigour, what life! They are preposterous, but they have panache. There is humour, too."

He laid down the *Adventures of Arsene Lupin* and picked up another book. " And there is *The Mystery of the Yellow Room*. That—ah, that is really a *classic*! I approve of it from start to finish. Such a logical approach! There were criticisms of it, I remember, which said that it was unfair. But it is not unfair, my dear Colin. No, no. Very nearly so, perhaps, but not quite. There is the hair's breadth of difference. No. All through there is truth, concealed with a careful and cunning use of words. Everything should be clear at that supreme moment when the men meet at the angle of three corridors." He laid it down reverently. " Definitely a masterpiece, and, I gather, almost forgotten nowadays."

Poirot skipped twenty years or so, to approach the works of somewhat later authors.

"I have read also," he said, "some of the early works of Mrs. Ariadne Oliver. She is by way of being a friend of mine, and of yours, I think. I do not wholly approve of her works, mind you. The happenings in them are highly improbable. The long arm of coincidence is far too freely employed. And, being young at the time, she was foolish enough to make her detective a Finn, and it is clear that she knows nothing about Finns or Finland except possibly the works of Sibelius. Still, she has an original habit of mind, she makes an occasional shrewd deduction, and of later years she has learnt a good deal about things which she did not know before. Police procedure for instance. She is also now a little more reliable on the subject of firearms. What was even more needed, she has possibly acquired a solicitor or a barrister friend who has put her right on certain points of the law."

He laid aside Mrs. Ariadne Oliver and picked up another book.

"Now here is Mr. Cyril Quain. Ah, he is a master, Mr. Quain, of the *alibi*."

"He's a deadly dull writer if I remember rightly," I said.

"It is true," said Poirot, "that nothing particularly thrilling happens in his books. There is a corpse, of course. Occasionally more than one. But the whole point is always the *alibi*, the railway time-table, the bus routes, the plans of the cross-country roads. I confess I enjoy this intricate, this elaborate use of the *alibi*. I enjoy trying to catch Mr. Cyril Quain out."

"And I suppose you always succeed," I said.

Poirot was honest.

"Not always," he admitted. "No, not always. Of course, after a time one realises that one book of his is almost exactly like another. The *alibis* resemble each other every time, even though they are not exactly the same. You know, *mon cher* Colin, I imagine this Cyril Quain sitting in his room, smoking his pipe as he is represented to do in his photographs, sitting there with around him the A.B.C.s, the continental Bradshaws, the air-line brochures, the time-tables of every kind. Even the movements of liners. Say what you will, Colin, there is order and method in Mr. Cyril Quain."

He laid Mr. Quain down and picked up another book.

all authors from the top 87

"Now here is Mr. Garry Gregson, a prodigious writer of thrillers. He has written at least sixty-four, I understand. He is almost the exact opposite of Mr. Quain. In Mr. Quain's books nothing much happens, in Garry Gregson's far too many things happen. They happen implausibly and in mass confusion. They are all highly coloured. It is melodrama stirred up with a stick. Bloodshed—bodies—clues—thrills piled up and bulging over. All lurid, all very unlike life. He is not quite, as you would say, my cup of tea. He is, in fact, not a cup of tea at all. He is more like one of these American cocktails of the more obscure kind, whose ingredients are highly suspect."

Poirot paused, sighed and resumed his lecture. "Then we turn to America." He plucked a book from the left-hand pile. "Florence Elks, now. There is order and method there, colourful happenings, yes, but plenty of point in them. Gay and alive. She has wit, this lady, though perhaps, like so many American writers, a little too obsessed with drink. I am, as you know, *mon ami*, a connoisseur of wine. A claret or a burgundy introduced into a story, with its vintage and date properly authenticated I always find pleasing. But the exact amounts of rye and bourbon that are consumed on every other page by the detective in an American thriller do not seem to me interesting at all. Whether he drinks a pint or a half-pint which he takes from his collar drawer does not seem to me really to affect the action of the story in any way. This drink motive in American books is very much what King Charles's head was to poor Mr. Dick when he tried to write his memoirs. Impossible to keep it out."

"What about the tough school?" I asked.

Poirot waved aside the tough school much as he would have waved an intruding fly or mosquito.

"Violence for violence' sake? Since when has that been interesting? I have seen plenty of violence in my early career as a police officer. Bah, you might as well read a medical text book. *Tout de même*, I give American crime fiction on the whole a pretty high place. I think it is more ingenious, more imaginative than English writing. It is less atmospheric and over-laden with atmosphere than most French writers. Now take Louisa O'Malley for instance."

He dived once more for a book.

"What a model of fine scholarly writing is hers, yet what excitement, what mounting apprehension she arouses in her reader. Those brownstone mansions in New York. *Enfin,* what *is* a brownstone mansion—I have never known? Those exclusive apartments, and soulful snobberies, and underneath, deep unsuspected seams of crime run their uncharted course. It *could* happen so, and it *does* happen so. She is very good, this Louisa O'Malley, she is very good indeed."

He sighed, leaned back, shook his head and drank off the remainder of his tisane.

"And then—there are always the old favourites."

Again he dived for a book.

"*The Adventures of Sherlock Holmes,*" he murmured lovingly, and even uttered reverently the one word, "*Maître!*"

"Sherlock Holmes?" I asked.

"Ah, *non, non,* not Sherlock Holmes! It is the author, Sir Arthur Conan Doyle, that I salute. These tales of Sherlock Holmes are in reality far-fetched, full of fallacies and most artificially contrived. But the art of the writing—ah, that is entirely different. The pleasure of the language, the creation above all of that magnificent character, Dr. Watson. Ah, that was indeed a triumph."

He sighed and shook his head, and murmured, obviously by a natural association of ideas,

"*Ce cher* Hastings. My friend Hastings of whom you have often heard me speak. It is a long time since I have had news of him. What an absurdity to go and bury oneself in South America, where they are always having revolutions."

"That's not confined to South America," I pointed out. "They're having revolutions all over the world nowadays."

"Let us not discuss the Bomb," said Hercule Poirot. "If it has to be, it has to be, but let us not discuss it."

"Actually," I said, "I came to discuss something quite different with you."

"Ah! You are about to be married, is that it? I am delighted, *mon cher,* delighted."

"What on earth put that in your head, Poirot?" I asked. "Nothing of the kind."

"It happens," said Poirot, "it happens every day."

"Perhaps," I said firmly, "but not to me. Actually I came

to tell you that I'd run across rather a pretty little problem in murder."

"Indeed? A pretty problem in murder, you say? And you have brought it to *me*. Why?"

"Well——" I was slightly embarrassed. "I—I thought you might enjoy it," I said.

Poirot looked at me thoughtfully. He caressed his moustache with a loving hand, then he spoke.

"A master," he said, "is often kind to his dog. He goes out and throws a ball for the dog. A dog, however, is also capable of being kind to its master. A dog kills a rabbit or a rat and he brings it and lays it at his master's feet. And what does he do then? He wags his tail."

I laughed in spite of myself. "Am I wagging my tail?"

"I think you are, my friend. Yes, I think you are."

"All right then," I said. "And what does master say? Does he want to see doggy's rat? Does he want to know all about it?"

"Of course. Naturally. It is a crime that you think will interest me. Is that right?"

"The whole point of it is," I said, "that it just doesn't make sense."

"That is impossible," said Poirot. "Everything makes sense. Everything."

"Well, you try and make sense of this. *I* can't. Not that it's really anything to do with me. I just happened to come in on it. Mind you, it may turn out to be quite straightforward, once the dead man is identified."

"You are talking without method or order," said Poirot severely. "Let me beg of you to let me have the facts. You say it is a murder, yes?"

"It's a murder all right," I assured him. "Well, here we go."

I described to him in detail the events that had taken place at 19, Wilbraham Crescent. Hercule Poirot leant back in his chair. He closed his eyes and gently tapped with a forefinger the arm of his chair while he listened to my recital. When I finally stopped, he did not speak for a moment. Then he asked, without opening his eyes:

"*Sans blague?*"

incroyable, amazing!

"Oh, absolutely," I said.

"*Epatant*," said Hercule Poirot. He savoured the word on his tongue and repeated it syllable by syllable. "*E-pa-tant*." After that he continued his tapping on the arm of his chair and gently nodded his head.

"Well," I said impatiently, after waiting a few moments more. "What have you got to say?"

"But what do you want me to say?"

"I want you to give me the solution. I've always understood from you that it was perfectly possible to lie back in one's chair, just think about it all, and come up with the answer. That it was quite unnecessary to go and question people and run about looking for clues."

"It is what I have always maintained."

"Well, I'm calling your bluff," I said. "I've given you the facts, and now I want the answer."

"Just like that, hein? But then there is a lot more to be known, *mon ami*. We are only at the *beginning* of the facts. Is that not so?"

"I still want you to come up with *something*."

"I see." He reflected a moment. "One thing is certain," he pronounced. "It must be a very simple crime."

"Simple?" I demanded in some astonishment.

"Naturally."

"Why must it be simple?"

"Because it appears so complex. If it has necessarily to appear complex, it *must* be simple. You comprehend that?"

"I don't really know that I do."

"Curious," mused Poirot, "what you have told me—I think—yes, there is something familiar to me there. Now where—when—have I come across something . . ." He paused.

"Your memory," I said, "must be one vast reservoir of crimes. But you can't possibly remember them all, can you?"

"Unfortunately no," said Poirot, "but from time to time these reminiscences are helpful. There was a soap boiler, I remember, once, at Liége. He poisoned his wife in order to marry a blonde stenographer. The crime made a pattern. Later, much later, that pattern recurred. I recognised it. This time it was an affair of a kidnapped pekinese dog, but the *pattern* was the same. I looked for the equivalent of the blonde stenographer and the soap boiler, and *voilà*! That is the kind of thing. And here again in what you have told me I have that feeling of recognition."

"Clocks?" I suggested hopefully. "Bogus insurance agents?"

"No, no," Poirot shook his head.

"Blind women?"

"No, no, no. Do not confuse me."

"I'm disappointed in you, Poirot," I said. "I thought you'd give me the answer straight away."

"But, my friend, at present you have presented me only with a *pattern*. There are many more things to find out. Presumably this man will be identified. In that kind of thing the police are excellent. They have their criminal records, they can advertise the man's picture, they have access to a list of missing persons, there is scientific examination of the dead man's clothing, and so on and so on. Oh, yes, there are a hundred other ways and means at their disposal. Undoubtedly, this man will be identified."

"So there's nothing to do at the moment. Is that what you think?"

"There is always something to do," said Hercule Poirot, severely.

"Such as?"

He wagged an emphatic forefinger at me.

"Talk to the neighbours," he said.

"I've done that," I said. "I went with Hardcastle when he was questioning them. They don't know anything useful."

"Ah, tcha, tcha, that is what *you* think. But I assure you, that cannot be so. You go to them, you ask them: 'Have you seen anything suspicious?' and they say no, and you think that that is all there is to it. But that is not what I mean when I say talk to the neighbours. I say *talk* to them. Let them talk to *you*. And from their conversation always, somewhere, you will find a clue. They may be talking about their gardens or their pets or their hairdressing or their dress-maker, or their friends, or the kind of food they like. Always somewhere there will be a word that sheds light. You say there was nothing in those conversations that was useful. I say that cannot be so. If you could repeat them to me word for word . . ."

"Well, that's practically what I can do," I said. "I took shorthand transcripts of what was said, acting in my role of assistant police officer. I've had them transcribed and typed and I've brought them along to you. Here they are."

"Ah, but you are a good boy, you are a very good boy indeed! What you have done is exactly right. Exactly. *Je vous remercie infiniment*."

I felt quite embarrassed.

"Have you any more suggestions?" I asked.

"Yes, always I have suggestions. There is this girl. You can talk to this girl. Go and see her. Already you are friends, are you not? Have you not clasped her in your arms when she flew from the house in terror?"

"You've been affected by reading Garry Gregson," I said. "You've caught the melodramatic style."

"Perhaps you are right," Poirot admitted. "One gets infected, it is true, by the style of a work that one has been reading."

"As for the girl——" I said, then paused.

Poirot looked at me inquiringly.

"Yes?" he said.

"I shouldn't like—I don't want . . ."

"Ah, so that is it. At the back of your mind you think she is concerned somehow in this case."

"No, I don't. It was absolutely pure chance that she happened to be there."

"No, no, *mon ami*, it was not pure chance. You know that very well. You've told me so. She was asked for over the telephone. Asked for specially."

"But she doesn't know why."

"You cannot be sure that she does not know why. Very likely she *does* know why and is hiding the fact."

"I don't think so," I said obstinately.

"It is even possible you may find out why by talking to her, even if she herself does not realise the truth."

"I don't see very well how—I mean—I hardly know her."

Hercule Poirot shut his eyes again.

"There is a time," he said, " in the course of an attraction between two persons of the opposite sex, when that particular statement is bound to be true. She is an attractive girl, I suppose?"

"Well—yes," I said, "Quite attractive."

"You will talk to her," Poirot ordered, "because you are already friends, and you will go and see again this blind woman with some excuse. And you will talk to *her*. And you will go to the typewriting bureau on the pretence perhaps of having some manuscript typed. You will make friends, perhaps, with one of the other young ladies who works there. You will talk to all these people and then you will come and see me again and you will tell me all the things that they will say."

"Have mercy!" I said.

"Not at all," said Poirot, "you will enjoy it."

"You don't seem to realise that I've got my own work to do."

"You will work all the better for having a certain amount of relaxation," Poirot assured me.

I got up and laughed.

"Well," I said, "you're the doctor! Any more words of wisdom for me? What do you feel about this strange business of the clocks?"

Poirot leaned back in his chair again and closed his eyes. The words he spoke were quite unexpected.

>   "'The time has come, the Walrus said,
>   To talk of many things.
>   Of shoes and ships and sealing wax,
>   And cabbages and kings.
>   And why the sea is boiling hot
>   And whether pigs have wings.'"

He opened his eyes again and nodded his head.

"Do you understand?" he said.

"Quotation from 'The Walrus and the Carpenter,' *Alice Through the Looking Glass*."

"Exactly. For the moment, that is the best I can do for you, *mon cher*. Reflect upon it."

CHAPTER 15

The inquest was well attended by the general public. Thrilled by a murder in their midst, Crowdean turned out with eager hopes of sensational disclosures. The proceedings, however, were as dry as they could be. Sheila Webb need not have dreaded her ordeal, it was over in a couple of minutes.

There had been a telephone message to the Cavendish Bureau directing her to go to 19, Wilbraham Crescent. She had gone, acting as told to do, by entering the sitting-room. She had found the dead man there and had screamed and rushed out of the house to summon assistance. There were no questions or elaborations. Miss Martindale, who also gave evidence, was questioned for an even shorter time. She had received a message purporting to be from Miss Pebmarsh asking her to send a shorthand typist, preferably Miss Sheila Webb, to 19, Wilbraham Crescent, and giving certain directions. She had noted down the exact time of the telephone call as 1.49. That disposed of Miss Martindale.

Miss Pebmarsh, called next, denied categorically that she had asked for *any* typist to be sent to her that day from the Cavendish Bureau. Detective Inspector Hardcastle made a short emotionless statement. On receipt of a telephone call, he had gone to 19, Wilbraham Crescent where he had found the body of a dead man. The coroner then asked him:

" Have you been able to identify the dead man? "

" Not as yet, sir. For that reason, I would ask for this inquest to be adjourned."

" Quite so."

Then came the medical evidence. Doctor Rigg, the police surgeon, having described himself and his qualifications, told of his arrival at 19, Wilbraham Crescent, and of his examination of the dead man.

" Can you give us an approximate idea of the time of death, Doctor? "

" I examined him at half past three. I should put the time of death as between half past one and half past two."

" You cannot put it nearer than that? "

" I should prefer not to do so. At a guess, the most likely time would be two o'clock or rather earlier, but there are many factors which have to be taken into account. Age, state of health, and so on."

" You performed an autopsy?"

" I did."

" The cause of death?"

" The man had been stabbed with a thin, sharp knife. Something in the nature, perhaps, of a French cooking-knife with a tapering blade. The point of the knife entered . . ." Here the doctor became technical as he explained the exact position where the knife had entered the heart.

" Would death have been instantaneous?"

" It would have occurred within a very few minutes."

" The man would not have cried out or struggled?"

" Not under the circumstances in which he was stabbed."

" Will you explain to us, Doctor, what you mean by that phrase?"

" I made an examination of certain organs and made certain tests. I would say that when he was killed he was in a state of coma due to the administration of a drug."

" Can you tell us what this drug was, Doctor?"

" Yes. It was chloral hydrate."

" Can you tell how this was administered?"

" I should say presumably in alcohol of some kind. The effect of chloral hydrate is very rapid."

" Known in certain quarters as a Mickey Finn, I believe," murmured the coroner.

" That is quite correct," said Doctor Rigg. " He would drink the liquid unsuspectingly, and a few moments later he would reel over and fall unconscious."

" And he was stabbed, in your opinion, while unconscious?"

" That is my belief. It would account for there being no sign of a struggle and for his peaceful appearance."

" How long after becoming unconscious was he killed?"

" That I cannot say with any accuracy. There again it depends on the personal idiosyncrasy of the victim. He would certainly not come round under half an hour and it might be a good deal more than that."

" Thank you, Doctor Rigg. Have you any evidence as to when this man last had a meal?"

" He had not lunched if that is what you mean. He had eaten no solid food for at least four hours."

" Thank you, Doctor Rigg. I think that is all."

The coroner then looked round and said,

" The inquest will be adjourned for a fortnight, until September 28th."

The inquest concluded, people began to move out of the court. Edna Brent who, with most of the other girls at the Cavendish Bureau, had been present, hesitated as she got outside the door. The Cavendish Secretarial Bureau had been closed for the morning. Maureen West, one of the other girls, spoke to her.

" What about it, Edna? Shall we go to the Bluebird for lunch? We've got heaps of time. At any rate, *you* have."

" I haven't got any more time than you have," said Edna in an injured voice. " Sandy Cat told me I'd better take the first interval for lunch. Mean of her. I thought I'd get a good extra hour for shopping and things."

" Just like Sandy Cat," said Maureen. " Mean as hell, isn't she? We open up again at two and we've all got to be there. Are you looking for anyone?"

" Only Sheila. I didn't see her come out."

" She went away earlier," said Maureen, " after she'd finished giving her evidence. She went off with a young man —but I didn't see who he was. Are you coming?"

Edna still hovered uncertainly, and said, " You go on— I've got shopping to do anyway."

Maureen and another girl went off together. Edna lingered. Finally she nerved herself to speak to the fair-haired young policeman who stood at the entrance.

" Could I go in again?" she murmured timidly, " and speak to—to the one who came to the office—Inspector something."

" Inspector Hardcastle?"

" That's right. The one who was giving evidence this morning."

" Well——" the young policeman looked into the court and observed the inspector in deep consultation with the coroner and with the chief constable of the county.

" He looks busy at the moment, miss," he said. " If you

called round at the station later, or if you'd like to give me a message . . . Is it anything important?"

"Oh, it doesn't matter really," said Edna. "It's—well—just that I don't see how what she said could have been true because I mean . . ." She turned away, still frowning perplexedly.

She wandered away from the Cornmarket and along the High Street. She was still frowning perplexedly and trying to think. Thinking had never been Edna's strong point. The more she tried to get things clear in her mind, the more muddled her mind became.

Once she said aloud:

"But it couldn't have been like that . . . It couldn't have been like she said . . ."

Suddenly, with an air of one making a resolution, she turned off from the High Street and along Albany Road in the direction of Wilbraham Crescent.

Since the day that the Press had announced that a murder had been committed at 19, Wilbraham Crescent, large numbers of people had gathered in front of the house every day to have a good look at it. The fascination mere bricks and mortar can have for the general public under certain circumstances is a truly mysterious thing. For the first twenty-four hours a policeman had been stationed there to pass people along in an authoritative manner. Since then interest had lessened; but had still not ceased entirely. Tradesmen's delivery vans would slacken speed a little as they passed, women wheeling prams would come to a four or five minute stop on the opposite pavement and stare their eyes out as they contemplated Miss Pebmarsh's neat residence. Shopping women with baskets would pause with avid eyes and exchange pleasurable gossip with friends.

"That's the house—that one there . . ."

"The body was in the sitting-room . . . No, I think the sitting-room's the room at the front, the one on the left . . ."

"The grocer's man told me it was the one on the right."

"Well, of course it might be, I've been into Number 10 once and there, I distinctly remember the *dining*-room was on the right, and the sitting-room was on the left . . ."

"It doesn't look a bit as though there had been a murder done there, does it . . .?"

" The girl, I believe, came out of the gate screaming her head off . . ."

" They say she's not been right in her head since . . . Terrible shock, of course . . ."

" He broke in by a back window, so they say. He was putting the silver in a bag when this girl came in and found him there . . ."

" The poor woman who owns the house, she's *blind*, poor soul. So, of course, *she* couldn't know what was going on."

" Oh, but she wasn't *there* at the time . . ."

" Oh, I thought she *was*. I thought she was upstairs and heard him. Oh, dear, I *must* get on to the shops."

These and similar conversations went on most of the time. Drawn as though by a magnet, the most unlikely people arrived in Wilbraham Crescent, paused, stared, and then passed on, some inner need satisfied.

Here, still puzzling in her mind—Edna Brent found herself jostling a small group of five or six people who were engaged in the favourite pastime of looking at the murder house.

Edna, always suggestible, stared also.

So that was the house where it happened! Net curtains in the windows. Looked ever so nice. And yet a man had been killed there. Killed with a kitchen knife. An ordinary kitchen knife. Nearly everybody had got a kitchen knife . . .

Mesmerised by the behaviour of the people round her, Edna, too, stared and ceased to think . . .

She had almost forgotten what had brought her here . . .

She started when a voice spoke in her ear.

She turned her head in surprised recognition.

CHAPTER 16

COLIN'S NARRATIVE

I noticed when Sheila Webb slipped quietly out of the Coroner's Court. She'd given her evidence very well. She had looked nervous but not unduly nervous. Just natural, in fact. (What would Beck say? " Quite a good performance." I could hear him say it!)

I took in the surprise finish of Doctor Rigg's evidence, (Dick Hardcastle hadn't told me that, but he must have known) and then I went after her.

"It wasn't so bad after all, was it?" I said, when I had caught her up.

"No. It was quite easy really. The coroner was very nice." She hesitated. "What will happen next?"

"He'll adjourn the inquest—for further evidence. A fortnight probably or until they can identify the dead man."

"You think they *will* identify him?"

"Oh, yes," I said. "They'll identify him all right. No doubt of that."

She shivered. "It's cold to-day."

It wasn't particularly cold. In fact I thought it was rather warm.

"What about an early lunch?" I suggested. "You haven't got to go back to your typewriting place, have you?"

"No. It's closed until two o'clock."

"Come along then. How do you react to Chinese food? I see there's a little Chinese restaurant just down the street."

Sheila looked hesitant.

"I've really got to do some shopping."

"You can do it afterwards."

"No, I can't—some of the shops close between one and two."

"All right then. Will you meet me there? In half an hour's time?"

She said she would.

I went along to the sea front and sat there in a shelter. As the wind was blowing straight in from the sea, I had it to myself.

I wanted to think. It always infuriates one when other people know more about you than you know about yourself. But old Beck and Hercule Poirot and Dick Hardcastle, they all had seen quite clearly what I was now forced to admit to myself was true.

I minded about this girl—minded in a way I had never minded about a girl before.

It wasn't her beauty—she was pretty, pretty in rather an unusual way, no more. It wasn't her sex appeal—I had met that often enough—had been given the full treatment.

It was just that, almost from the first, I had recognised that she was *my* girl.

And I didn't know the first damned thing about her!

It was just after two o'clock that I walked into the station and asked for Dick. I found him at his desk leafing over a pile of stuff. He looked up and asked me what I had thought of the inquest.

I told him I thought it had been a very nicely managed and gentlemanly performance.

" We do this sort of thing so well in this country."

" What did you think of the medical evidence?"

" Rather a facer. Why didn't you tell me about it?"

" You were away. Did you consult your specialist?"

" Yes, I did."

" I believe I remember him vaguely. A lot of moustache."

" Oceans of it," I agreed. " He's very proud of that moustache."

" He must be quite old."

" Old but not ga-ga," I said.

" Why did you really go to see him? Was it purely the milk of human kindness?"

" You have such a suspicious policeman's mind, Dick! It was mainly that. But I admit to curiosity, too. I wanted to hear what he had to say about our own particular set-up. You see, he's always talked what I call a lot of cock about its being easy to solve a case by just sitting in your chair, bringing the tips of your fingers symmetrically together, closing your eyes and thinking. I wanted to call his bluff."

" Did he go through that procedure for you?"

" He did."

" And what did he say?" Dick asked with some curiosity.

" He said," I told him, " that it must be a very *simple* murder."

" Simple, my God!" said Hardcastle, roused. " Why simple?"

" As far as I could gather," I said, " because the whole set-up was so complex."

Hardcastle shook his head. "I don't see it," he said. "It sounds like one of those clever things that young people in Chelsea say, but I don't see it. Anything else?"

"Well, he told me to talk to the neighbours. I assured him we had done so."

"The neighbours are even more important now in view of the medical evidence."

"The presumption being that he was doped somewhere else and brought to Number 19 to be killed?"

Something familiar about the words struck me.

"That's more or less what Mrs. What's-her-name, the cat woman said. It struck me at the time as a rather interesting remark."

"Those cats," said Dick, and shuddered. He went on: "We've found the weapon, by the way. Yesterday."

"You have? Where?"

"In the cattery. Presumably thrown there by the murderer after the crime."

"No fingerprints, I suppose?"

"Carefully wiped. And it could be anybody's knife—slightly used—recently sharpened."

"So it goes like this. He was doped—then brought to Number 19—in a car? Or how?"

"He *could* have been brought from one of the houses with an adjoining garden."

"Bit risky, wouldn't it have been?"

"It would need audacity," Hardcastle agreed, "and it would need a very good knowledge of the neighbourhood's habits. It's more likely that he would have been brought in a car."

"That would have been risky too. People notice a car."

"Nobody did. But I agree that the murderer couldn't know that they wouldn't. Passers-by would have noted a car stopping at Number 19 that day——"

"I wonder if they *would* notice," I said. "Everyone's so used to cars. Unless, of course, it had been a very lush car—something unusual, but that's not likely——"

"And of course it was the lunch hour. You realise, Colin, that this brings Miss Millicent Pebmarsh back into the picture? It seems far-fetched to think of an able-bodied man being stabbed by a blind woman—but if he was doped——"

" In other words ' if he came there to be killed,' as our Mrs. Hemming put it, he arrived by appointment quite unsuspiciously, was offered a sherry or a cocktail—the Mickey Finn took effect and Miss Pebmarsh got to work. Then she washed up the Mickey Finn glass, arranged the body neatly on the floor, threw the knife into her neighbour's garden, and tripped out as usual."

" Telephoning to the Cavendish Secretarial Bureau on the way——"

" And why should she do that? And ask particularly for Sheila Webb?"

" I wish we knew." Hardcastle looked at me. " Does *she* know? The girl herself?"

" She says not."

" She says not," Hardcastle repeated tonelessly. " I'm asking you what *you* think about it?"

I didn't speak for a moment or two. What *did* I think? I had to decide right now on my course of action. The truth would come out in the end. It would do Sheila no harm if she were what I believed her to be.

With a brusque movement I pulled a postcard out of my pocket and shoved it across the table.

" Sheila got this through the post."

Hardcastle scanned it. It was one of a series of postcards of London buildings. It represented the Central Criminal Court. Hardcastle turned it over. On the right was the address—in neat printing. Miss R. S. Webb, 14, Palmerston Road, Crowdean, Sussex. On the left hand side, also printed, was the word REMEMBER! and below it 4.13.

" 4.13," said Hardcastle. " That was the time the clocks showed that day." He shook his head. " A picture of the Old Bailey, the word ' Remember ' and a time—4.13. It *must* tie up with something."

" She says she doesn't know what it means." I added; " I believe her."

Hardcastle nodded.

" I'm keeping this. We may get something from it."

" I hope you do."

There was embarrassment between us. To relieve it, I said:

useless info

"You've got a lot of bumf there."

"All the usual. And most of it no damned good. The dead man hadn't got a criminal record, his fingerprints aren't on file. Practically all this stuff is from people who claim to have recognised him." He read:

"'Dear Sir, the picture that was in the paper I'm almost sure is the same as a man who was catching a train at Willesden Junction the other day. He was muttering to himself and looking very wild and excited, I thought when I saw him there must be something wrong.'

"'Dear Sir, I think this man looks very like my husband's cousin John. He went abroad to South Africa but it may be that he's come back. He had a moustache when he went away but of course he could have shaved that off.'

"'Dear Sir, I saw the man in the paper in a tube train last night. I thought at the time there was something peculiar about him.'

"And of course there are all the women who recognise husbands. Women don't really seem to know what their husbands look like! There are hopeful mothers who recognise sons they have not seen for twenty years.

"And here's the list of missing persons. Nothing here likely to help us. 'George Barlow, 65, missing from home. His wife thinks he must have lost his memory.' And a note below 'Owes a lot of money. Has been seen going about with a red-haired widow. Almost certain to have done a bunk.'

"Next one; 'Professor Hargraves, expected to deliver a lecture last Tuesday. Did not turn up and sent no wire or note of excuse.'"

Hardcastle did not appear to consider Professor Hargraves seriously.

"Thought the lecture was the week before or the week after," he said. "Probably thought he had told his housekeeper where he was going but hasn't done so. We get a lot of that."

The buzzer on Hardcastle's table sounded. He picked up the receiver.

"Yes? . . . What? . . . Who found her? Did she give her name? . . . I see. Carry on." He put down the receiver again. His face as he turned to me was a changed face. It was stern, almost vindictive.

"They've found a girl dead in a telephone box on Wilbraham Crescent," he said.

"Dead?" I stared at him. "How?"

"Strangled. With her own scarf!"

I felt suddenly cold.

"What girl? It's not——"

Hardcastle looked at me with a cold, appraising glance that I didn't like.

"It's not your girl friend," he said, "if that's what you're afraid of. The constable there seems to know who she is. He says she's a girl who works in the same office as Sheila Webb. Edna Brent her name is."

"Who found her? The constable?"

"She was found by Miss Waterhouse, the woman from Number 18. It seems she went to the box to make a telephone call as her phone was out of order and found the girl there huddled down in a heap."

The door opened and a police constable said,

"Doctor Rigg telephones that he's on his way, sir. He'll meet you at Wilbraham Crescent."

CHAPTER 17

It was an hour and a half later and Detective Inspector Hardcastle sat down behind his desk and accepted with relief an official cup of tea. His face still held its bleak, angry look.

"Excuse me, sir, Pierce would like a word with you."

Hardcastle roused himself.

"Pierce? Oh, all right. Send him in."

Pierce entered, a nervous-looking young constable.

"Excuse me, sir, I thought per'aps as I ought to tell you."

"Yes? Tell me what?"

"It was after the inquest, sir. I was on duty at the door. This girl—this girl that's been killed. She—she spoke to me."

"Spoke to you, did she? What did she say?"

"She wanted to have a word with you, sir."

Hardcastle sat up, suddenly alert.

"She wanted to have a word with me? Did she say why?"

"Not exactly, sir. I'm sorry, sir, if I—if I ought to have

done something about it. I asked her if she could give me a message or—or if perhaps she could come to the station later on. You see, you were busy with the chief constable and the coroner and I thought——"

"Damn!" said Hardcastle, under his breath. "Couldn't you have told her just to wait until I was free?"

"I'm sorry, sir." The young man flushed. "I suppose if I'd known, I ought to have done so. But I didn't think it was anything important. I don't think *she* thought it was important. It was just something she said she was worried about."

"Worried?" said Hardcastle. He was silent for quite a minute turning over in his mind certain facts. This was the girl he had passed in the street when he was going to Mrs. Lawton's house, the girl who had wanted to see Sheila Webb. The girl who had recognised him as she passed him and had hesitated a moment as though uncertain whether to stop him or not. She'd had something on her mind. Yes, that was it. Something on her mind. He'd slipped up. He'd not been quick enough on the ball. Filled with his own purpose of finding out a little more about Sheila Webb's background, he had overlooked a valuable point. The girl had been worried? Why? Now, probably, they'd never know why.

"Go on, Pierce," he said, "tell me all you can remember." He added kindly, for he was a fair man: "You couldn't know that it was important."

It wasn't, he knew, any good to pass on his own anger and frustration by blaming it on this boy. How should the boy have known? Part of his training was to uphold discipline, to make sure that his superiors were only accosted at the proper times and in the proper places. If the girl had said it was important or urgent, that would have been different. But she hadn't been, he thought, remembering his first view of her in the office, that kind of girl. A slow thinker. A girl probably distrustful of her own mental processes.

"Can you remember exactly what happened, and what she said to you, Pierce?" he asked.

Pierce was looking at him with a kind of eager gratitude.

"Well, sir, she just come up to me when everyone was leaving and she sort of hesitated a moment and looked round just as though she were looking for someone. Not you, sir, I don't think. Somebody else. Then she come up to me and said could she speak to the police officer, and she said the one that had given evidence. So, as I said, I saw you were busy with the chief constable so I explained to her that you were engaged just now, could she give me a message or contact you later at the station. And I think she said that would do quite well. I said was it anything particular . . ."

"Yes?" Hardcastle leaned forward.

"And she said well not really. It was just something, she said, that she didn't see how it could have been the way she'd said it was."

"She didn't see how what she said could have been like that?" Hardcastle repeated.

"That's right, sir. I'm not sure of the exact words. Perhaps it was: 'I don't see how what she said can have been true.' She was frowning and looking puzzled-like. But when I asked her, she said it wasn't really important."

Not really important, the girl had said. The same girl who had been found not long afterwards strangled in a telephone box . . .

"Was anybody near you at the time she was talking to you?" he asked.

"Well, there were a good many people, sir, filing out, you know. There'd been a lot of people attending the inquest. It's caused quite a stir, this murder has, what with the way the Press have taken it up and all."

"You don't remember anyone in particular who was near you at the time—any of the people who'd given evidence, for instance?"

"I'm afraid I don't recall anyone in particular, sir."

"Well," said Hardcastle, "it can't be helped. All right, Pierce, if you remember anything further, come to me at once with it."

Left alone he made an effort to subdue his rising anger and self-condemnation. That girl, that rabbity-looking girl, had known something. No, perhaps not put it as high as *known*, but she had seen something, heard something. Something that had worried her; and the worry had been intensified after attending the inquest. What could it have been? Something in the evidence? Something, in all probability, in Sheila Webb's evidence? Had she gone to Sheila's aunt's house two days before on purpose to see Sheila. Surely she could have talked to Sheila at the office? Why did she want to see her privately? Did she know something about Sheila Webb that perplexed her? Did she want to ask Sheila for an explanation of whatever it was, somewhere in private—not in front of the other girls? It looked that way. It certainly looked like it.

He dismissed Pierce. Then he gave a few directions to Sergeant Cray.

"What do you think the girl went to Wilbraham Crescent *for*?" Sergeant Cray asked.

"I've been wondering about that," said Hardcastle. "It's possible, of course, that she just suffered from curiosity— wanted to see what the place looked like. There's nothing unusual about that—half the population of Crowdean seems to feel the same."

"Don't we know it," said Sergeant Cray with feeling.

"On the other hand," said Hardcastle slowly, "she may have gone to see someone who lived there . . ."

When Sergeant Cray had gone out again, Hardcastle wrote down three numbers on his blotting pad.

"20," he wrote, and put a query after it. He added: "19?" and then "18?" He wrote names to correspond. Hemming, Pebmarsh, Waterhouse. The three houses in the higher crescent were out of it. To visit one of them Edna Brent would not have gone along the lower road at all.

Hardcastle studied the three possibilities.

He took No. 20 first. The knife used in the original murder had been found there. It seemed more likely that the knife had been thrown there from the garden of No. 19 but they didn't *know* that it had. It *could* have been thrust into the shrubbery by the owner of No. 20 herself. When questioned, Mrs. Hemming's only reaction had been indignation. "How wicked of someone to throw a nasty knife like that at my cats!" she had said. How did Mrs. Hemming connect up with Edna Brent? She didn't, Inspector Hardcastle decided. He went on to consider Miss Pebmarsh.

Had Edna Brent gone to Wilbraham Crescent to call on Miss Pebmarsh? Miss Pebmarsh had given evidence at the inquest. Had there been something in that evidence which had aroused disbelief in Edna? But she had been worried *before* the inquest. Had she already known something about

Miss Pebmarsh? Had she known, for instance, that there was a link of some kind between Miss Pebmarsh and Sheila Webb? That would fit in with her words to Pierce. " It couldn't have been true what she said."

" Conjecture, all conjecture," he thought angrily.

And No. 18? Miss Waterhouse had found the body. Inspector Hardcastle was professionally prejudiced against people who found bodies. Finding the body avoided so many difficulties for a murderer—it saved the hazards of arranging an alibi, it accounted for any overlooked fingerprints. In many ways it was a cast-iron position—with one proviso only. There must be no obvious motive. There was certainly no apparent motive for Miss Waterhouse to do away with little Edna Brent. Miss Waterhouse had not given evidence at the inquest. She might have been there, though. Did Edna perhaps have some reason for knowing, or believing, that it was Miss Waterhouse who had impersonated Miss Pebmarsh over the telephone and asked for a shorthand typist to be sent to No. 19?

More conjecture.

And there was, of course, Sheila Webb herself. . . .

Hardcastle's hand went to the telephone. He got on to the hotel where Colin Lamb was staying. Presently he got Colin himself on the wire.

" Hardcastle here—what time was it when you lunched with Sheila Webb to-day?"

There was a pause before Colin answered:

" How do you know that we lunched together?"

" A damned good guess. You did, didn't you?"

" Why shouldn't I have lunch with her?"

" No reason at all. I'm merely asking you the time. Did you go off to lunch straight from the inquest?"

" No. She had shopping to do. We met at the Chinese place in Market Street at one o'clock."

" I see."

Hardcastle looked down at his notes. Edna Brent had died between 12.30 and one o'clock.

" Don't you want to know what we had for lunch?"

" Keep your hair on. I just wanted the exact time. For the record."

" I see. It's like that."

E

There was a pause. Hardcastle said, endeavouring to ease the strain,

"If you're not doing anything this evening——"

The other interrupted.

"I'm off. Just packing up. I found a message waiting for me. I've got to go abroad."

"When will you be back?"

"That's anybody's guess. A week at least—perhaps longer —possibly never!"

"Bad luck—or isn't it?"

"I'm not sure," said Colin, and rang off.

CHAPTER 18

Hardcastle arrived at No. 19, Wilbraham Crescent just as Miss Pebmarsh was coming out of the house.

"Excuse me a minute, Miss Pebmarsh."

"Oh. Is it—Detective Inspector Hardcastle?"

"Yes. Can I have a word with you?"

"I don't want to be late at the Institute. Will it take long?"

"I assure you only three or four minutes."

She went into the house and he followed.

"You've heard what happened this afternoon?" he said.

"Has anything happened?"

"I thought you might have heard. A girl was killed in the telephone box just down the road."

"Killed? When?"

"Two hours and three quarters ago." He looked at the grandfather clock.

"I've heard nothing about it. Nothing," said Miss Pebmarsh. A kind of anger sounded momentarily in her voice. It was as though her disability had been brought home to her in some particularly wounding way. "A girl—killed! What girl?"

"Her name is Edna Brent and she worked at the Cavendish Secretarial Bureau."

"Another girl from there! Had she been sent for like this girl, Sheila what's-her-name was?"

"I don't think so," said the inspector. "She did not come to see you here, at your house?"

"Here? No. Certainly not."

"Would you have been in if she had come here?"

"I'm not sure. What time did you say?"

"Approximately twelve-thirty or a little later."

"Yes," said Miss Pebmarsh. "I would have been home by then."

"Where did you go after the inquest?"

"I came straight back here." She paused and then asked, "Why did you think this girl might have come to see me?"

"Well, she had been at the inquest this morning and she had seen you there, and she must have had *some* reason for coming to Wilbraham Crescent. As far as we know, she was not acquainted with anyone in this road."

"But why should she come to see me just because she had seen me at the inquest?"

"Well——" the inspector smiled a little, then hastily tried to put the smile into his voice as he realised that Miss Pebmarsh could not appreciate its disarming quality. "One never knows with these girls. She might just have wanted an autograph. Something like that."

"An autograph!" Miss Pebmarsh sounded scornful. Then she said, "Yes . . . Yes, I suppose you're right. That sort of thing does happen." Then she shook her head briskly. "I can only assure you, Inspector Hardcastle, that it did *not* happen to-day. Nobody has been here since I came back from the inquest."

"Well, thank you, Miss Pebmarsh. We thought we had better check up on every possibility."

"How old was she?" asked Miss Pebmarsh.

"I believe she was nineteen."

"Nineteen? Very young." Her voice changed slightly. "Very young . . . Poor child. Who could want to kill a girl of that age?"

"It happens," said Hardcastle.

"Was she pretty—attractive—sexy?"

"No," said Hardcastle. "She would have liked to be, I think, but she was not." - brutal

"Then that was not the reason," said Miss Pebmarsh.

She shook her head again. " I'm sorry. More sorry than I can say, Inspector Hardcastle, that I can't help you."

He went out, impressed as he always was impressed, by Miss Pebmarsh's personality.

II

Miss Waterhouse was also at home. She was also true to type, opening the door with a suddenness which displayed a desire to trap someone doing what they should not do.

" Oh, it's *you!* " she said. " Really, I've told your people all I know."

" I'm sure you've replied to all the questions that were asked you," said Hardcastle, " but they can't all be asked at once, you know. We have to go into a few more details."

" I don't see why. The whole thing was a most terrible shock," said Miss Waterhouse, looking at him in a censorious way as though it had been all his doing. " Come in, come in. You can't stand on the mat all day. Come in and sit down and ask me any questions you want to, though really what questions there can be, I cannot see. As I told you, I went out to make a telephone call. I opened the door of the box and there was the girl. Never had such a shock in my life. I hurried down and got the police constable. And after that, in case you want to know, I came back here and I gave myself a medicinal dose of brandy. *Medicinal*," said Miss Waterhouse fiercely.

" Very wise of you, madam," said Inspector Hardcastle.

" And that's that," said Miss Waterhouse with finality.

" I wanted to ask you if you were quite sure you had never seen this girl before?"

" May have seen her a dozen times," said Miss Waterhouse, " but not to remember. I mean, she may have served me in Woolworth's, or sat next to me in a bus, or sold me tickets in a cinema."

" She was a shorthand typist in the Cavendish Bureau."

" I don't think I've ever had occasion to use a shorthand typist. Perhaps she worked in my brother's office at Gainsford and Swettenham. Is that what you're driving at?"

" Oh, no," said Inspector Hardcastle, " there appears to be

no connection of that kind. But I just wondered if she'd come to see you this morning before being killed."

"Come to *see* me? No, of course not. Why should she?"

"Well, that we wouldn't know," said Inspector Hardcastle, "but you would say, would you, that anyone who saw her coming in at your gate this morning was mistaken?" He looked at her with innocent eyes.

"Somebody saw her coming in at my gate? Nonsense," said Miss Waterhouse. She hesitated. "At least——"

"Yes?" said Hardcastle, alert though he did not show it.

"Well, I suppose she may have pushed a leaflet or something through the door . . . There *was* a leaflet there at lunch time. Something about a meeting for nuclear disarmament, I think. There's always something every day. I suppose conceivably she might have come and pushed something through the letter box; but you can't blame me for that, can you?"

"Of course not. Now as to your telephone call—you say your own telephone was out of order. According to the exchange, that was not so."

"Exchanges will say anything! I dialled and got a *most* peculiar noise, not the engaged signal, so I went out to the call-box."

Hardcastle got up.

"I'm sorry, Miss Waterhouse, for bothering you in this way, but there is some idea that this girl *did* come to call on someone in the crescent and that she went to a house not very far from here."

"And so you have to inquire all along the crescent," said Miss Waterhouse. "I should think the most likely thing is that she went to the house next door—Miss Pebmarsh's, I mean."

"Why should you consider that the most likely?"

"You said she was a shorthand typist and came from the Cavendish Bureau. Surely, if I remember rightly, it was said that Miss Pebmarsh asked for a shorthand typist to come to her house the other day when that man was killed."

"It was said so, yes, but she denied it."

"Well, if you ask me," said Miss Waterhouse, "not that anyone ever listens to what *I* say until it's too late, I should say that she'd gone a little batty. Miss Pebmarsh, I mean. I think, perhaps, that she *does* ring up bureaux and ask for shorthand typists to come. Then, perhaps, she forgets all about it."

"But you don't think that she would do murder?"

"I never suggested murder or anything of that kind. I know a man was killed in her house, but I'm not for a moment suggesting that Miss Pebmarsh had anything to do with it. No. I just thought that she might have one of those curious fixations like people do. I knew a woman once who was always ringing up a confectioner's and ordering a dozen meringues. She didn't want them, and when they came she said she hadn't ordered them. That sort of thing."

"Of course, anything is possible," said Hardcastle. He said good-bye to Miss Waterhouse and left.

He thought she'd hardly done herself justice by her last suggestion. On the other hand, if she believed that the girl had been seen entering her house, and that that had in fact been the case, then the suggestion that the girl had gone to No. 19 was quite an adroit one under the circumstances.

Hardcastle glanced at his watch and decided that he had still time to tackle the Cavendish Secretarial Bureau. It had, he knew, been reopened at two o'clock this afternoon. He might get some help from the girls there. And he would find Sheila Webb there too.

III

One of the girls rose at once as he entered the office.

"It's Detective Inspector Hardcastle, isn't it," she said. "Miss Martindale is expecting you."

She ushered him into the inner office. Miss Martindale did not wait a moment before attacking him.

"It's disgraceful, Inspector Hardcastle, absolutely disgraceful! You must get to the bottom of this. You must get to the bottom of it *at once*. No dilly-dallying about. The police are supposed to give protection and that is what we need here at this office. *Protection*. I want protection for my girls and I mean to get it."

"I'm sure, Miss Martindale, that——"

" Are you going to deny that two of my girls, *two* of them, have been victimised? There is clearly some irresponsible person about who has got some kind of—what do they call it nowadays—a fixture or a complex—about shorthand typists or secretarial bureaux. They are deliberately martyrising this institute. First Sheila Webb was summoned by a heartless trick to find a dead body—the kind of thing that might send a nervous girl off her head—and now this. A perfectly nice harmless girl murdered in a telephone box. You must get to the bottom of it, Inspector."

" There's nothing I want more than to get to the bottom of it, Miss Martindale. I've come to see if you can give me any help."

" Help! What help can I give you? Do you think if I had any help, I wouldn't have rushed to you with it before now? You've got to find who killed that poor girl, Edna, and who played that heartless trick on Sheila. I'm strict with my girls, Inspector, I keep them up to their work and I won't allow them to be late or slipshod. But I don't stand for their being victimised or murdered. I intend to defend them, and I intend to see that people who are paid by the State to defend them do their work." She glared at him and looked rather like a tigress in human form.

" Give us time, Miss Martindale," he said.

" Time? Just because that silly child is dead, I suppose you think you've all the time in the world. The next thing that happens will be one of the other girls is murdered."

" I don't think you need fear that, Miss Martindale."

" I don't suppose you thought this girl was going to be killed when you got up this morning, Inspector. If so, you'd have taken a few precautions, I suppose, to look after her. And when one of my girls gets killed or is put in some terribly compromising position, you'll be equally surprised. The whole thing is extraordinary, *crazy*! You must admit yourself it's a crazy set-up. That is, if the things one reads in the paper were true. All those clocks, for instance. They weren't mentioned this morning at the inquest, I noticed."

" As little as possible was mentioned this morning, Miss Martindale. It was only an *adjourned* inquest, you know."

" All I say is," said Miss Martindale, glaring at him again, " you must *do* something about it."

" And there's nothing you can tell me, no hint Edna might have given to you? She didn't appear worried by anything, she didn't consult you?"

" I don't suppose she'd have consulted me if she *was* worried," said Miss Martindale. " But what had she to be worried about?"

That was exactly the question that Inspector Hardcastle would have liked to have had answered for him, but he could see that it was not likely that he would get the answer from Miss Martindale. Instead he said,

" I'd like to talk to as many of your girls here as I can. I can see that it is not likely that Edna Brent would have confided any fears or worries to you, but she *might* have spoken of them to her fellow employees."

" That's possible enough, I expect," said Miss Martindale. " They spend their time gossiping—these girls. The moment they hear my step in the passage outside all the typewriters begin to rattle. But what have they been doing just before? Talking. Chat, chat, chitter-chat!" Calming down a little, she said, " There are only three of them in the office at present. Would you like to speak to them while you're here? The others are out on assignments. I can give you their names and their home addresses, if you like."

" Thank you, Miss Martindale."

" I expect you'd like to speak to them alone," said Miss Martindale. " They wouldn't talk as freely if I was standing there looking on. They'd have to admit, you see, that they *had* been gossiping and wasting their time."

She got up from her seat and opened the door into the outer office.

" Girls," she said, " Detective Inspector Hardcastle wants to talk things over with you. You can stop work for the moment. Try and tell him anything you know that can help him to find out who killed Edna Brent."

She went back into her own private office and shut the door firmly. Three startled girlish faces looked at the inspector. He summed them up quickly and superficially, but sufficiently to make up his mind as to the quality of the material with which he was about to deal. A fair solid-looking girl with spectacles. Dependable, he thought, but not particularly bright. A rather rakish-looking brunette with the kind of hair-do that suggested she'd been out in a blizzard lately. Eyes that noticed things here, perhaps, but probably highly unreliable in her recollection of events. Everything would be suitably touched up. The third was a born giggler who would, he was sure, agree with whatever anyone else said.

He spoke quietly, informally.

"I suppose you've all heard what has happened to Edna Brent who worked here?"

Three heads nodded violently.

"By the way, how did you hear?"

They looked at each other as if trying to decide who should be spokesman. By common consent it appeared to be the fair girl, whose name, it seemed, was Janet.

"Edna didn't come to work at two o'clock, as she should have done," she explained.

"And Sandy Cat was very annoyed," began the dark-haired girl, Maureen, and then stopped herself. "Miss Martindale, I mean."

The third girl giggled. "Sandy Cat is just what we call her," she explained.

"And not a bad name," the inspector thought.

"She's a perfect terror when she likes," said Maureen. "Fairly jumps on you. She asked if Edna had said anything to us about not coming back to the office this afternoon, and that she ought to have at least sent an excuse."

The fair girl said: "I told Miss Martindale that she'd been at the inquest with the rest of us, but that we hadn't seen her afterwards and didn't know where she'd gone."

"That was true, was it?" asked Hardcastle. "You've no idea where she did go when she left the inquest."

"I suggested she should come and have some lunch with me," said Maureen, "but she seemed to have something on her mind. She said she wasn't sure that she'd bother to have any lunch. Just buy something and eat it in the office."

"So she meant, then, to come back to the office?"

"Oh, yes, of course. We all knew we'd got to do that."

"Have any of you noticed anything different about Edna Brent these last few days? Did she seem to you worried at all, as though she had something on her mind? Did she tell you anything to that effect? If there is anything at all you know, I must beg of you to tell me."

They looked at each other but not in a conspiratorial manner. It seemed to be merely vague conjecture.

"She was always worried about something," said Maureen. "She gets things muddled up, and makes mistakes. She was a bit slow in the uptake."

"Things always seemed to happen to Edna," said the giggler. "Remember when that stiletto heel of hers came off the other day? Just the sort of thing that *would* happen to Edna."

"I remember," said Hardcastle.

He remembered how the girl had stood looking down ruefully at the shoe in her hand.

"You know, I had a feeling something awful had happened this afternoon when Edna didn't get here at two o'clock," said Janet. She nodded with a solemn face.

Hardcastle looked at her with some dislike. He always disliked people who were wise after the event. He was quite sure that the girl in question had thought nothing of the kind. Far more likely, he thought to himself, that she had said, "Edna will catch it from Sandy Cat when she does come in."

"When did you hear what had happened?" he asked again.

They looked at each other. The giggler flushed guiltily. Her eyes shot sideways to the door into Miss Martindale's private office.

"Well, I—er—I just slipped out for a minute," she said. "I wanted some pastries to take home and I knew they'd all be gone by the time we left. And when I got to the shop—it's on the corner and they know me quite well there—the woman said 'She worked at your place, didn't she, ducks?' and I said 'Who do you mean?' And then she said 'This girl they've just found dead in a telephone box.' Oh, it gave me ever such a turn! So I came rushing back and I told the others and in the end we all said we'd have to tell Miss Martindale about it, and just at that moment she came bouncing out of her office and said to us, '*Now* what are you doing? Not a single typewriter going'."

The fair girl took up the saga.

"And I said, 'Really it's not *our* fault. We've heard some terrible news about Edna, Miss Martindale.'"

" And what did Miss Martindale say or do?"

" Well, she wouldn't believe it at first," said the brunette. " She said ' Nonsense. You've just been picking up some silly gossip in a shop. It must be some other girl. Why should it be Edna?' And she marched back into her room and rang up the police station and found out it *was* true."

" But I don't see," said Janet almost dreamily, " I don't see why *anyone* should want to kill Edna."

" It's not as though she had a boy or anything," said the brunette.

All three looked at Hardcastle hopefully as though he could give them the answer to the problem. He sighed. There was nothing here for him. Perhaps one of the other girls might be more helpful. And there was Sheila Webb herself.

" Were Sheila Webb and Edna Brent particular friends?" he asked.

They looked at each other vaguely.

" Not special, I don't think."

" Where is Miss Webb, by the way?"

He was told that Sheila Webb was at the Curlew Hotel, attending on Professor Purdy.

CHAPTER 19

Professor Purdy sounded irritated as he broke off dictating and answered the telephone.

" Who? What? You mean he is here *now*? Well, ask him if to-morrow will do?——Oh, very well—very well—Tell him to come up."

" Always something," he said with vexation. " How one can ever be expected to do any serious work with these constant interruptions." He looked with mild displeasure at Sheila Webb and said: " Now where were we, my dear?"

Sheila was about to reply when there was a knock at the door. Professor Purdy brought himself back with some difficulty from the chronological difficulties of approximately three thousand years ago.

"Yes?" he said testily, "yes, come in, what is it? I may say I mentioned particularly that I was *not* to be disturbed this afternoon."

"I'm very sorry, sir, very sorry indeed that it has been necessary to do so. Good evening, Miss Webb."

Sheila Webb had risen to her feet, setting aside her note-book. Hardcastle wondered if he only fancied that he saw sudden apprehension come into her eyes.

"Well, what is it?" said the professor again, sharply.

"I am Detective Inspector Hardcastle, as Miss Webb here will tell you."

"Quite," said the professor. "Quite."

"What I really wanted was a few words with Miss Webb."

"Can't you wait? It is really *most* awkward at this moment. Most awkward. We were just at a critical point. Miss Webb will be disengaged in about a quarter of an hour—oh, well, perhaps half an hour. Something like that. Oh, dear me, is it six o'clock *already*?"

"I'm very sorry, Professor Purdy," Hardcastle's tone was firm.

"Oh, very well, very well. What is it—some motoring offence, I suppose? How very officious these traffic wardens are. One insisted the other day that I had left my car four and a half hours at a parking meter. I'm sure that could not possibly be so."

"It's a little more serious than a parking, offence, sir."

"Oh, yes. Oh, yes. And you don't have a car, do you, my dear?" He looked vaguely at Sheila Webb. "Yes, I remember, you come here by bus. Well, Inspector, what is it?"

"It's about a girl called Edna Brent." He turned to Sheila Webb. "I expect you've heard about it."

She stared at him. Beautiful eyes. Cornflower-blue eyes. Eyes that reminded him of someone.

"Edna Brent, did you say?" She raised her eyebrows. "Oh, yes, I know her, of course. What about her?"

"I see the news hasn't got to you yet. Where did you lunch, Miss Webb?"

Colour came up in her cheeks.

"I lunched with a friend at the Ho Tung restaurant, if— if it's really any business of yours."

"You didn't go on afterwards to the office?"

"To the Cavendish Bureau, you mean? I called in there and was told it had been arranged that I was to come straight here to Professor Purdy at half past two."

"That's right," said the professor, nodding his head. "*Half past two*. And we have been working ever since. Ever since. Dear me, I should have ordered tea. I am very sorry, Miss Webb, I'm afraid you must have missed having your tea. You should have reminded me."

"Oh, it didn't matter, Professor Purdy, it didn't matter at all."

"Very remiss of me," said the professor, "very remiss. But there. I mustn't interrupt, since the inspector wants to ask you some questions."

"So you don't know what's happened to Edna Brent?"

"*Happened* to her?" asked Sheila, sharply, her voice rising. "Happened to her? What do you mean? Has she had an accident or something—been run over?"

"Very dangerous, all this speeding," put in the professor.

"Yes," said Hardcastle, "something's happened to her." He paused and then said, putting it as brutally as possible, "She was strangled about half past twelve, in a telephone box."

"In a telephone box?" said the professor, rising to the occasion by showing some interest.

Sheila Webb said nothing. She stared at him. Her mouth opened slightly, her eyes widened. "Either this is the first you've heard of it or you're a damn' good actress," thought Hardcastle to himself.

"Dear, dear," said the professor. "Strangled in a telephone box. That seems *very* extraordinary to me. Very extraordinary. Not the sort of place I would choose myself. I mean, if I were to do such a thing. No, indeed. Well, well. Poor girl. Most unfortunate for her."

"Edna—*killed*! But why?"

"Did you know, Miss Webb, that Edna Brent was very anxious to see you the day before yesterday, that she came to your aunt's house, and waited for some time for you to come back?"

"My fault again," said the professor guiltily. "I kept Miss

Webb very late that evening, I remember. Very late indeed. I really still feel very apologetic about it. You *must* always remind me of the time, my dear. You really must."

" My aunt told me about that," said Sheila, " but I didn't know it was anything special. Was it? Was Edna in trouble of any kind?"

" We don't know," said the inspector. " We probably never shall know. Unless *you* can tell us?"

" *I* tell you? How should I know?"

" You might have had some idea, perhaps, of what Edna Brent wanted to see you about?"

She shook her head. " I've no idea, no idea at all."

" Hasn't she hinted anything to you, spoken to you in the office at all about whatever the trouble was?"

" No. No, indeed she hasn't—hadn't—I wasn't at the office at all yesterday. I had to go over to Landis Bay to one of our authors for the whole day."

" You didn't think that she'd been worried lately?"

" Well, Edna always looked worried or puzzled. She had a very—what shall I say—diffident, uncertain kind of mind. I mean, she was never quite sure that what she thought of doing was the right thing or not. She missed out two whole pages in typing Armand Levine's book once and she was terribly worried about what to do then, because she'd sent it off to him before she realised what had happened."

" I see. And she asked you all your advice as to what she should do about it?"

" Yes. I told her she'd better write a note to him quickly because people don't always start reading their typescript at once for correction. She could write and say what had happened and ask him not to complain to Miss Martindale. But she said she didn't quite like to do that."

" She usually came and asked for advice when one of these problems arose?"

" Oh, yes, always. But the trouble was, of course, that we didn't always all agree as to what she should do. Then she got puzzled again."

" So it would be quite natural that she should come to one of you if she *had* a problem? It happened quite frequently?"

" Yes. Yes, it did."

"You don't think it might have been something more serious this time?"

"I don't suppose so. What sort of serious thing could it be?"

Was Sheila Webb, the inspector wondered, quite as much at ease as she tried to appear?

"I don't know what she wanted to talk to me about," she went on, speaking faster and rather breathlessly. "I've no idea. And I certainly can't imagine why she wanted to come out to my aunt's house and speak to me *there*."

"It would seem, wouldn't it, that it was something she did not want to speak to you about at the Cavendish Bureau? Before the other girls, shall we say? Something, perhaps, that she felt ought to be kept private between you and her. Could that have been the case?"

"I think it's very unlikely. I'm sure it couldn't have been at all like that." Her breath came quickly.

"So you can't help me, Miss Webb?"

"No. I'm sorry. I'm *very* sorry about Edna, but I don't know anything that could help you."

"Nothing that might have a connection or a tie-up with what happened on the 9th of September?"

"You mean—that man—that man in Wilbraham Crescent?"

"That's what I mean."

"How could it have been? What *could* Edna have known about that?"

"Nothing very important, perhaps," said the inspector, "but *something*. And anything would help. *Anything*, however small." He paused. "The telephone box where she was killed was in Wilbraham Crescent. Does that convey anything to you, Miss Webb?"

"Nothing at all."

"Were you yourself in Wilbraham Crescent to-day?"

"No, I wasn't," she said vehemently. "I never went near it. I'm beginning to feel that it's a horrible place. I wish I'd never gone there in the first place, I wish I'd never got mixed up in all this. Why did they send for me, ask for me specially, that day? Why did Edna have to get killed near there? You *must* find out, Inspector, you must, you *must*!"

"We mean to find out, Miss Webb," the inspector said. There was a faint menace in his voice as he went on: "I can assure you of that."

"You're trembling, my dear," said Professor Purdy. "I think, I really *do* think that you ought to have a glass of sherry."

CHAPTER 20

COLIN'S NARRATIVE

I reported to Beck as soon as I got to London.

He waved his cigar at me.

"There might have been something in that idiotic crescent idea of yours after all," he allowed.

"I've turned up something at last, have I?"

"I won't go as far as that, but I'll just say that you *may* have. Our construction engineer, Mr. Ramsay of 62, Wilbraham Crescent, is not all he seems. Some very curious assignments he's taken on lately. Genuine firms, but firms without much back history, and what history they have, rather a peculiar one. Ramsay went off at a moment's notice about five weeks ago. He went to Rumania."

"That's not what he told his wife."

"Possibly not, but that's where he went. And that's where he is now. We'd like to know a bit more about him. So you can stir your stumps, my lad, and get going. I've got all the visas ready for you, and a nice new passport. Nigel Trench it will be this time. Rub up your knowledge of rare plants in the Balkans. You're a botanist."

"Any special instructions?"

"No. We'll give you your contact when you pick up your papers. Find out all you can about our Mr. Ramsay." He looked at me keenly. "You don't sound as pleased as you might be." He peered through the cigar smoke.

"It's always pleasant when a hunch pays off," I said evasively.

"Right Crescent, wrong number. 61 is occupied by a

perfectly blameless builder. Blameless in our sense, that is. Poor old Hanbury got the number wrong, but he wasn't far off."

"Have you vetted the others? Or only Ramsay?"

"Diana Lodge seems to be as pure as Diana. A long history of cats. McNaughton was vaguely interesting. He's a retired professor, as you know. Mathematics. Quite brilliant, it seems. Resigned his Chair quite suddenly on the grounds of ill-health. I suppose that *may* be true—but he seems quite hale and hearty. He seems to have cut himself off from all his old friends, which is rather odd."

"The trouble is," I said, "that we get to thinking that everything that *everybody* does is highly suspicious."

"You may have got something there," said Colonel Beck. "There are times when I suspect *you*, Colin, of having changed over to the other side. There are times when I suspect *myself* of having changed over to the other side, and then having changed back again to this one! All a jolly mix-up."

My plane left at ten p.m. I went to see Hercule Poirot first. This time he was drinking a *sirop de cassis*. (Blackcurrant to you and me.) He offered me some. I refused. George brought me whisky. Everything as usual.

"You look depressed," said Poirot.

"Not at all. I'm just off abroad."

He looked at me. I nodded.

"So it is like that?"

"Yes, it is like that."

"I wish you all success."

"Thank you. And what about you, Poirot, how are you getting along with your homework?"

"*Pardon?*"

"What about the Crowdean Clocks Murder—Have you leaned back, closed your eyes and come up with all the answers?"

"I have read what you left here with great interest," said Poirot.

"Not much there, was there? I told you these particular neighbours were a wash-out——"

"On the contrary. In the case of at least *two* of these people very illuminating remarks were made——"

"Which of them? And what were the remarks?"

Poirot told me in an irritating fashion that I must reread my notes carefully.

" You will see for yourself then——It leaps to the eye. The thing to do now is to talk to more neighbours."

" There aren't any more."

" There must be. *Somebody* has always seen something. It is an axiom. *principle taken to be true.*

" It may be an axiom but it isn't so in this case. And I've got further details for you. There has been another murder."

" Indeed? So soon? That is interesting. Tell me."

I told him. He questioned me closely until he got every single detail out of me. I told him, too, of the postcard I had passed on to Hardcastle.

" Remember—four one three—or four thirteen," he repeated. " Yes—it is the same pattern."

" What do you mean by that?"

Poirot closed his eyes.

" That postcard lacks only one thing, a fingerprint dipped in blood."

I looked at him doubtfully.

" What do you really think of this business?"

" It grows much clearer—as usual, the murderer cannot let well alone."

" But who's the murderer?"

Poirot craftily did not reply to that.

" Whilst you are away, you permit that I make a few researches?"

" Such as?"

" To-morrow I shall instruct Miss Lemon to write a letter to an old lawyer friend of mine, Mr. Enderby. I shall ask her to consult the marriage records at Somerset House. She will also send for me a certain overseas cable."

" I'm not sure that's fair," I objected. " You're not just sitting and thinking."

" That is exactly what I am doing! What Miss Lemon is to do, is to verify for me the answers that I have already arrived at. I ask not for information, but for *confirmation*."

" I don't believe you know a thing, Poirot! This is all bluff. Why, nobody knows yet who the dead man is——"

" I know."

" What's his name?"

"I have no idea. His name is not important. I know, if you can understand, not *who* he is but who he *is*."

"A blackmailer?"

Poirot closed his eyes.

"A private detective?"

Poirot opened his eyes.

"I say to you a little quotation. As I did last time. And after that I say no more."

He recited with the utmost solemnity:

"*Dilly, dilly, dilly——Come and be killed.*"

CHAPTER 21

Detective Inspector Hardcastle looked at the calendar on his desk. September the 20th. Just over ten days. They hadn't been able to make as much progress as he would have liked because they were held up with that initial difficulty: the identification of a dead body. It had taken longer than he would have thought possible. All the leads seemed to have petered out, failed. The laboratory examination of the clothes had brought in nothing particularly helpful. The clothes themselves had yielded no clues. They were good quality clothes, export quality, not new but well cared for. Dentists had not helped, nor laundries, nor cleaners. The dead man remained a "mystery man!" And yet, so Hardcastle felt, he was not really a "mystery man." There was nothing spectacular or dramatic about him. He was just a man whom nobody had been able to come forward and recognise. That was the pattern of it, he was sure. Hardcastle sighed as he thought of the telephone calls and letters that had necessarily poured in after the publication in the public press of the photograph with the caption below it: DO YOU KNOW THIS MAN? Astonishing the amount of people who thought they did know this man. Daughters who wrote in a hopeful vein of fathers from whom they'd been estranged for years. An old woman of ninety was sure that the photograph in question was her son who had left home thirty years ago. Innumerable wives had been sure that it was a missing husband. Sisters had not been quite so anxious to claim brothers.

Sisters, perhaps, were less hopeful thinkers. And, of course, there were vast numbers of people who had seen that very man in Lincolnshire, Newcastle, Devon, London, on a tube, in a bus, lurking on a pier, looking sinister at the corner of a road, trying to hide his face as he came out of the cinema. Hundreds of leads, the more promising of them patiently followed up and not yielding anything.

But to-day, the inspector felt slightly more hopeful. He looked again at the letter on his desk. Merlina Rival. He didn't like the Christian name very much. Nobody in their senses, he thought, could christen a child Merlina. No doubt it was a fancy name adopted by the lady herself. But he liked the feel of the letter. It was not extravagant or over-confident. It merely said that the writer thought it possible that the man in question was her husband from whom she had parted several years ago. She was due this morning. He pressed his buzzer and Sergeant Cray came in.

"That Mrs. Rival not arrived yet?"

"Just come this minute," said Cray. "I was coming to tell you."

"What's she like?"

"Bit theatrical-looking," said Cray, after reflecting a moment. "Lot of make-up—not very good make-up. Fairly reliable sort of woman on the whole, I should say."

"Did she seem upset?"

"No. Not noticeably."

"All right," said Hardcastle, "let's have her in."

Cray departed and presently returned saying as he did so, "Mrs. Rival, sir."

The inspector got up and shook hands with her. About fifty, he would judge, but from a long way away—quite a long way—she might have looked thirty. Close at hand, the result of make-up carelessly applied made her look rather older than fifty but on the whole he put it at fifty. Dark hair heavily hennaed. No hat, medium height and build, wearing a dark coat and skirt and a white blouse. Carrying a large tartan bag. A jingly bracelet or two, several rings. On the whole, he thought, making moral judgments on the basis of his experience, rather a good sort. Not over-scrupulous, probably, but easy to live with, reasonably generous, possibly kind. Reliable? That was the question. He wouldn't bank on it, but then he couldn't afford to bank on that kind of thing anyway.

" I'm very glad to see you, Mrs. Rival," he said, " and I hope very much you'll be able to help us."

" Of course, I'm not at all sure," said Mrs. Rival. She spoke apologetically. " But it did look like Harry. Very much like Harry. Of course I'm quite prepared to find that it isn't, and I hope I shan't have taken up your time for nothing."

She seemed quite apologetic about it.

" You mustn't feel that in any case," said the inspector. " We want help very badly over this case."

" Yes, I see. I hope I'll be able to be sure. You see, it's a long time since I saw him."

" Shall we get down a few facts to help us? When did you last see your husband?"

" I've been trying to get it accurate," said Mrs. Rival, " all the way down in the train. It's terrible how one's memory goes when it comes to time. I believe I said in my letter to you it was about ten years ago, but it's more than that. D'you know, I think it's nearer fifteen. Time does go so fast. I suppose," she added shrewdly, " that one tends to think it's less than it is because it makes you yourself feel younger. Don't you think so?"

" I should think it could do," said the inspector. " Anyway you think it's roughly fifteen years since you saw him? When were you married?"

" It must have been about three years before that," said Mrs. Rival.

" And you were living then?"

" At a place called Shipton Bois in Suffolk. Nice town. Market town. Rather one-horse, if you know what I mean."

" And what did your husband do?"

" He was an insurance agent. At least——" she stopped herself "——that's what he said he was."

The inspector looked up sharply.

" You found out that that wasn't true?"

" Well, no, not exactly . . . Not at the time. It's only since then that I've thought that perhaps it wasn't true. It'd be an easy thing for a man to say, wouldn't it?"

" I suppose it would in certain circumstances."

"I mean, it gives a man an excuse for being away from home a good deal."

"Your husband was away from home a good deal, Mrs. Rival?"

"Yes. I never thought about it much to begin with——"

"But later?"

She did not answer at once then she said:

"Can't we get on with it? After all, if it *isn't* Harry . . ."

He wondered what exactly she was thinking. There was strain in her voice, possibly emotion? He was not sure.

"I can understand," he said, "that you'd like to get it over. We'll go now."

He rose and escorted her out of the room to the waiting car. Her nervousness when they got to where they were going, was no more than the nervousness of other people he had taken to this same place. He said the usual reassuring things.

"It'll be quite all right. Nothing distressing. It will only take a minute or two."

The tray was rolled out, the attendant lifted the sheet. She stood staring down for a few moments, her breath came a little faster, she made a faint gasping sound, then she turned away abruptly. She said:

"It's Harry. Yes. He's a lot older, he looks different . . . But it's Harry."

The inspector nodded to the attendant, then he laid his hand on her arm and took her out again to the car and they drove back to the station. He didn't say anything. He left her to pull herself together. When they got back to his room a constable came in almost at once with a tray of tea.

"There you are, Mrs. Rival. Have a cup, it'll pull you together. Then we'll talk."

"Thank you."

She put sugar in the tea, a good deal of it, and gulped it down quickly.

"That's better," she said. "It's not that I *mind* really. Only—only, well it does turn you up a bit, doesn't it?"

"You think this man is definitely your husband?"

"I'm sure he is. Of course, he's much older, but he hasn't changed really so much. He always looked—well, very neat. Nice, you know, good class."

Yes, thought Hardcastle, it was quite a good description. Good class. Presumably, Harry had looked much better class than he was. Some men did, and it was helpful to them for their particular purposes.

Mrs. Rival said, " He was very particular always about his clothes and everything. That's why, I think—they fell for him so easily. They never suspected anything."

" Who fell for him, Mrs. Rival?" Hardcastle's voice was gentle, sympathetic.

" Women," said Mrs. Rival. " Women. That's where he was most of the time."

" I see. And you got to know about it."

" Well, I—I suspected. I mean, he was away such a lot. Of course I knew what men are like. I thought probably there *was* a girl from time to time. But it's no good asking men about these things. They'll lie to you and that's all. But I didn't think—I really didn't think that he made a *business* of it."

" And did he?"

She nodded. " I think he must have done."

" How did you find out?"

She shrugged her shoulders.

" He came back one day from a trip he'd taken. To Newcastle, he *said*. Anyway, he came back and said he'd have to clear out quickly. He said that the game was up. There was some woman he'd got into trouble. A school teacher, he said, and there might be a bit of a stink about it. I asked him questions then. He didn't mind telling me. Probably he thought I knew more than I did. They used to fall for him, you know, easily enough, just as I did. He'd give her a ring and they'd get engaged—and then he'd say he'd invest money for them. They usually gave it him quite easily."

" Had he tried the same thing with you?"

" He had, as a matter of fact, only I didn't give him any."

" Why not? Didn't you trust him even then?"

" Well, I wasn't the kind that trusts anybody. I'd had what you'd call a bit of experience, you know, of men and their ways and the seamier side of things. Anyway, I didn't want him investing my money for me. What money I had I could invest for myself. Always keep your money in your hands and then you'll be sure you've got it! I've seen too many girls and women make fools of themselves."

"When did he want you to invest money? Before you were married or after?"

"I think he suggested something of the kind beforehand, but I didn't respond and he sheered off the subject at once. Then, after we were married, he told me about some wonderful opportunity he'd got. I said 'Nothing doing.' It wasn't only because I didn't trust him, but I'd often heard men say they're on to something wonderful and then it turned out that they'd been had for a mug themselves."

"Had your husband ever been in trouble with the police?"

"No fear," said Mrs. Rival. "Women don't like the world to know they've been duped. But this time, apparently, things might be different. This girl or woman, she was an educated woman. She wouldn't be as easy to deceive as the others may have been."

"She was going to have a child?"

"Yes."

"Had that happened on other occasions?"

"I rather think so." She added, "I don't honestly know what it was used to start him off in the first place. Whether it was *only* the money—a way of getting a living, as you might say—or whether he was the kind of man who just *had* to have women and he saw no reason why they shouldn't pay the expenses of his fun." There was bitterness now in her voice.

Hardcastle said gently:

"You were fond of him, Mrs. Rival?"

"I don't know. I honestly don't know. I suppose I was in a way, or I wouldn't have married him . . ."

"You *were*—excuse me—married to him?"

"I don't even know that for sure," said Mrs. Rival frankly. "We were married all right. In a church, too, but I don't know if he had married other women as well, using a different name, I suppose. His name was Castleton when I married him. I don't think it was his own name."

"Harry Castleton. Is that right?"

"Yes."

"And you lived in this place, Shipton Bois, as man and wife—for how long?"

"We'd been there about two years. Before that we lived near Doncaster. I don't say I was really surprised when he came back that day and told me. I think I'd known he was a wrong 'un for some time. One just couldn't believe it because, you see, he always seemed so respectable. So absolutely the gentleman!"

"And what happened then?"

"He said he'd got to get out of there quick and I said he could go and good riddance, that I wasn't standing for all this!" She added thoughtfully, "I gave him ten pounds. It was all I had in the house. He said he was short of money . . . I've never seen or heard of him since. Until to-day. Or rather, until I saw his picture in the paper."

"He didn't have any special distinguishing marks? Scars? An operation—or a fracture—anything like that?"

She shook her head.

"I don't think so."

"Did he ever use the name Curry?"

"Curry? No, I don't think so. Not that I know of, anyway."

Hardcastle slipped the card across the table to her.

"This was in his pocket," he said.

"Still saying he's an insurance agent, I see," she remarked. "I expect he uses—used, I mean—all sorts of different names."

"You say you've never heard of him for the last fifteen years?"

"He hasn't sent me a Christmas card, if that's what you mean," said Mrs. Rival, with a sudden glint of humour. "I don't suppose he'd know where I was, anyway. I went back to the stage for a bit after we parted. On tour mostly. It wasn't much of a life and I dropped the name of Castleton too. Went back to Merlina Rival."

"Merlina's—er—not your real name, I suppose?"

She shook her head and a faint, cheerful smile appeared on her face.

"I thought it up. Unusual. My real name's Flossie Gapp. Florence, I suppose I must have been christened, but everyone always calls me Flossie or Flo. Flossie Gapp. Not very romantic, is it?"

"What are you doing now? Are you still acting, Mrs. Rival?"

"Occasionally," said Mrs. Rival with a touch of reticence. "On and off, as you might say."

Hardcastle was tactful.

"I see," he said.

"I do odd jobs here and there," she said. "Help out at parties, a bit of hostess work, that sort of thing. It's not a bad life. At any rate you meet people. Things get near the bone now and again."

"You've never heard anything of Henry Castleton since you parted—or about him?"

"Not a word. I thought perhaps he'd gone abroad—or was dead."

"The only other thing I can ask you, Mrs. Rival, is if you have any idea why Harry Castleton should have come to this neighbourhood?"

"No. Of course I've no idea. I don't even know what he's been doing all these years."

"Would it be likely that he would be selling fraudulent insurance—something of that kind?"

"I simply don't know. It doesn't seem to me terribly likely. I mean, Harry was very careful of himself always. He wouldn't stick his neck out doing something that he might be brought to book for. I should have thought it more likely it was some racket with women."

"Might it have been, do you think, Mrs. Rival, some form of blackmail?"

"Well, I don't know . . . I suppose, yes, in a way. Some woman, perhaps, that wouldn't want something in her past raked up. He'd feel pretty safe over that, I think. Mind you, I don't say it *is* so, but it might be. I don't think he'd want very much money, you know. I don't think he'd drive anyone desperate, but he might just collect in a small way." She nodded in affirmation. "Yes."

"Women liked him, did they?"

"Yes. They always fell for him rather easily. Mainly, I think, because he always seemed so good class and respectable. They were proud of having made a conquest of a man like that. They looked forward to a nice safe future with him.

That's the nearest way I can put it. I felt the same way myself," added Mrs. Rival with some frankness.

"There's just one more small point." Hardcastle spoke to his subordinate. "Just bring those clocks in, will you?"

They were brought in on a tray with a cloth over them. Hardcastle whipped off the cloth and exposed them to Mrs. Rival's gaze. She inspected them with frank interest and approbation.

"Pretty, aren't they? I like that one." She touched the ormolu clock.

"You haven't seen any of them before. They don't mean anything to you?"

"Can't say they do. Ought they to?"

"Can you think of any connection between your husband and the name Rosemary?"

"Rosemary? Let me think. There was a red-head—No, her name was Rosalie. I'm afraid I can't think of anyone. But then I probably wouldn't know, would I? Harry kept his affairs very dark."

"If you saw a clock with the hands pointing to four-thirteen——" Hardcastle paused.

Mrs. Rival gave a cheerful chuckle.

"I'd think it was getting on for tea-time."

Hardcastle sighed.

"Well, Mrs. Rival," he said, "we are very grateful to you. The adjourned inquest, as I told you, will be the day after to-morrow. You won't mind giving evidence of identification, will you?"

"No. No, that will be all right. I'll just have to say who he was, is that it? I shan't have to go into things? I won't have to go into the manner of his life—anything of that kind?"

"That will not be necessary at present. All you will have to swear to is that he is the man, Harry Castleton, to whom you were married. The exact date will be on record at Somerset House. Where were you married? Can you remember that?"

"Place called Donbrook—St. Michael's, I think was the name of the church. I hope it isn't *more* than twenty years ago. That *would* make me feel I had one foot in the grave," said Mrs. Rival.

She got up and held out her hand. Hardcastle said good-bye. He went back to his desk and sat there tapping it with a pencil. Presently Sergeant Cray came in.

"Satisfactory?" he asked.

"Seems so," said the inspector. "Name of Harry Castleton —possibly an alias. We'll have to see what we can find out about the fellow. It seems likely that more than one woman might have reason to want revenge on him."

"Looks so respectable, too," said Cray.

"That," said Hardcastle, "seems to have been his principal stock-in-trade."

He thought again about the clock with Rosemary written on it. Remembrance?

—Harry ridei's dad?

CHAPTER 22

COLIN LAMB'S NARRATIVE

"So you have returned," said Hercule Poirot.

He placed a bookmarker carefully to mark his place in the book he was reading. This time a cup of hot chocolate stood on the table by his elbow. Poirot certainly has the most terrible taste in drinks! For once he did not urge me to join him.

"How are you?" I asked.

"I am disturbed. I am much disturbed. They make the renovations, the redecorations, even the structural alteration in these flats."

"Won't that improve them?"

"It will improve them, yes—but it will be most vexatious to *me*. I shall have to disarrange myself. There will be a smell of paint!" He looked at me with an air of outrage.

Then, dismissing his difficulties with a wave of his hand, he asked:

"You have had the success, yes?"

I said slowly: "I don't know."

"Ah—it is like that."

"I found out what I was sent to find out. I did not find

the man himself. I myself do not know what was wanted. Information? Or a body?"

"Speaking of bodies, I read the account of the adjourned inquest at Crowdean. Wilful murder by a person or persons unknown. And your body has been given a name at last."

I nodded.

"Harry Castleton, whoever he may be."

"Identified by his wife. You have been to Crowdean?"

"Not yet. I thought of going down to-morrow."

"Oh, you have some leisure time?"

"Not yet. I'm still on the job. My job takes me there——" I paused a moment and then said: "I don't know much about what's been happening while I've been abroad— just the mere fact of identification—what do you think of it?"

Poirot shrugged his shoulders.

"It was to be expected."

"Yes—the police are very good——"

"And wives are very obliging."

"Mrs. Merlina Rival! What a name!"

"It reminds me of something," said Poirot. "Now of what does it remind me?"

He looked at me thoughtfully but I couldn't help him. Knowing Poirot, it might have reminded him of anything.

"A visit to a friend—in a country house," mused Poirot, then shook his head. "No—it is so long ago."

"When I come back to London, I'll come and tell you all I can find out from Hardcastle about Mrs. Merlina Rival," I promised.

Poirot waved a hand and said: "It is not necessary."

"You mean you know all about her already without being told?"

"No. I mean that I am not interested in her——"

"You're not interested—but why not? I don't get it." I shook my head.

"One must concentrate on the essentials. Tell me instead of the girl Edna—who died in the telephone box in Wilbraham Crescent."

"I can't tell you more than I've told you already—I know nothing about the girl."

"So all you know," said Poirot accusingly, "or all you can tell me is that the girl was a poor little rabbit, whom you saw in a typewriting office, where she had torn the heel off her shoe in a grating——" he broke off. " Where was that grating, by the way?"

" Really, Poirot, how should I know?"

" You could have known if you had *asked*. How do you expect to know *anything* if you do not ask the proper questions?"

" But how can it matter *where* the heel came off?"

" It may not matter. On the other hand, we should know a definite spot where this girl had been, and that might connect up with a person she had seen there—or with an event of some kind which took place there."

" You are being rather far-fetched. Anyway I do know it was quite near the office because she said so and that she bought a bun and hobbled back on her stocking feet to eat the bun in the office and she ended up by saying how on earth was she to get home like that?"

" Ah, and how *did* she get home?" Poirot asked with interest.

I stared at him.

" I've no idea."

" Ah—but it is impossible, the way you never ask the right questions! As a result you know nothing of what is important."

" You'd better come down to Crowdean and ask questions yourself," I said, nettled.

" That is impossible at the moment. There is a most interesting sale of authors' manuscripts next week——"

" Still on your hobby?"

" But, yes, indeed." His eyes brightened. " Take the works of John Dickson Carr or Carter Dickson, as he calls himself sometimes——"

I escaped before he could get under way, pleading an urgent appointment. I was in no mood to listen to lectures on past masters of the art of crime fiction.

II

I was sitting on the front step of Hardcastle's house, and rose out of the gloom to greet him when he got home on the following evening.

"Hallo, Colin? Is that you? So you've appeared out of the blue again, have you?"

"If you called it out of the *red*, it would be much more appropriate."

"How long have you been here, sitting on my front door-step?"

"Oh, half an hour or so."

"Sorry you couldn't get into the house."

"I could have got into the house with perfect ease," I said indignantly. "You don't know our training!"

"Then why didn't you get in?"

"I wouldn't like to lower your prestige in any way," I explained. "A detective inspector of police would be bound to lose face if his house were entered burglariously with complete ease."

Hardcastle took his keys from his pocket and opened the front door.

"Come on in," he said, "and don't talk nonsense."

He led the way into the sitting-room, and proceeded to supply liquid refreshment.

"Say when."

I said it, not too soon, and we settled ourselves with our drinks.

"Things are moving at last," said Hardcastle. "We've identified our corpse."

"I know. I looked up the newspaper files—who was Harry Castleton?"

"A man of apparently the utmost respectability and who made his living by going through a form of marriage or merely getting engaged to well-to-do credulous women. They en-trusted their savings to him, impressed by his superior know-ledge of finance and shortly afterwards he quietly faded into the blue."

"He didn't look that kind of man," I said, casting my mind back.

"That was his chief asset."

"Wasn't he ever prosecuted?"

"No—we've made inquiries but it isn't easy to get much

information. He changed his name fairly often. And although they think at the Yard that Harry Castleton, Raymond Blair, Lawrence Dalton, Roger Byron were all one and the same person, they never could prove it. The women, you see, wouldn't tell. They preferred to lose their money. The man was really more of a name than anything—cropping up here and there—always the same pattern—but incredibly elusive. Roger Byron, say, would disappear from Southend, and a man called Lawrence Dalton would commence operations in Newcastle on Tyne. He was shy of being photographed—eluded his lady friends' desire to snapshot him. All this goes quite a long time back—fifteen to twenty years. About that time he seemed really to disappear. The rumour spread about that he was dead—but some people said he had gone abroad——"

" Anyway, nothing was heard of him until he turned up, dead, on Miss Pebmarsh's sitting-room carpet?" I said.

" Exactly."

" It certainly opens up possibilities."

" It certainly does."

" A woman scorned who never forgot?" I suggested.

" It does happen, you know. There *are* women with long memories who don't forget——"

" And if such a woman were to go blind—a second affliction on top of the other——"

" That's only conjecture. Nothing to substantiate it as yet."

" What was the wife like—Mrs.—what was it?—Merlina Rival? What a name! It can't be her own."

" Her real name is Flossie Gapp. The other she invented. More suitable for her way of life."

" What is she? A tart?"

" Not a professional."

" What used to be called, tactfully, a lady of easy virtue?"

" I should say she was a good-natured woman, and one willing to oblige her friends. Described herself as an ex-actress. Occasionally did ' hostess ' work. Quite likeable."

" Reliable?"

" As reliable as most. Her recognition was quite positive. No hesitation."

" That's a blessing."

"Yes. I was beginning to despair. The amount of wives I've had here! I'd begun to think it's a wise woman who knows her own husband. Mind you, I think Mrs. Rival might have known a little more about her husband than she lets on."

"Has she herself ever been mixed up in criminal activities?"

"Not for the record. I think she may have had, perhaps still has, some shady friends. Nothing serious—just fiddles— that kind of thing."

"What about the clocks?"

"Didn't mean a thing to her. I think she was speaking the truth. We've traced where they came from—Portobello Market. That's the ormolu and the Dresden china. And very little help *that* is! You know what it's like on a Saturday there. Bought by an American lady, the stall keeper *thinks*— but I'd say that's just a guess. Portobello Market is full of American tourists. His wife says it was a man bought them. She can't remember what he looked like. The silver one came from a silversmith in Bournemouth. A tall lady who wanted a present for her little girl! All she can remember about her is she wore a green hat."

"And the fourth clock? The one that disappeared?"

"No comment," said Hardcastle.

I knew just what he meant by that.

CHAPTER 23

COLIN LAMB'S NARRATIVE

The hotel I was staying in was a poky little place by the station. It served a decent grill but that was all that could be said for it. Except, of course, that it was cheap.

At ten o'clock the following morning I rang the Cavendish Secretarial Bureau and said that I wanted a shorthand typist to take down some letters and retype a business agreement. My name was Douglas Weatherby and I was staying at the Clarendon Hotel (extraordinarily tatty hotels always have grand names). Was Miss Sheila Webb available? A friend of mine had found her very efficient.

I was in luck. Sheila could come straight away. She had,

however, an appointment at twelve o'clock. I said that I would have finished with her well before that as I had an appointment myself.

I was outside the swing doors of the Clarendon when Sheila appeared. I stepped forward.

" Mr. Douglas Weatherby at your service," I said.

" Was it *you* rang up?"

" It was."

" But you can't do things like that." She looked scandalised.

" Why not? I'm prepared to pay the Cavendish Bureau for your services. What does it matter to them if we spend your valuable and expensive time in the Buttercup Café just across the street instead of dictating dull letters beginning ' Yours of the 3rd prontissimo to hand,' etc. Come on, let's go and drink indifferent coffee in peaceful surroundings."

The Buttercup Café lived up to its name by being violently and aggressively yellow. Formica table tops, plastic cushions and cups and saucers were all canary colour

I ordered coffee and scones for two. It was early enough for us to have the place practically to ourselves.

When the waitress had taken the order and gone away, we looked across the table at each other.

" Are you all right, Sheila?"

" What do you mean—am I all right?"

Her eyes had such dark circles under them that they looked violet rather than blue.

" Have you been having a bad time?"

" Yes—no—I don't know. I thought you had gone away?"

" I had. I've come back."

" Why?"

" You know why."

Her eyes dropped.

" I'm afraid of him," she said after a pause of at least a minute, which is a long time.

" Who are you afraid of?"

" That friend of yours—that inspector. He thinks . . . he thinks I killed that man, and that I killed Edna too . . ."

" Oh, that's just his manner," I said reassuringly. " He always goes about looking as though he suspected everybody."

" No, Colin, it's not like that at all. It's no good saying things just to cheer me up. He's thought that I had something to do with it right from the beginning."

" My dear girl, there's no evidence against you. Just because you were there on the spot that day, because someone put you on the spot . . ."

She interrupted.

" He thinks I put myself on the spot. He thinks it's all a trumped-up story. He thinks that Edna in some way knew about it. He thinks that Edna recognised my voice on the telephone pretending to be Miss Pebmarsh."

" *Was* it your voice?" I asked.

" No, of course it wasn't. I *never* made that telephone call. I've always told you so."

" Look here, Sheila," I said. " Whatever you tell anyone else, you've got to tell *me* the truth."

" So you don't believe a word I say!"

" Yes, I do. You *might* have made that telephone call that day for some quite innocent reason. Someone may have *asked* you to make it, perhaps told you it was part of a joke, and then you got scared and once you'd lied about it, you had to go on lying. Was it like that?"

" No, no, *no*! How often have I got to tell you?"

" It's all very well, Sheila, but there's *something* you're not telling me. I want you to trust me. If Hardcastle *has* got something against you, something that he hasn't told me about——"

She interrupted again.

" Do you expect him to tell you everything?"

" Well, there's no reason why he shouldn't. We're roughly members of the same profession."

The waitress brought our order at this point. The coffee was as pale as the latest fashionable shade of mink.

" I didn't know you had anything to do with the police," Sheila said, slowly stirring her coffee round and round.

" It's not exactly the police. It's an entirely different branch. But what I was getting at was, that if Dick *doesn't* tell me things he knows about you, it's for a special reason. It's because he thinks I'm interested in you. Well, I am interested in you. I'm more than that. I'm *for* you, Sheila, whatever you've done. You came out of that house that day scared to death. You were really scared. You weren't pretending. You couldn't have acted a part the way you did."

"Of course I was scared. I was terrified."

"Was it only finding the dead body that scared you? Or was there something else?"

"What else should there be?"

I braced myself.

"Why did you pinch that clock with Rosemary written across it?"

"What do you mean? Why should I pinch it?"

"I'm asking you *why* you did."

"I never touched it."

"You went back into that room because you'd left your gloves there, you said. You weren't wearing any gloves that day. A fine September day. I've never seen you wear gloves. All right then, you went back into that room and you picked up that clock. Don't lie to me about that. That's what you did, isn't it?"

She was silent for a moment or two, crumbling up the scones on her plate.

"All right," she said in a voice that was almost a whisper. "All right. I did. I picked up the clock and I shoved it into my bag and I came out again."

"But why did you do it?"

"Because of the name—Rosemary. It's my name."

"Your name is Rosemary, not Sheila?"

"It's both. Rosemary Sheila."

"And that was enough, just that? The fact that you'd the same name as was written on one of those clocks?"

She heard my disbelief, but she stuck to it.

"I was scared, I tell you."

I looked at her. Sheila was *my* girl—the girl I wanted—and wanted for keeps. But it wasn't any use having illusions about her. Sheila was a liar and probably always would be a liar. It was her way of fighting for survival—the quick easy glib denial. It was a child's weapon—and she'd probably never got out of using it. If I wanted Sheila I must accept her as she was—be at hand to prop up the weak places. We've all got our weak places. Mine were different from Sheila's but they were there.

I made up my mind and attacked. It was the only way.

"It was *your* clock, wasn't it?" I said. "It belonged to you?"

She gasped.

"How did you know?"

"Tell me about it."

The story tumbled out then in a helter-skelter of words. She'd had the clock nearly all her life. Until she was about six years old she'd always gone by the name of Rosemary—but she hated it and had insisted on being called Sheila. Lately the clock had been giving trouble. She'd taken it with her to leave at a clock-repairing shop not far from the Bureau. But she'd left it somewhere—in the bus, perhaps, or in the milk bar where she went for a sandwich at lunch time.

"How long was this before the murder at 19, Wilbraham Crescent?"

About a week, she thought. She hadn't bothered much, because the clock was old and always going wrong and it would really be better to get a new one.

And then:

"I didn't notice it at first," she said. "Not when I went into the room. And then I—found the dead man. I was paralysed. I straightened up after touching him and I just stood there staring and my clock was facing me on a table by the fire—*my* clock—and there was blood on my hand—and then she came in and I forgot everything because she was going to tread on him. And—and so—I bolted. To get away—that's all I wanted."

I nodded.

"And later?"

"I began to think. She said *she* hadn't telephoned for me—then who had—who'd got me there and put *my* clock there? I—I said that about leaving gloves and—and stuffed it into my bag. I suppose it was—stupid of me."

"You couldn't have done anything sillier," I told her. "In some ways, Sheila, you've got no sense at all."

"But someone is trying to involve me. That postcard. It must have been sent by someone who knows I took that clock. And the postcard itself—the Old Bailey. If my father was a criminal——"

"What do you know about your father and mother?"

"My father and mother died in an accident when I was a

baby. That's what my aunt told me, what I've always been told. But she never speaks about them, she never tells me anything *about* them. Sometimes, once or twice when I asked, she's told me things about them that aren't the same as what she's told me before. So I've always known, you see, that there's something *wrong*."

" Go on."

" So I think that perhaps my father was some kind of criminal—perhaps even, a murderer. Or perhaps it was my mother. People don't say your parents are dead and can't or won't tell you anything about those parents, unless the real reason is something—something that they think would be too awful for you to know."

" So you got yourself all worked up. It's probably quite simple. You may just have been an illegitimate child."

" I thought of that, too. People do sometimes try and hide that kind of thing from children. It's very stupid. They'd much better just tell them the real truth. It doesn't matter as much nowadays. But the whole point is, you see, that I don't *know*. I don't know what's *behind* all this. Why was I called Rosemary? It's not a family name. It means remembrance, doesn't it?"

" Which could be a nice meaning," I pointed out.

" Yes, it could . . . But I don't feel it was. Anyway, after the inspector had asked me questions that day, I began to think. Why had someone wanted to get me there? To get me there with a strange man who was dead? Or was it the dead man who had wanted me to meet him there? Was he, perhaps—my father, and he wanted me to do something for him? And then someone had come along and killed him instead. Or did someone want to make out from the beginning that it was I who had killed him? Oh, I was all mixed up, frightened. It seemed somehow as if everything was being made to point at *me*. Getting me there, and a dead man, and my name—Rosemary—on my own clock that didn't belong there. So I got in a panic and did something that was stupid, as you say."

I shook my head at her.

" You've been reading or typing too many thrillers and mystery stories," I said accusingly. " What about Edna? Haven't you any idea at all what she'd got into her head about you? Why did she come all the way to your house to talk to you when she saw you every day at the office?"

"I've no idea. She couldn't have thought *I* had anything to do with the murder. She couldn't."

"Could it have been something she overheard and made a mistake about?"

"There was nothing, I tell you. Nothing!"

I wondered. I couldn't help wondering . . . Even now, I didn't trust Sheila to tell the truth.

"Have you got any personal enemies? Disgruntled young men, jealous girls, someone or other a bit unbalanced who might have it in for you?"

It sounded most unconvincing as I said it.

"Of course not."

So there it was. Even now I wasn't sure about that clock. It was a fantastic story. 413. What did those figures mean? Why write them on a postcard with the word: REMEMBER unless they would mean *something* to the person to whom the postcard was sent?

I sighed, paid the bill and got up.

"Don't worry," I said. (Surely the most fatuous words in the English or any other language.) "The Colin Lamb Personal Service is on the job. You're going to be all right, and we're going to be married and live happily ever after on practically nothing a year. By the way," I said, unable to stop myself, though I knew it would have been better to end on the romantic note, but the Colin Lamb Personal Curiosity drove me on. "What have you actually done with that clock? Hidden it in your stocking drawer?"

She waited just a moment before she said:

"I put it in the dustbin of the house next door."

I was quite impressed. It was simple and probably effective. To think of that had been clever of her. Perhaps I had under-estimated Sheila.

CHAPTER 24

When Sheila had gone, I went across to the Clarendon, packed my bag and left it ready with the porter. It was the kind of hotel where they are particular about your checking out before noon.

Then I set out. My route took me past the police station, and after hesitating a moment, I went in. I asked for Hardcastle and he was there. I found him frowning down at a letter in his hand.

"I'm off again this evening, Dick," I said. "Back to London."

He looked up at me with a thoughtful expression.

"Will you take a piece of advice from me?"

"No," I said immediately.

He paid no attention. People never do when they want to give you advice.

"I should get away—and stay away—if you know what's best for you."

"Nobody can judge what's best for anyone else."

"I doubt that."

"I'll tell you something, Dick. When I've tidied up my present assignment, I'm quitting. At least—I think I am."

"Why?"

"I'm like an old-fashioned Victorian clergyman. I have Doubts."

"Give yourself time."

I wasn't sure what he meant by that. I asked him what he himself was looking so worried about.

"Read that." He passed me the letter he had been studying.

Dear Sir,

I've just thought of something. You asked me if my husband had any identifying marks and I said he hadn't. But I was wrong. Actually he has a kind of scar behind

168

his left ear. He cut himself with a razor when a dog we had jumped up at him, and he had to have it stitched up. It was so small and unimportant I never thought of it the other day.

Yours truly,
Merlina Rival

" She writes a nice dashing hand," I said, " though I've never really fancied purple ink. Did the deceased have a scar?"

" He had a scar all right. Just where she says."

" Didn't she see it when she was shown the body?"

Hardcastle shook his head.

" The ear covers it. You have to bend the ear forward before you can see it."

" Then that's all right. Nice piece of corroboration. What's eating you?"

Hardcastle said gloomily that this case was the devil! He asked if I would be seeing my French or Belgian friend in London.

" Probably. Why?"

" I mentioned him to the chief constable who says he remembers him quite well—that Girl Guide murder case. I was to extend a very cordial welcome to him if he is thinking of coming down here."

" Not he," I said. " The man is practically a limpet."

aquatic snail

II

It was a quarter past twelve when I rang the bell at 62, Wilbraham Crescent. Mrs. Ramsay opened the door. She hardly raised her eyes to look at me.

" What is it?" she said.

" Can I speak to you for a moment? I was here about ten days ago. You may not remember."

She lifted her eyes to study me further. A faint frown appeared between her eyebrows.

" You came—you were with that police inspector, weren't you?"

" That's right, Mrs. Ramsay. Can I come in?"

" If you want to, I suppose. One doesn't refuse to let the

police in. They'd take a very poor view of it if you did."

She led the way into the sitting-room, made a brusque gesture towards a chair and sat down opposite me. There had been a faint acerbity in her voice, but her manner now resumed a listlessness which I had not noted in it previously.

I said:

" It seems quiet here to-day . . . I suppose your boys have gone back to school?"

" Yes. It does make a difference." She went on, " I suppose you want to ask some more questions, do you, about this last murder? The girl who was killed in the telephone box."

" No, not exactly that. I'm not really connected with the police, you know."

She looked faintly surprised.

" I thought you were Sergeant—Lamb, wasn't it?"

" My name is Lamb, yes, but I work in an entirely different department."

The listlessness vanished from Mrs. Ramsay's manner. She gave me a quick, hard, direct stare.

" Oh," she said, " well, what is it?"

" Your husband is still abroad?"

" Yes."

" He's been gone rather a long time, hasn't he, Mrs. Ramsay? And gone rather a long way?"

" What do you know about it?"

" Well, he's gone beyond the Iron Curtain, hasn't he?" She was silent for a moment or two, and then she said in a quiet, toneless voice:

" Yes. Yes, that's quite right."

" Did you know he was going?"

" More or less." She paused a minute and then said, " He wanted me to join him there."

" Had he been thinking of it for some time?"

" I suppose so. He didn't tell me until lately."

" You are not in sympathy with his views?"

" I was once, I suppose. But you must know that already . . . You check up pretty thoroughly on things like that, don't you? Go back into the past, find out who was a fellow traveller, who was a party member, all that sort of thing."

" You might be able to give us information that would be very useful to us," I said.

She shook her head.

"No. I can't do that. I don't mean that I won't. You see, he never told me anything definite. I didn't want to know. I was sick and tired of the whole thing! When Michael told me that he was leaving this country, clearing out, and going to Moscow, it didn't really startle me. I had to decide then, what *I* wanted to do."

"And you decided you were not sufficiently in sympathy with your husband's aims?"

"No, I wouldn't put it like that at all! My view is entirely personal. I believe it always is with women in the end, unless of course one is a fanatic. And then women can be *very* fanatical, but I wasn't. I've never been anything more than mildly left-wing."

"Was your husband mixed up in the Larkin business?"

"I don't know. I suppose he might have been. He never told me anything or spoke to me about it."

She looked at me suddenly with more animation.

"We'd better get it quite clear, Mr. Lamb. Or Mr. Wolf in Lamb's clothing, or whatever you are. I loved my husband. I might have been fond enough of him to go with him to Moscow, whether I agreed with what his politics were or not. He wanted me to bring the boys. I didn't want to bring the boys! It was as simple as that. And so I decided I'd have to stay with them. Whether I shall ever see Michael again or not I don't know. He's got to choose his way of life and I've got to choose mine, but I did know one thing quite definitely. After he talked about it to me. I wanted the boys brought up here in their own country. They're English. I want them to be brought up as ordinary English boys."

"I see."

"And that I think is all," said Mrs. Ramsay, as she got up. There was now a sudden decision in her manner.

"It must have been a hard choice," I said gently. "I'm very sorry for you."

I was, too. Perhaps the real sympathy in my voice got through to her. She smiled very slightly.

"Perhaps you really are . . . I suppose in your job you have to try and get more or less under people's skins, know what they're feeling and thinking. It's been rather a knock-out blow for me, but I'm over the worst of it . . . I've got to make plans now, what to do, where to go, whether to stay here or go somewhere else. I shall have to get a job. I used to do secretarial work once. Probably I'll take a refresher course in shorthand and typing."

"Well, don't go and work for the Cavendish Bureau," I said.

"Why not?"

"Girls who are employed there seem to have rather unfortunate things happen to them."

"If you think I know anything at all about that, you're wrong. I don't."

I wished her luck and went. I hadn't learnt anything from her. I hadn't really thought I should. But one has to tidy up the loose ends.

III

Going out of the gate I almost cannoned into Mrs. McNaughton. She was carrying a shopping-bag and seemed very wobbly on her feet.

"Let me," I said and took it from her. She was inclined to clutch it from me at first, then she leaned her head forward, peering at me, and relaxed her grip.

"You're the young man from the police," she said. "I didn't recognise you at first."

I carried the shopping-bag to her front door and she teetered beside me. The shopping-bag was unexpectedly heavy. I wondered what was in it. Pounds of potatoes?

"Don't ring," she said. "The door isn't locked."

Nobody's door seemed ever to be locked in Wilbraham Crescent.

"And how are you getting on with things?" she asked chattily. "He seems to have married very much below him."

I didn't know what she was talking about.

"Who did—I've been away," I explained.

"Oh, I see. *Shadowing* someone, I suppose. I meant that Mrs. Rival. I went to the inquest. Such a *common*-looking woman. I must say she didn't seem much upset by her husband's death."

"She hadn't seen him for fifteen years," I explained.

"Angus and I have been married for twenty years." She

sighed. " It's a long time. And so much gardening now that
he isn't at the university . . . It makes it difficult to know
what to do with oneself."

At that moment, Mr. McNaughton, spade in hand, came
round the corner of the house.

" Oh, you're back, my dear. Let me take the things——"

" Just put it in the kitchen," said Mrs. McNaughton to me
swiftly—her elbow nudged me. " Just the Cornflakes and the
eggs and a melon," she said to her husband, smiling brightly.

I deposited the bag on the kitchen table. It clinked.

Cornflakes, my foot! I let my spy's instincts take over.
Under a camouflage of sheet gelatine were three bottles of
whisky.

I understood why Mrs. McNaughton was sometimes so
bright and garrulous and why she was occasionally a little
unsteady on her feet. And possibly why McNaughton had
resigned his Chair.

It was a morning for neighbours. I met Mr. Bland as
I was going along the crescent towards Albany Road. Mr.
Bland seemed in very good form. He recognised me at once.

" How are you? How's crime? Got your dead body identified, I see. Seems to have treated that wife of his rather badly.
By the way, excuse me, you're not one of the locals, are
you?"

I said evasively I had come down from London.

" So the Yard was interested, was it?"

" Well——" I drew the word out in a noncommittal way.

" I understand. Mustn't tell tales out of school. You
weren't at the inquest, though."

I said I had been abroad.

" So have I, my boy. So have I!" He winked at me.

" Gay Paree?" I asked, winking back.

" Wish it had been. No, only a day trip to Boulogne."
He dug me in the side with his elbow (quite like Mrs.
McNaughton!).

" Didn't take the wife. Teamed up with a very nice little
bit. Blonde. Quite a hot number."

" Business trip?" I said. We both laughed like men of
the world.

He went on towards No. 61 and I walked on towards
Albany Road.

I was dissatisfied with myself. As Poirot had said, there should have been more to be got out of the neighbours. It was positively unnatural that *nobody* should have seen anything! Perhaps Hardcastle had asked the wrong questions. But could I think of any better ones? As I turned into Albany Road I made a mental list of questions. It went something like this:

Mr. Curry (Castleton) had been doped—When?
        ditto   had been killed—Where?
Mr. Curry (Castleton) had been taken to No. 19—How?
Somebody must have seen something!—Who?
        ditto   —What?

I turned to the left again. Now I was walking along Wilbraham Crescent just as I had walked on September 9th. Should I call on Miss Pebmarsh? Ring the bell and say—well, what should I say?

Call on Miss Waterhouse? But what on earth could I say to *her*?

Mrs. Hemming perhaps? It wouldn't much matter what one said to Mrs. Hemming. She wouldn't be listening, and what *she* said, however haphazard and irrelevant, *might* lead to something.

I walked along, mentally noting the numbers as I had before. Had the late Mr. Curry come along here, also noting numbers, until he came to the number he meant to visit?

Wilbraham Crescent had never looked primmer. I almost found myself exclaiming in Victorian fashion, "Oh! if these stones could speak!" It was a favourite quotation in those days, so it seemed. But stones don't speak, no more do bricks and mortar, nor even plaster nor stucco. Wilbraham Crescent remained silently itself. Old-fashioned, aloof, rather shabby, and not given to conversation. Disapproving, I was sure, of itinerant prowlers who didn't even know what they were looking for.

There were few people about, a couple of boys on bicycles passed me, two women with shopping-bags. The houses themselves might have been embalmed like mummies for all the signs of life there were in them. I knew why that was. It was already, or close upon, the sacred hour of one, an hour sanctified by English traditions to the consuming of a midday meal. In one or two houses I could see through the uncurtained windows a group of one or two people round a dining table, but even that was exceedingly rare. Either the windows were discreetly screened with nylon netting, as opposed to the once popular Nottingham lace, or—which was far more probable—anyone who was at home was eating in the "modern" kitchen, according to the custom of the 1960's.

It was, I reflected, a perfect hour of day for a murder. Had the murderer thought of that, I wondered? Was it part of the murderer's plan? I came at last to No. 19.

Like so many other moronic members of the populace I stood and stared. There was, by now, no other human being in sight. "No neighbours," I said sadly, "no intelligent onlookers."

I felt a sharp pain in my shoulder. I had been wrong. There *was* a neighbour here, all right, a very useful neighbour if the neighbour had only been able to speak. I had been leaning against the post of No. 20, and the same large orange cat I had seen before was sitting on the gate post. I stopped and exchanged a few words with him, first detaching his playful claw from my shoulder.

"If cats could speak," I offered him as a conversational opening.

The orange cat opened his mouth, gave a loud melodious miaow.

"I know you can," I said. "I know you can speak just as well as I can. But you're not speaking my language. Were you sitting here that day? Did you see who went into that house or came out of it? Do you know all about what happened? I wouldn't put it past you, puss."

The cat took my remark in poor part. He turned his back on me and began to switch his tail.

"I'm sorry, your Majesty," I said.

He gave me a cold look over his shoulder and started industriously to wash himself. Neighbours, I reflected bitterly! There was no doubt about it, neighbours were in short supply in Wilbraham Crescent. What I wanted—what Hardcastle wanted—was some nice gossipy, prying, peering old lady with time hanging heavy on her hands. Always hoping to look out and see something scandalous. The trouble is that that kind of old lady seems to have died out nowadays. They are all sitting grouped together in Old Ladies' Homes with every comfort for the aged, or crowding up hospitals where beds are needed urgently for the really sick. The lame and the halt and the old didn't live in their own houses any more, attended by a faithful domestic or by some half-witted poor relation glad of a good home. It was a serious setback to criminal investigation.

I looked across the road. Why couldn't there be any neighbours there? Why couldn't there be a neat row of houses facing me instead of that great, inhuman-looking concrete block. A kind of human beehive, no doubt, tenanted by worker bees who were out all day and only came back in the evening to wash their smalls or make up their faces and go out to meet their young men. By contrast with the inhumanity of that block of flats I began almost to have a kindly feeling for the faded Victorian gentility of Wilbraham Crescent.

My eye was caught by a flash of light somewhere half-way up the building. It puzzled me. I stared up. Yes, there it came again. An open window and someone looking through it. A face slightly obliterated by something that was being held up to it. The flash of light came again. I dropped a hand into my pocket. I keep a good many things in my pockets, things that may be useful. You'd be surprised at what is ueful sometimes. A little adhesive tape. A few quite innocent-looking instruments which are quite capable of opening most locked doors, a tin of grey powder labelled something which it isn't and an insufflator to use with it, and one or two other little gadgets which most people wouldn't recognise for what they are. Amongst other things I had a pocket bird watcher. Not a high-powered one but just good enough to be useful. I took this out and raised it to my eye.

There was a child at the window. I could see a long plait of hair lying over one shoulder. She had a pair of small opera glasses and she was studying me with what might have been flattering attention. As there was nothing else for her to look at, however, it might not be as flattering as it seemed. At that moment, however, there was another midday distraction in Wilbraham Crescent.

A very old Rolls-Royce came with dignity along the road driven by a very elderly chauffeur. He looked dignified but rather disgusted with life. He passed me with the solemnity of a whole procession of cars. My child observer, I noticed, was now training her opera glasses on him. I stood there, thinking.

It is always my belief that if you wait long enough, you're bound to have *some* stroke of luck. Something that you can't count upon and that you would never have thought of, but which just *happens*. Was it possible that this might be mine? Looking up again at the big square block, I noted carefully the position of the particular window I was interested in, counting from it to each end and up from the ground. Third floor. Then I walked along the street till I came to the entrance to the block of flats. It had a wide carriage-drive sweeping round the block with neatly spaced flower-beds at strategic positions in the grass.

It's always well, I find, to go through all the motions, so I stepped off the carriage-drive towards the block, looked up over my head as though startled, bent down to the grass, pretended to hunt about and finally straightened up, apparently transferring something from my hand to my pocket. Then I walked round the block until I came to the entrance.

At most times of day I should think there was a porter here, but between the sacred hours of one and two the entrance hall was empty. There was a bell with a large sign above it, saying PORTER, but I did not ring it. There was an automatic lift and I went to it and pressed a button for the third floor. After that I had to check things pretty carefully.

It looks simple enough from the outside to place one particular room, but the inside of a building is confusing. However, I've had a good deal of practice at that sort of thing in my time, and I was fairly sure that I'd got the right door. The number on it, for better or worse, was No. 77. 'Well,' I thought, 'sevens are lucky. Here goes.' I pressed the bell and stood back to await events.

CHAPTER 25

COLIN'S NARRATIVE

I had to wait just a minute or two, then the door opened.

A big blonde Nordic girl with a flushed face and wearing gay-coloured clothing, looked at me inquiringly. Her hands had been hastily wiped but there were traces of flour on them and there was a slight smear of flour on her nose so it was easy for me to guess what she had been doing.

"Excuse me," I said, "but you have a little girl here, I think. She dropped something out of the window."

She smiled at me encouragingly. The English language was not as yet her strong point.

"I am sorry—what you say?"

"A child here—a little girl."

"Yes, yes." She nodded.

"Dropped something—out of the window."

Here I did a little gesticulation.

"I picked it up and brought it here."

I held out an open hand. In it was a silver fruit knife. She looked at it without recognition.

"I do not think—I have not seen . . ."

"You're busy cooking," I said sympathetically.

"Yes, yes, I cook. That is so," she nodded vigorously.

"I don't want to disturb you," I said. "If you let me just take it to her."

"Excuse?"

My meaning seemed to come to her. She led the way across the hall and opened a door. It led into a pleasant sitting-room. By the window a couch had been drawn up and on it there was a child of about nine or ten years old, with a leg done up in plaster.

"This gentleman, he say you—you drop . . ."

At this moment, rather fortunately, a strong smell of burning came from the kitchen. My guide uttered an exclamation of dismay.

"Excuse, please excuse."

" You go along," I said heartily. " I can manage this."

She fled with alacrity. I entered the room, shut the door behind me and came across to the couch.

" How d'you do?" I said.

The child said " How d'you do?" and proceeded to sum me up with a long, penetrating glance that almost unnerved me. She was rather a plain child with straight mousy hair arranged in two plaits. She had a bulging forehead, a sharp chin and a pair of very intelligent grey eyes.

" I'm Colin Lamb," I said. " What's your name?"

She gave me the information promptly.

" Geraldine Mary Alexandra Brown."

" Dear me," I said, " that's quite a bit of a name. What do they call you?"

" Geraldine. Sometimes Gerry, but I don't like that. And Daddy doesn't approve of abbreviations."

One of the great advantages of dealing with children is that they have their own logic. Anyone of adult years would at once have asked me what I wanted. Geraldine was quite ready to enter into conversation without resorting to foolish questions. She was alone and bored and the onset of any kind of visitor was an agreeable novelty. Until I proved myself a dull and unamusing fellow, she would be quite ready to converse.

" Your daddy's out, I suppose," I said.

She replied with the same promptness and fullness of detail which she had already shown.

" Cartinghaven Engineering Works, Beaverbridge," she said. " It's fourteen and three-quarter miles from here exactly."

" And your mother?"

" Mummy's dead," said Geraldine, with no diminution of cheerfulness. " She died when I was a baby two months old. She was in a plane coming from France. It crashed. Everyone was killed."

She spoke with a certain satisfaction and I perceived that to a child, if her mother *is* dead, it reflects a certain kudos if she has been killed in a complete and devastating accident.

" I see," I said. " So you have——" I looked towards the door.

" That's Ingrid. She comes from Norway. She's only been

here a fortnight. She doesn't know any English to speak of yet. I'm teaching her English."

" And she is teaching you Norwegian?"

" Not very much," said Geraldine.

" Do you like her?"

" Yes. She's all right. The things she cooks are rather odd sometimes. Do you know, she likes eating raw fish."

" I've eaten raw fish in Norway," I said. " It's very good sometimes."

Geraldine looked extremely doubtful about that.

" She is trying to make a treacle tart to-day," she said.

" That sounds good."

" Umm—yes, I like treacle tart." She added politely, " Have you come to lunch?"

" Not exactly. As a matter of fact I was passing down below out there, and I think you dropped something out of the window."

" Me?"

" Yes." I advanced the silver fruit knife.

Geraldine looked at it, at first suspiciously and then with signs of approval.

" It's rather nice," she said. " What is it?"

" It's a fruit knife."

I opened it.

" Oh, I see. You mean you can peel apples with it and things like that."

" Yes."

Geraldine sighed.

" It's not mine. I didn't drop it. What made you think I did?"

" Well, you were looking out of the window, and . . ."

" I look out of the window most of the time," said Geraldine. " I fell down and broke my leg, you see."

" Hard luck."

" Yes, wasn't it. I didn't break it in a very interesting way, though. I was getting out of a bus and it went on suddenly. It hurt rather at first and it ached a bit, but it doesn't now."

" Must be rather dull for you," I said.

" Yes, it is. But Daddy brings me things. Plasticine, you know, and books and crayons and jigsaw puzzles and things

like that, but you get tired of *doing* things, so I spend a lot of
time looking out of the window with these."

She produced with enormous pride a small pair of opera
glasses.

" May I look? " I said.

I took them from her, adjusted them to my eyes and looked
out of the window.

" They're jolly good," I said appreciatively.

They were indeed, excellent. Geraldine's daddy, if it had
been he who supplied them, had not spared expense. It was
astonishing how clearly you could see No. 19, Wilbraham
Crescent and its neighbouring houses. I handed them back
to her.

" They're excellent," I said. " First-class."

" They're proper ones," said Geraldine, with pride. " Not
just for babies and pretending."

" No . . . I can see that."

" I keep a little book," said Geraldine.

She showed me.

" I write down things in it and the times. It's like train
spotting," she added. " I've got a cousin called Dick and he
does train spotting. We do motor-car numbers too. You
know, you start at 1 and see how far you can get."

" It's rather a good sport," I said.

" Yes, it is. Unfortunately there aren't many cars come
down this road so I've rather given that up for the time
being."

" I suppose you must know all about those houses down
there, who lives in them and all that sort of thing."

I threw it out casually enough but Geraldine was quick to
respond.

" Oh, yes. Of course I don't know their real names, so I
have to give them names of my own."

" That must be rather fun," I said.

" That's the Marchioness of Carrabas down there," said
Geraldine, pointing. " That one with all the untidy trees.
You know, like Puss in Boots. She has masses and masses of
cats."

" I was talking to one just now," I said, " an orange
one."

" Yes, I saw you," said Geraldine.

"You must be very sharp," I said. "I don't expect you miss much, do you?"

Geraldine smiled in a pleased way. Ingrid opened the door and came in breathless.

"You are all right, yes?"

"We're quite all right," said Geraldine firmly. "You needn't worry, Ingrid."

She nodded violently and pantomimed with her hands.

"You go back, you cook."

"Very well, I go. It is nice that you have a visitor."

"She gets nervous when she cooks," explained Geraldine, "when she's trying anything new, I mean. And sometimes we have meals very late because of that. I'm glad you've come. It's nice to have someone to distract you, then you don't think about being hungry."

"Tell me more about the people in the houses there," I said, "and what you see. Who lives in the next house—the neat one?"

"Oh, there's a blind woman there. She's quite blind and yet she walks just as well as though she could see. The porter told me that. Harry. He's very nice, Harry is. He tells me a lot of things. He told me about the murder."

"The murder?" I said, sounding suitably astonished.

Geraldine nodded. Her eyes shone with importance at the information she was about to convey.

"There was a murder in that house. I practically *saw* it."

"How very interesting."

"Yes, isn't it? I've never seen a murder before. I mean I've never seen a place where a murder happened."

"What did you—er—see?"

"Well, there wasn't very much going on just then. You know, it's rather an empty time of day. The exciting thing was when somebody came rushing out of the house screaming. And then of course I knew something must have happened."

"Who was screaming?"

"Just a woman. She was quite young, rather pretty really. She came out of the door and she screamed and she screamed. There was a young man coming along the road. She came out of the gate and sort of clutched him—like this." She made a motion with her arms. She fixed me with a sudden glance. "He looked rather like you."

"I must have a double," I said lightly. "What happened next? This is very exciting."

"Well, he sort of plumped her down. You know, on the ground there and then he went back into the house and the Emperor—that's the orange cat, I always call him the Emperor because he looks so proud—stopped washing himself and he looked quite surprised, and then Miss Pikestaff came out of her house—that's the one there, Number 18—she came out and stood on the steps staring."

"Miss Pikestaff?"

"I call her Miss Pikestaff because she's so plain. She's got a brother and she bullies him."

"Go on," I said with interest.

"And then all sorts of things happened. The man came out of the house again—are you sure it wasn't you?"

"I'm a very ordinary-looking chap," I said modestly, "there are lots like me."

"Yes, I suppose that's true," said Geraldine, somewhat unflatteringly. "Well, anyway, this man, he went off down the road and telephoned from the call-box down there. Presently police began arriving." Her eyes sparkled. "Lots of police. And they took the dead body away in a sort of ambulance thing. Of course there were lots of people by that time, staring, you know. I saw Harry there, too. That's the porter from these flats. He told me about it afterwards."

"Did he tell you who was murdered?"

"He just said it was a man. Nobody knew his name."

"It's all very interesting," I said.

I prayed fervently that Ingrid would not choose this moment to come in again with a delectable treacle tart or other delicacy.

"But go back a little, do. Tell me earlier. Did you see this man—the man who was murdered—did you see him arrive at the house?"

"No, I didn't. I suppose he must have been there all along."

"You mean he lived there?"

"Oh, no, nobody lives there except Miss Pebmarsh."

"So you know her real name?"

"Oh, yes, it was in the papers. About the murder. And the screaming girl was called Sheila Webb. Harry told me that the man who was murdered was called Mr. Curry. That's a funny name, isn't it, like the thing you eat. And there was a second murder, you know. Not the same day— later—in the telephone box down the road. I can see it from here, just, but I have to get my head right out of the window and turn it round. Of course I didn't really *see* it, because I mean if I'd known it was going to happen, I would have looked out. But, of course, I didn't know it was going to happen, so I didn't. There were a lot of people that morning just standing there in the street, looking at the house opposite. I think that's rather stupid, don't you?"

" Yes," I said, " very stupid."

Here Ingrid made her appearance once more.

" I come soon," she said reassuringly. " I come very soon now."

She departed again. Geraldine said:

" We don't really want her. She gets worried about meals. Of course this is the only one she has to cook except breakfast. Daddy goes down to the restaurant in the evening and he has something sent up for me from there. Just fish or something. Not a real dinner." Her voice sounded wistful.

" What time do you usually have your lunch, Geraldine?"

" My dinner, you mean? This is my dinner. I don't have dinner in the evening, it's supper. Well, I really have my dinner at any time Ingrid happens to have cooked it. She's rather funny about time. She has to get breakfast ready at the right time because Daddy gets so cross, but midday dinner we have any time. Sometimes we have it at twelve o'clock and sometimes I don't get it till two. Ingrid says you don't have meals at a particular time, you just have them when they're ready."

" Well, it's an easy idea," I said. " What time did you have your lunch—dinner, I mean—on the day of the murder?"

" That was one of the twelve o'clock days. You see, Ingrid goes out that day. She goes to the cinema or to have her hair done and a Mrs. Perry comes and keeps me company. She's terrible, really. She pats one."

" Pats one?" I said, slightly puzzled.

" You know, on the head. Says things like ' dear little girlie.' She's not," said Geraldine, " the kind of person you can have *any* proper conversation with. But she brings me sweets and that sort of thing."

" How old are you, Geraldine?"

" I'm ten. Ten and three months."

" You seem to me very good at intelligent conversation," I said.

" That's because I have to talk to Daddy a lot," said Geraldine seriously.

" So you had your dinner early on that day of the murder?"

" Yes, so Ingrid could get washed up and go off just after one."

" Then you were looking out of the window that morning, watching people."

" Oh, yes. Part of the time. Earlier, about ten o'clock, I was doing a crossword puzzle."

" I've been wondering whether you could possibly have seen Mr. Curry arriving at the house?"

Geraldine shook her head.

" No. I didn't. It is rather odd, I agree."

" Well, perhaps he got there quite early."

" He didn't go to the front door and ring the bell. I'd have seen him."

" Perhaps he came in through the garden. I mean through the other side of the house."

" Oh, no," said Geraldine. " It backs on other houses. They wouldn't like anyone coming through their garden."

" No, no, I suppose they wouldn't."

" I wish I knew what he'd looked like," said Geraldine.

" Well, he was quite old. About sixty. He was clean-shaven and he had on a dark grey suit."

Geraldine shook her head.

" It sounds terribly ordinary," she said with disapprobation.

" Anyway," I said, " I suppose it's difficult for you to remember one day from another when you're lying here and always looking."

" It's not at all difficult." She rose to the challenge. " I can tell you everything about that morning. I know when Mrs. Crab came and when she left."

" That's the daily cleaning woman, is it?"

"Yes. She scuttles, just like a crab. She's got a little boy. Sometimes she brings him with her, but she didn't that day. And then Miss Pebmarsh goes out about ten o'clock. She goes to teach children at a blind school. Mrs. Crab goes away about twelve. Sometimes she has a parcel with her that she didn't have when she came. Bits of butter, I expect, and cheese because Miss Pebmarsh can't see. I know particularly well what happened that day because you see Ingrid and I were having a little quarrel so she wouldn't talk to me. I'm teaching her English and she wanted to know how to say 'until we meet again.' She had to tell it me in German. *Auf Wiedersehen*. I know that because I once went to Switzerland and people said that there. And they said *Grüss Gott*, too. That's rude if you say it in English."

"So what did you tell Ingrid to say?"

Geraldine began to laugh, a deep malicious chuckle. She started to speak but her chuckles prevented her, but at last she got it out.

"I told her to say 'Get the hell out of here'! So she said it to Miss Bulstrode next door and Miss Bulstrode was *furious*. So Ingrid found out and was very cross with me and we didn't make friends until nearly tea-time the next day."

I digested this information.

"So you concentrated on your opera glasses."

Geraldine nodded.

"So that's how I know Mr. Curry didn't go in by the front door. I think perhaps he got in somehow in the night and hid in an attic. Do you think that's likely?"

"I suppose anything really is possible," I said, "but it doesn't seem to me very probable."

"No," said Geraldine, "he would have got hungry, wouldn't he? And he couldn't have asked Miss Pebmarsh for breakfast, not if he was hiding from her."

"And nobody came to the house?" I said. "Nobody at all? Nobody in a car—a tradesman—callers?"

"The grocer comes Mondays and Thursdays," said Geraldine, "and the milk comes at half past eight in the morning."

The child was a positive encyclopaedia.

"The cauliflowers and things Miss Pebmarsh buys herself. Nobody called at all except the laundry. It was a new laundry," she added.

" A new laundry?"

"Yes. It's usually the Southern Downs Laundry. Most people have the Southern Downs. It was a new laundry that day—the Snowflake Laundry. I've never seen the Snowflake Laundry. They must have just started."

I fought hard to keep any undue interest out of my voice. I didn't want to start her romancing.

" Did it deliver laundry or call for it?" I asked.

" Deliver it," said Geraldine. " In a great big basket, too. Much bigger than the usual one."

" Did Miss Pebmarsh take it in?"

" No, of course not, she'd gone out again."

" What time was this, Geraldine?"

" 1.35 exactly," said Geraldine. " I wrote it down," she added proudly.

She motioned towards a small note-book and opening it pointed with a rather dirty forefinger to an entry. 1.35 *laundry came. No. 19.*

" You ought to be at Scotland Yard," I said.

" Do they have women detectives? I'd quite like that. I don't mean police women. I think police women are silly."

" You haven't told me exactly what happened when the laundry came."

" Nothing happened," said Geraldine. " The driver got down, opened the van, took out this basket and staggered along round the side of the house to the back door. I expect he couldn't get in. Miss Pebmarsh probably locks it, so he probably left it there and came back."

" What did he look like?"

" Just ordinary," said Geraldine.

" Like me?" I asked.

" Oh, no, much older than you," said Geraldine, " but I didn't really see him properly because he drove up to the house—this way." She pointed to the right. " He drew up in front of 19 although he was on the wrong side of the road. But it doesn't matter in a street like this. And then he went in through the gate bent over the basket. I could only see the back of his head and when he came out again he was rubbing his face. I expect he found it a bit hot and trying, carrying that basket."

" And then he drove off again?"

" Yes. Why do you think it so interesting? "

" Well, I don't know," I said. " I thought perhaps *he* might have seen something interesting."

Ingrid flung the door open. She was wheeling a trolley.

" We eat dinner now," she said, nodding brightly.

" Goody," said Geraldine, " I'm starving."

I got up.

" I must be going now," I said. " Goodbye, Geraldine."

" Goodbye. What about this thing? " She picked up the fruit knife. " It's not mine." Her voice became wistful. " I wish it were."

" It looks as though it's nobody's in particular, doesn't it? "

" Would that make it treasure trove, or whatever it is? "

" Something of the kind," I said. " I think you'd better hang on to it. That is, hang on to it until someone else claims it. But I don't think," I said truthfully, " that anybody will."

" Get me an apple, Ingrid," said Geraldine.

" Apple? "

" *Pomme! Apfel!* "

She did her linguistic best. I left them to it.

CHAPTER 26

Mrs. Rival pushed open the door of the Peacock's Arms and made a slightly unsteady progress towards the bar. She was murmuring under her breath. She was no stranger to this particular hostelry and was greeted quite affectionately by the barman.

" How do, Flo," he said, " how's tricks? "

" It's not right," said Mrs. Rival. " It's not fair. No, it's not right. I know what I'm talking about, Fred, and I say it's not right."

" Of course it isn't right," said Fred, soothingly. " What is, I'd like to know? Want the usual, dear? "

Mrs. Rival nodded assent. She paid and began to sip from her glass. Fred moved away to attend to another customer. Her drink cheered Mrs. Rival slightly. She still muttered under her breath but with a more good-humoured expression.

When Fred was near her once more she addressed him again with a slightly softened manner.

"All the same, I'm not going to put up with it," she said. "No, I'm not. If there's one thing I can't bear, it's deceit. I don't stand for deceit, I never did."

"Of course you didn't," said Fred.

He surveyed her with a practised eye. 'Had a good few already,' he thought to himself. 'Still, she can stand a couple more, I expect. Something's upset her.'

"Deceit," said Mrs. Rival. "Prevari—prevari—well, you know the word I mean."

"Sure I know," said Fred.

He turned to greet another acquaintance. The unsatisfactory performance of certain dogs came under review. Mrs. Rival continued to murmur.

"I don't like it and I won't stand for it. I shall say so. People can't think they can go around treating me like that. No, indeed they can't. I mean, it's not right and if you don't stick up for yourself, who'll stick up for you? Give me another, dearie," she added in a louder voice.

Fred obliged.

"I should go home after that one, if I were you," he advised.

He wondered what had upset the old girl so much. She was usually fairly even-tempered. A friendly soul, always good for a laugh.

"It'll get me in bad, Fred, you see," she said. "When people ask you to do a thing, they should tell you all about it. They should tell you what it means and what they're doing. Liars. Dirty liars, that's what I say. And I won't stand for it."

"I should cut along home, if I were you," said Fred, as he observed a tear about to trickle down the mascaraed splendour. "Going to come on to rain soon, it is, and rain hard, too. Spoil that pretty hat of yours."

Mrs. Rival gave one faint appreciative smile.

"I always was fond of cornflowers," she said. "Oh, dear me, I don't know *what* to do, I'm sure."

"I should go home and have a nice kip," said the barman, kindly.

"Well, perhaps, but——"

"Come on, now, you don't want to spoil that hat."

"That's very true," said Mrs. Rival. "Yes, that's very true. That's a very prof—profumed—no I don't mean that—what do I mean?"

"Profound remark of yours, Fred."

"Thank you very much."

"You're welcome," said Fred.

Mrs. Rival slipped down from her high seat and went not too unsteadily towards the door.

"Something seems to have upset old Flo to-night," said one of the customers.

"She's usually a cheerful bird—but we all have our ups and downs," said another man, a gloomy-looking individual.

"If anyone had told me," said the first man, "that Jerry Grainger would come in fifth, way behind Queen Caroline, I wouldn't have believed it. If you ask me, there's been hanky-panky. Racing's not straight nowadays. Dope the horses, they do. All of 'em."

Mrs. Rival had come out of the Peacock's Arms. She looked up uncertainly at the sky. Yes, perhaps it *was* going to rain. She walked along the street, hurrying slightly, took a turn to the left, a turn to the right and stopped before a rather dingy-looking house. As she took out a key and went up the front steps a voice spoke from the area below, and a head poked round a corner of the door and looked up at her.

"Gentleman waiting for you upstairs."

"For me?"

Mrs. Rival sounded faintly surprised.

"Well, if you call him a gentleman. Well dressed and all that, but not quite Lord Algernon Vere de Vere, I would say."

Mrs. Rival succeeded in finding the keyhole, turned the key in it and entered.

The house smelled of cabbage and fish and eucalyptus. The latter smell was almost permanent in this particular hall. Mrs. Rival's landlady was a great believer in taking care of her chest in winter weather and began the good work in mid-September. Mrs. Rival climbed the stairs, aiding herself with the banisters. She pushed open the door on the first floor and went in, then she stopped dead and took a step backwards.

"Oh," she said, "it's you."

Detective Inspector Hardcastle rose from the chair where he was sitting.

"Good evening, Mrs. Rival."

"What do *you* want?" asked Mrs. Rival with less *finesse* than she would normally have shown.

"Well, I had to come up to London on duty," said Inspector Hardcastle, "and there were just one or two things I thought I'd like to take up with you, so I came along on the chance of finding you. The—er—the woman downstairs seemed to think you might be in before long."

"Oh," said Mrs. Rival. "Well, I don't see—well——"

Inspector Hardcastle pushed forward a chair.

"Do sit down," he said politely.

Their positions might have been reversed, he the host and she the guest. Mrs. Rival sat down. She stared at him very hard.

"What did you mean by one or two things?" she said.

"Little points," said Inspector Hardcastle, "little points that come up."

"You mean—about Harry?"

"That's right."

"Now look here," said Mrs. Rival, a slight belligerence coming into her voice; at the same time as an aroma of spirits came clearly to Inspector Hardcastle's nostrils. "I've *had* Harry. I don't want to think of him any more. I came forward, didn't I, when I saw his picture in the paper? I came and told you about him. It's all a long time ago and I don't want to be reminded of it. There's nothing more I can tell you. I've told you everything I could remember and now I don't want to hear any more about it."

"It's quite a small point," said Inspector Hardcastle. He spoke gently and apologetically.

"Oh, very well," said Mrs. Rival, rather ungraciously. "What is it? Let's have it."

"You recognised the man as your husband or the man you'd gone through a form of marriage with about fifteen years ago. That is right, is it not?"

"I should have thought that by this time you would have known exactly how many years ago it was."

"Sharper than I thought," Inspector Hardcastle said to himself. He went on,

"Yes, you're quite right there. We looked it up. You were married on May 15th, 1948."

"It's always unlucky to be a May bride, so they say," said Mrs. Rival gloomily. "It didn't bring me any luck."

"In spite of the years that have elapsed, you were able to identify your husband quite easily."

Mrs. Rival moved with some slight uneasiness.

"He hadn't aged much," she said, "always took care of himself, Harry did."

"And you were able to give us some additional identification. You wrote to me, I think, about a scar."

"That's right. Behind his left ear it was. Here," Mrs. Rival raised a hand and pointed to the place.

"Behind his *left* ear?" Hardcastle stressed the word.

"Well——" she looked momentarily doubtful, "yes. Well, I think so. Yes I'm sure it was. Of course one never does know one's left from one's right in a hurry, does one? But, yes, it was the left side of his neck. Here." She placed her hand on the same spot again.

"And he did it shaving, you say?"

"That's right. The dog jumped up on him. A very bouncy dog we had at the time. He kept rushing in—affectionate dog. He jumped up on Harry and he'd got the razor in his hand, and it went in deep. It bled a lot. It healed up but he never lost the mark." She was speaking now with more assurance.

"That's a very valuable point, Mrs. Rival. After all, one man sometimes looks very like another man, especially when a good many years have passed. But to find a man closely resembling your husband who has a scar in the identical place—well that makes the identification very nice and safe, doesn't it? It seems that we really have something to go on."

"I'm glad you're pleased," said Mrs. Rival.

"And this accident with the razor happened—when?"

Mrs. Rival considered a moment.

"It must have been about—oh, about six months after we were married. Yes, that was it. We got the dog that summer, I remember."

" So it took place about October or November, 1948. Is that right? "

" That's right. "

" And after your husband left you in 1951 . . . "

" He didn't so much leave me as I turned him out," said Mrs. Rival with dignity.

" Quite so. Whichever way you like to put it. Anyway, after you turned your husband out in 1951 you never saw him again until you saw his picture in the paper? "

" Yes. That's what I told you. "

" And you're quite sure about that, Mrs. Rival? "

" Of course I'm sure. I never set eyes on Harry Castleton since that day until I saw him dead. "

" That's odd, you know," said Inspector Hardcastle, " that's very odd. "

" Why—what do you mean? "

" Well, it's a very curious thing, scar tissue. Of course, it wouldn't mean much to you or me. A scar's a scar. But doctors can tell a lot from it. They can tell roughly, you know, how long a man has *had* a scar. "

" I don't know what you're getting at. "

" Well, simply this, Mrs. Rival. According to our police surgeon and to another doctor whom we consulted, that scar tissue behind your husband's ear shows very clearly that the wound in question could not be older than about five to six years ago. "

" Nonsense," said Mrs. Rival. " I don't believe it. I— nobody can tell. Anyway that wasn't when . . . "

" So you see," proceeded Hardcastle in a smooth voice, " if that wound made a scar only five or six years ago, it means that if the man *was* your husband he had no scar at the time when he left you in 1951. "

" Perhaps he didn't. But anyway it was Harry. "

" But you've never seen him since, Mrs. Rival. So if you've never seen him since, how would you know that he had acquired a scar five or six years ago. "

" You mix me up," said Mrs. Rival, " you mix me up badly. Perhaps it wasn't as long ago as 1948—You can't remember all these things. Anyway, Harry had that scar and I know it. "

" I see," said Inspector Hardcastle and he rose to his feet.

G

" I think you'd better think over that statement of yours very carefully, Mrs. Rival. You don't want to get into trouble, you know."

" How do you mean, get into trouble?"

" Well," Inspector Hardcastle spoke almost apologetically, " perjury."

" Perjury. Me!"

" Yes. It's quite a serious offence in law, you know. You could get into trouble, even go to prison. Of course, you've not been on oath in a coroner's court, but you may have to swear to this evidence of yours in a proper court sometime. Then—well, I'd like you to think it over very carefully, Mrs. Rival. It may be that somebody—suggested to you that you should tell us this story about a scar?"

Mrs. Rival got up. She drew herself to her full height, her eyes flashed. She was at that moment almost magnificent.

" I never heard such nonsense in my life," she said. " Absolute nonsense. I try and do my duty. I come and help you, I tell you all I can remember. If I've made a mistake I'm sure it's natural enough. After all I meet a good many—well, gentlemen friends, and one may get things a little wrong sometimes. But I don't think I *did* make a mistake. That man was Harry and Harry had a scar behind his left ear, I'm quite sure of it. And now, perhaps, Inspector Hardcastle, you'll go away instead of coming here and insinuating that I've been telling lies."

Inspector Hardcastle got up promptly.

" Good night, Mrs. Rival," he said. " Just think it over. That's all."

Mrs. Rival tossed her head. Hardcastle went out of the door. With his departure, Mrs. Rival's attitude altered immediately, The fine defiance of her attitude collapsed. She looked frightened and worried.

" Getting me into this," she murmured, " getting me into this. I'll—I'll not go on with it. I'll—I'll—I'm not going to get into trouble for anybody. Telling me things, lying to me, deceiving me. It's monstrous. Quite monstrous. I shall say so."

She walked up and down unsteadily, then finally making up her mind, she took an umbrella from the corner and went

out again. She walked along to the end of the street, hesitated at a call-box, then went on to a post office. She went in
there, asked for change and went into one of the call-boxes.
She dialled Directory and asked for a number. She stood
there waiting till the call came through.

" Go ahead please. Your party is on the line."

She spoke.

" Hallo . . . oh, it's you. Flo here. No, I know you told
me not to but I've had to. You've not been straight with
me. You never told me what I was getting into. You just
said it would be awkward for you if this man was identified.
I didn't dream for a moment that I would get mixed up in a
murder . . . Well, of course you'd say that, but at any
rate it wasn't what you told me . . . Yes, I do. I think you
are mixed up in it in some way . . . Well, I'm not going to
stand for it, I tell you . . . There's something about being
an—ac—well, you know the word I mean—accessory,
something like that. Though I always thought that that was
costume jewellery. Anyway, it's something like being a something after the fact, and I'm frightened, I tell you . . . telling
me to write and tell them that bit about the scar. Now it
seems he'd only got that scar a year or two ago and here's me
swearing he had it when he left me years ago . . . And that's
perjury and I might go to prison for it. Well, it's no good
your trying to talk me round . . . No . . . Obliging someone is one thing . . . Well I know . . . I know you paid
me for it. And not very much either . . . Well, all right, I'll
listen to you, but I'm not going to . . . All right, all right,
I'll keep quiet . . . What did you say? . . . How much?
. . . That's a lot of money. How do I know that you've got
it even . . . Well, yes, of course it would make a difference.
You swear you didn't have anything to do with it?—I mean
with killing anyone . . . No, well I'm sure you wouldn't. Of
course, I see that . . . Sometimes you get mixed up with a
crowd of people—and they go further than you would and it's
not your fault . . . You always make things sound so
plausible . . . You always did . . . Well, all right, I'll think
it over but it's got to be soon . . . To-morrow? What time?
. . . Yes . . . yes, I'll come but no cheque. It might bounce
. . . I don't know really that I ought to go on getting

myself mixed up in things even . . . all right. Well, if you say so . . . Well, I didn't mean to be nasty about it . . . All right then."

She came out of the post office weaving from side to side of the pavement and smiling to herself.

It was worth risking a little trouble with the police for that amount of money. It would set her up nicely. And it wasn't very much risk really. She'd only got to say she'd forgotten or couldn't remember. Lots of women couldn't remember things that had only happened a year ago. She'd say she got mixed up between Harry and another man. Oh, she could think up lots of things to say.

Mrs. Rival was a naturally mercurial type. Her spirits rose as much now as they had been depressed before. She began to think seriously and intently of the first things she would spend the money on . . .

CHAPTER 27

COLIN'S NARRATIVE

"You don't seem to have got much out of that Ramsay woman?" complained Colonel Beck.

"There wasn't much to get."

"Sure of that?"

"Yes."

"She's not an active party?"

"No."

Beck gave me a searching glance.

"Satisfied?" he asked.

"Not really."

"You hoped for more?"

"It doesn't fill the gap."

"Well—we'll have to look elsewhere . . . give up crescents—eh?"

"Yes."

"You're very monosyllabic. Got a hangover?"

"I'm no good at this job," I said slowly.

" Want me to pat you on the head and say ' There, there '?"
In spite of myself I laughed.

" That's better," said Beck. " Now then, what's it all
about? Girl trouble, I suppose."

I shook my head. " It's been coming on for some time."

" As a matter of fact I've noticed it," said Beck unexpectedly. " The world's in a confusing state nowadays. The
issues aren't clear as they used to be. When discouragement
sets in, it's like dry rot. Whacking great mushrooms bursting
through the walls! If that's so, your usefulness to us is over.
You've done some first-class work, boy. Be content with that.
Go back to those damned seaweeds of. yours."

He paused and said: " You really *like* the beastly things,
don't you?"

" I find the whole subject passionately interesting."

" I should find it repulsive. Splendid variation in nature,
isn't there? Tastes, I mean. How's that patent murder of
yours? I bet you the girl did it."

" You're wrong," I said.

Beck shook his finger at me in an admonitory and avuncular
manner.

" What I say to you is: ' Be prepared.' And I don't mean
it in the Boy Scout sense."

I walked down Charing Cross Road deep in thought.

At the tube station I bought a paper.

I read that a woman, supposed to have collapsed in the
rush hour at Victoria Station yesterday, had been taken to
hospital. On arrival there she was found to have been
stabbed. She had died without recovering consciousness.

Her name was Mrs. Merlina Rival.

II

I rang Hardcastle.

" Yes," he said in answer to my questions. " It's just as
they say."

His voice sounded hard and bitter.

" I went to see her night before last. I told her her story
about the scar just wouldn't jell. That the scar tissue was
comparatively recent. Funny how people slip up. Just by
trying to overdo things. Somebody paid that woman to iden-

tify the corpse as being that of her husband, who ran out on her years ago.

"Very well she did it, too! I believed her all right. And then whoever it was tried to be a little too clever. If she remembered that unimportant little scar as an *afterthought*, it would carry conviction and clinch the identification. If she had plumped out with it straight away, it might have sounded a bit too glib."

"So Merlina Rival was in it up to the neck?"

"Do you know, I rather doubt that. Suppose an old friend or acquaintance goes to her and says: 'Look here, I'm in a bit of a spot. A chap I've had business dealings with has been murdered. If they identify him and all our dealings come to light, it will be absolute disaster. But if you were to come along and say it's that husband of yours, Harry Castleton, who did a bunk years ago, then the whole case will peter out '."

"Surely she'd jib at that—say it was too risky?"

"If so, that someone would say: 'What's the risk? At the worst, you've made a mistake. Any woman can make a mistake after fifteen years.' And probably at that point a nice little sum would have been mentioned. And she says O.K. she'll be a sport! and do it."

"With no suspicions?"

"She wasn't a suspicious woman. Why, good lord, Colin, every time we catch a murderer there are people who've known him well, and simply can't believe he could do anything like that!"

"What happened when you went up to see her?"

"I put the wind up her. After I left, she did what I expected she'd do—tried to get in touch with the man or woman who'd got her into this. I had a tail on her, of course. She went to a post office and put through a call from an automatic call-box. Unfortunately, it wasn't the box I'd expected her to use at the end of her own street. She had to get change. She came out of the call-box looking pleased with herself. She was kept under observation, but nothing of interest happened until yesterday evening. She went to Victoria Station and took a ticket to Crowdean. It was half past six, the rush hour. She wasn't on her guard. She thought she was going to meet whoever it was at Crowdean. But the cunning devil was a step ahead of her. Easiest thing in the world to gang up behind someone in a crowd, and press the knife in . . . Don't suppose she even knew she had been stabbed. People don't, you know. Remember that case of Barton in the Levitti Gang robbery? Walked the length of a street before he fell down dead. Just a sudden sharp pain—then you think you're all right again. But you're not. You're dead on your feet although you don't know it."

He finished up: " Damn and damn and damn!"

" Have you—checked on—anybody?"

I had to ask. I couldn't help myself.

His reply came swift and sharp.

" The Pebmarsh woman was in London yesterday. She did some business for the Institute and returned to Crowdean by the 7.40 train." He paused. " And Sheila Webb took up a typescript to check over with a foreign author who was in London on his way to New York. She left the Ritz Hotel at 5.30 approx. and took in a cinema—alone—before returning."

" Look here, Hardcastle," I said, " I've got something for you. Vouched for by an eye witness. A laundry van drew up at 19, Wilbraham Crescent at 1.35 on September the 9th. The man who drove it delivered a big laundry basket at the back door of the house. It was a particularly large laundry basket."

" Laundry? What laundry?"

" The Snowflake Laundry. Know it?"

" Not off-hand. New laundries are always starting up. It's an ordinary sort of name for a laundry."

" Well—you check up. A *man* drove it—and a *man* took the basket into the house——"

Hardcastle's voice came suddenly, alert with suspicion.

" Are you making this up, Colin?"

" No. I told you I've got an eye witness. Check up, Dick. Get on with it."

I rang off before he could badger me further.

I walked out from the box and looked at my watch. I had a good deal to do—and I wanted to be out of Hardcastle's reach whilst I did it. I had my future life to arrange.

CHAPTER 28

I arrived at Crowdean at eleven o'clock at night, five days later. I went to the Clarendon Hotel, got a room, and went to bed. I'd been tired the night before and I overslept. I woke up at a quarter to ten.

I sent for coffee and toast and a daily paper. It came and with it a large square note addressed to me with the words BY HAND in the top left-hand corner.

I examined it with some surprise. It was unexpected. The paper was thick and expensive, the superscription neatly printed.

After turning it over and playing with it, I finally opened it.

Inside was a sheet of paper. Printed on it in large letters were the words:

CURLEW HOTEL 11.30
ROOM 413
(*Knock three times*)

I stared at it, turned it over in my hand—what was all this?

I noted the room number—413—the same as the clocks. A coincidence? Or *not* a coincidence.

I had thoughts of ringing the Curlew Hotel. Then I thought of ringing Dick Hardcastle. I didn't do either.

My lethargy was gone. I got up, shaved, washed, dressed and walked along the front to the Curlew Hotel and got there at the appointed time.

The summer season was pretty well over now. There weren't many people about inside the hotel.

I didn't make any inquiries at the desk. I went up in the lift to the fourth floor and walked along the corridor to No. 413.

I stood there for a moment or two: then, feeling a complete fool, I knocked three times . . .

A voice said, " Come in."

I turned the handle, the door wasn't locked. I stepped inside and stopped dead.

I was looking at the last person on earth I would have expected to see.

Hercule Poirot sat facing me. He beamed at me.

" *Une petite surprise, n'est-ce pas*?" he said. " But a pleasing one, I hope."

" Poirot, you old fox," I shouted. " How did *you* get here?"

" I got here in a Daimler limousine—most comfortable."

" But what are you *doing* here?"

" It was most vexing. They insisted, positively insisted, on the redecoration of my apartment. Imagine my difficulty. What can I do? Where can I go?"

" Lots of places," I said coldly.

" Possibly, but it is suggested to me by my doctor that the air of the sea will be good for me."

" One of those obliging doctors who finds out where his patient wants to go, and advises him to go there! Was it you who sent me *this*?" I brandished the letter I had received.

" Naturally—who else?"

" Is it a coincidence that you have a room whose number is 413?"

" It is not a coincidence. I asked for it specially."

" Why?"

Poirot put his head on one side and twinkled at me.

" It seemed to be appropriate."

" And knocking three times?"

" I could not resist it. If I could have enclosed a sprig of rosemary it would have been better still. I thought of cutting my finger and putting a bloodstained fingerprint on the door. But enough is enough! I might have got an infection."

" I suppose this is second childhood," I remarked coldly. " I'll buy you a balloon and a woolly rabbit this afternoon."

" I do not think you enjoy my surprise. You express no joy, no delight at seeing me."

" Did you expect me to?"

" *Pourquoi pas*? Come, let us be serious, now that I have had my little piece of foolery. I hope to be of assistance. I have called upon the chief constable who has been of the

utmost amiability, and at this moment I await your friend,
Detective Inspector Hardcastle."

" And what are you going to say to him?"

" It was in my mind that we might all three engage in
conversation."

I looked at him and laughed. He might call it conversation—but I knew who was going to do the talking.

Hercule Poirot!

II

Hardcastle had arrived. We had had the introduction and the
greetings. We were now settled down in a companionable
fashion, with Dick occasionally glancing surreptitiously at
Poirot with the air of a man at the Zoo studying a new and
surprising acquisition. I doubt if he had ever met anyone
quite like Hercule Poirot before!

Finally, the amenities and politeness having been observed,
Hardcastle cleared his throat and spoke.

" I suppose, M. Poirot," he said cautiously, " that you'll
want to see—well, the whole set-up for yourself? It won't
be exactly easy——" He hesitated. " The chief constable
told me to do everything I could for you. But you must
appreciate that there are difficulties, questions that may be
asked, objections. Still, as you have come down here
specially——"

Poirot interrupted him—with a touch of coldness.

" I came here," he said, " because of the reconstruction
and decoration of my apartment in London."

I gave a horse laugh and Poirot shot me a look of reproach.

" M. Poirot doesn't have to go and see things," I said. " He
has always insisted that you can do it all from an arm-chair.
But that's not quite true, is it, Poirot? Or why have you
come here?"

Poirot replied with dignity.

" I said that it was not necessary to be the foxhound, the
bloodhound, the tracking dog, running to and fro upon the
scent. But I will admit that for the chase a dog *is* necessary.
A retriever, my friend. A good retriever."

He turned towards the inspector. One hand twirled his
moustache in a satisfied gesture.

" Let me tell you," he said, " that I am not like the English, obsessed with dogs. I, personally, can live without the dog. But I accept, nevertheless, your ideal of the dog. The man loves and respects his dog. He indulges him, he boasts of the intelligence and sagacity of his dog to his friends. Now figure to yourself, the opposite may also come to pass! The dog is fond of his master. He indulges that master! He, too, boasts of his master, boasts of his master's sagacity and intelligence. And as a man will rouse himself when he does not really want to go out, and take his dog for a walk because the dog enjoys the walk so much, so will the dog endeavour to give his master what that master pines to have.

" It was so with my kind young friend Colin here. He came to see me, not to ask for help with his own problem ; that he was confident that he could solve for himself, and has, I gather, done so. No, he felt concern that I was unoccupied and lonely so he brought to me a problem that he felt would interest me and give me something to work upon. He challenged me with it—challenged me to do what I had so often told him it was possible to do—sit still in my chair and—in due course—resolve that problem. It may be, I suspect it is, that there was a *little* malice, just a small harmless amount, behind that challenge. He wanted, let us say, to prove to me that it was not so easy after all. *Mais oui, mon ami*, it is true, that! You wanted to mock yourself at me—just a little! I do not reproach you. All I say is, you did not know your Hercule Poirot."

He thrust out his chest and twirled his moustaches.

I looked at him and grinned affectionately.

" All right then," I said. " Give us the answer to the problem—if you know it." ·

" But of course I know it! "

Hardcastle stared at him incredulously.

" Are you saying you *know* who killed the man at 19, Wilbraham Crescent?"

" Certainly."

" And also who killed Edna Brent?"

" Of course."

" You know the identity of the dead man?"

" I know who he must be."

Hardcastle had a very doubtful expression on his face.

Mindful of the chief constable, he remained polite. But there was scepticism in his voice.

"Excuse me, M. Poirot, you claim that you know who killed three people. And why?"

"Yes."

"You've got an open and shut case?"

"That, no."

"All you mean is that you have a hunch," I said, unkindly.

"I will not quarrel with you over a word, *mon cher* Colin. All I say is, I *know*!"

Hardcastle sighed.

"But you see, M. Poirot, *I* have to have evidence."

"Naturally, but with the resources you have at your disposal, it will be possible for you, I think, to get that evidence."

"I'm not so sure about that."

"Come now, Inspector. If you know—really *know*—is not that the first step? Can you not, nearly always, go on from there?"

"Not always," said Hardcastle with a sigh. "There are men walking about to-day who ought to be in gaol. They know it and we know it."

"But that is a very small percentage, is it not——"

I interrupted.

"All right. All right. *You know* . . . Now let *us* know too!"

"I perceive you are still sceptical. But first let me say this: To be *sure* means that when the right solution is reached, everything falls into place. You perceive that *in no other way* could things have happened."

"For the love of Mike," I said, "get on with it! I grant you all the points you've made."

Poirot arranged himself comfortably in his chair and motioned to the inspector to replenish his glass.

"One thing, *mes amis*, must be clearly understood. To solve any problem one must have the *facts*. For that one needs the dog, the dog who is a retriever, who brings the pieces one by one and lays them at——"

"At the feet of the master," I said. "Admitted."

"One cannot from one's seat in a chair solve a case solely from reading about it in a newspaper. For one's facts must be accurate, and newspapers are seldom, if ever, accurate. They report something happened at four o'clock when it was a quarter past four, they say a man had a sister called Elizabeth when actually he had a sister-in-law called Alexandra. And so on. But in Colin here, I have a dog of remarkable ability— an ability, I may say, which has taken him far in his own career. He has always had a remarkable memory. He can repeat to you, even several days later, conversations that have taken place. He can repeat them accurately—that is, not transposing them, as nearly all of us do, to what the impression made on *him* was. To explain roughly—he would not say ' And at twenty past eleven the post came ' instead of describing what actually happened, namely a knock on the front door and someone coming into the room with letters in their hand. All this is very important. It means that he heard what *I* would have heard if I had been there and seen what I would have seen."

" Only the poor dog hasn't made the necessary deductions?"

" So, as far as can be, I have the facts—I am ' in the picture.' It is your war-time term, is it not? To ' put one in the picture.' The thing that struck me first of all, when Colin recounted the story to me, was its highly *fantastic* character. Four clocks, each roughly an hour ahead of the right time, and all introduced into the house without the knowledge of the owner, or so she *said*. For we must never, must we, believe what we are told, until such statements have been carefully checked?"

" Your mind works the way that mine does," said Hardcastle approvingly.

" On the floor lies a dead man—a respectable-looking elderly man. Nobody knows who he is (or again so they *say*). In his pocket is a card bearing the name of Mr. R. H. Curry, 7, Denvers Street. Metropolis Insurance Company. But there is no Metropolis Insurance Company. There is no Denvers Street and there seems to be no such person as Mr. Curry. That is negative evidence, but it *is* evidence. We now proceed further. Apparently at about ten minutes to two a secretarial agency is rung up, a Miss Millicent Pebmarsh asks for a stenographer to be sent to 19, Wilbraham Crescent at three o'clock. It is particularly asked that a Miss Sheila Webb should be sent. Miss Webb is sent. She arrives there at a few minutes before three; goes, according to instructions, into the sitting-room, finds a dead man on the floor and rushes out of the house screaming. She rushes into the arms of a young man."

Poirot paused and looked at me. I bowed.

"Enter our young hero," I said.

"You see," Poirot pointed out. "Even you cannot resist a farcical melodramatic tone when you speak of it. The whole thing is melodramatic, fantastic and completely unreal. It is the kind of thing that could occur in the writings of such people as Garry Gregson, for instance. I may mention that when my young friend arrived with this tale I was embarking on a course of thriller writers who had plied their craft over the last sixty years. Most interesting. One comes almost to regard actual crimes in the light of fiction. That is to say if I observe that a dog has not barked when he should bark, I say to myself 'Ha! A Sherlock Holmes crime!' Similarly if the corpse is found in a sealed room, naturally I say 'Ha! A Dickson Carr case!' Then there is my friend Mrs. Oliver. If I were to find—but I will say no more. You catch my meaning? So here is the setting of a crime in such wildly improbable circumstances that one feels at once 'This book is not true to life. All this is quite unreal.' But alas, that will not do here, for this *is* real. It *happened*. That gives one to think furiously, does it not?"

Hardcastle would not have put it like that, but he fully agreed with the sentiment, and nodded vigorously. Poirot went on:

"It is, as it were, the opposite of Chesterton's, 'Where would you hide a leaf? In a forest. Where would you hide a pebble? On a beach.' Here there is excess, fantasy, melodrama! When I say to myself in imitation of Chesterton, 'Where does a middle-aged woman hide her fading beauty?' I do not reply 'Amongst other faded middle-aged faces.' Not at all. She hides it under make-up, under rouge and mascara, with handsome furs wrapped round her and with jewels round her neck and hanging in her ears. You follow me?"

"Well——" said the inspector, disguising the fact that he didn't.

"Because then, you see, people will look at the furs and the jewels and the *coiffure* and the *haute couture*, and they will

not observe what the *woman herself* is like at all! So I say
to myself—and I say to my friend Colin ; Since this murder
has so many fantastic trappings to distract one it must really
be very simple. Did I not?"

"You did," I said. "But I still don't see how you can
possibly be right."

"For that you must wait. So, then, we discard the *trappings*
of the crime and we go to the *essentials*. A man has been
killed. Why has he been killed? And who is he? The answer
to the first question will obviously depend on the answer to
the second. And until you get the right answer to these two
questions you cannot possibly proceed. He could be a blackmailer, or a confidence trickster, or somebody's husband whose
existence was obnoxious or dangerous to his wife. He could
be one of a dozen things. The more I heard, the more everybody seems to agree that he *looked* a perfectly ordinary, well-
to-do, reputable elderly man. And suddenly I think to myself,
' You say this should be a simple crime? Very well, make it
so. Let this man be *exactly what he seems*—a well-to-do respectable elderly man '." He looked at the inspector. "You
see?"

"Well——" said the inspector again, and paused politely.

"So here is someone, an ordinary, pleasant, elderly man
whose removal is necessary to *someone*. To whom? And here
at last we can narrow the field a little. There is local knowledge—of Miss Pebmarsh and her habits, of the Cavendish
Secretarial Bureau, of a girl working there called Sheila Webb.
And so I say to my friend Colin ; ' The neighbours. Converse
with them. Find out about them. Their backgrounds. But
above all, engage in conversation. Because in conversation
you do not get merely the answers to questions—in ordinary
conversational prattle things slip out. People are on their
guard when the subject may be dangerous to them, but the
moment ordinary talk ensues they relax, they succumb to the
relief of speaking the truth, which is always very much easier
than lying. And so they let slip one little fact which unbe-
known to them makes all the difference."

"An admirable exposition," I said. "Unfortunately it
didn't happen in this case."

"But, *mon cher*, it *did*. One little sentence of inestimable
importance."

"What?" I demanded. "Who said it? When?"

"In due course, *mon cher*."

"You were saying, M. Poirot?" The inspector politely drew Poirot back to the subject.

"If you draw a circle round Number 19, anybody within it *might* have killed Mr. Curry. Mrs. Hemming, the Blands, the McNaughtons, Miss Waterhouse. But more important still, there are those already positioned on the spot. Miss Pebmarsh who could have killed him before she went out at 1.35 or thereabouts and Miss Webb who could have arranged to meet him there, and killed him before rushing from the house and giving the alarm."

"Ah," said the inspector. "You're coming down to brass tacks now."

"And of course," said Poirot, wheeling round, "*you*, my dear Colin. You also were on the spot. Looking for a high number where the low numbers were."

"Well, really," I said indignantly. "What will you say next?"

"Me, I say anything!" declared Poirot grandly.

"And yet *I* am the person who comes and dumps the whole thing in your lap!"

"Murderers are often conceited," Poirot pointed out. "And there too, it might have amused you—to have a joke like that at my expense."

"If you go on, you'll convince *me*," I said.

I was beginning to feel uncomfortable.

Poirot turned back to Inspector Hardcastle.

"Here, I say to myself, must be essentially a simple crime. The presence of irrelevant clocks, the advancing of time by an hour, the arrangements made so deliberately for the discovery of the body, all these must be set aside for the moment. They are, as is said in your immortal 'Alice' like '*shoes and ships and sealing wax and cabbages and kings*.' The vital point is that an ordinary elderly man is dead and that somebody wanted him dead. If we knew who the dead man was, it would give us a pointer to his killer. If he was a well-known blackmailer then we must look for a man who could be blackmailed. If he was a detective, then we look for a man who has a criminal secret ; if he is a man of wealth, then we look among his heirs. But if we do *not* know who the man is—then we have the more difficult task of hunting amongst those in the surrounding circle for a man who has a reason to kill.

"Setting aside Miss Pebmarsh and Sheila Webb, who is there who might not be what they seem to be? The answer was disappointing. With the exception of Mr. Ramsay who I understood was *not* what he seemed to be?" Here Poirot looked inquiringly at me and I nodded, "everybody's *bona fides* were genuine. Bland was a well-known local builder, McNaughton had had a Chair at Cambridge, Mrs. Hemming was the widow of a local auctioneer, the Waterhouses were respectable residents of long standing. So we come back to Mr. Curry. Where did he come *from*? What brought him to 19, Wilbraham Crescent? And here one very valuable remark was spoken by one of the neighbours, Mrs. Hemming. When told that the dead man did not live at Number 19, she said, 'Oh! I see. He just came there to be killed. How odd.' She had the gift, often possessed by those who are too occupied with their own thoughts to pay attention to what others are saying, to come to the heart of the problem. She summed up the whole crime. *Mr. Curry came to 19, Wilbraham Crescent to be killed.* It was as simple as that!"

"That remark of hers struck me at the time," I said.

Poirot took no notice of me.

"'*Dilly, dilly, dilly—come and be killed.*' Mr. Curry came —and he was killed. But that was not all. It was important *that he should not be identified*. He had no wallet, no papers, the tailor's marks were removed from his clothes. But that would not be enough. The printed card of Curry, Insurance Agent, was only a temporary measure. If the man's identity was to be concealed *permanently*, he must be given a false identity. Sooner or later, I was sure, somebody would turn up, recognise him positively and that would be that. A brother, a sister, a wife. It was a wife. Mrs. Rival—and the name alone might have aroused suspicion. There is a village in Somerset—I have stayed near there with friends—the village of Curry Rival—Subconsciously, without knowing why those two names suggested themselves, they were chosen. Mr. Curry —Mrs. Rival.

"So far—the plan is obvious, but what puzzled me was why our murderer took for granted that there would be no *real* identification. If the man had no family, there are at least landladies, servants, business associates. That led me to the next assumption—this man was *not known to be missing*. A further assumption was that he was not English, and was only visiting this country. That would tie in with the fact that the dental work done on his teeth did not correspond with any dental records here.

"I began to have a shadowy picture both of the victim and of the murderer. No more than that. The crime was well planned and intelligently carried out—but now there came that one piece of sheer bad luck that no murderer can foresee."

"And what was that?" asked Hardcastle.

Unexpectedly, Poirot threw his head back, and recited dramatically:

> "*For want of a nail the shoe was lost,*
> *For want of a shoe the horse was lost,*
> *For want of a horse the battle was lost,*
> *For want of a battle the Kingdom was lost,*
> *And all for the want of a horse shoe nail.*"

He leaned forward.

"A good many people *could* have killed Mr. Curry. But *only one person* could have killed, or could have had reason to kill, the girl Edna."

We both stared at him.

"Let us consider the Cavendish Secretarial Bureau. Eight girls work there. On the ninth of September, four of those girls were out on assignments some little distance away—that is, they were provided with lunch by the clients to whom they had gone. They were the four who normally took the first lunch period from 12.30 to 1.30. The remaining four, Sheila Webb, Edna Brent and two girls, Janet and Maureen, took the second period 1.30 to 2.30. But on that day Edna Brent had an accident quite soon after leaving the office. She tore the heel off her shoe in a grating. She could not walk like that. She bought some buns and came back to the office."

Poirot shook an emphatic finger at us.

"We have been told that Edna Brent was worried about something. She tried to see Sheila Webb out of the office, but failed. It has been assumed that something was connected with Sheila Webb, but there is no evidence of that. She might only have wanted to consult Sheila Webb about something that had puzzled her—but if so one thing was clear. She wanted to talk to Sheila Webb *away* from the bureau.

"Her words to the constable at the inquest are the only clue we have as to what was worrying her: She said something like: 'I don't see how what she said can have been true.' Three women had given evidence that morning. Edna could have been referring to Miss Pebmarsh. Or, as it has been generally assumed, she could have been referring to Sheila Webb. But there is a third possibility—*she could have been referring to Miss Martindale*."

"Miss Martindale? But her evidence only lasted a few minutes."

"Exactly. It consisted only of the telephone call she had received purporting to be from Miss Pebmarsh."

"Do you mean that Edna knew that it *wasn't* from Miss Pebmarsh?"

"I think it was simpler than that. I am suggesting that there was *no* telephone call at all."

He went on:

"The heel of Edna's shoe came off. The grating was quite close to the office. She came back to the bureau. But Miss Martindale, in her private office, did not know that Edna had come back. As far as she knew there was nobody but herself in the bureau. All she need do was to *say* a telephone call had come through at 1.49. Edna does not see the significance of what she knows at first. Sheila is called in to Miss Martindale and told to go out on an appointment. How and when that appointment was made is not mentioned to Edna. News of the murder comes through and little by little the story gets more definite. Miss Pebmarsh *rang up* and asked for Sheila Webb to be sent. But Miss Pebmarsh says it was not she who rang up. The call is said to have come through at ten minutes to two. *But Edna knows that couldn't be true.* No telephone call came through then. Miss Martindale must have made a mistake—But Miss Martindale definitely doesn't make mistakes. The more Edna thinks about it, the more puzzling it is. She must ask Sheila about it. Sheila will know.

"And then comes the inquest. And the girls all go to it. Miss Martindale repeats her story of the telephone call and Edna knows definitely now that that evidence Miss Martindale gives so clearly, with such precision as to the exact time, is untrue. It was then that she asked the constable if she could speak to the inspector. I think probably that Miss Martindale, leaving the Cornmarket in a crowd of people, overheard her asking that. Perhaps by then she had heard the girls chaffing Edna about her shoe accident without realising what it involved. Anyway, she followed the girl to Wilbraham Crescent. Why did Edna go there, I wonder?"

"Just to stare at the place where it happened, I expect," said Hardcastle with a sigh. "People do."

"Yes, that is true enough. Perhaps Miss Martindale speaks to her there, walks with her down the road and Edna plumps out her question. Miss Martindale acts quickly. They are just by the telephone box. She says, 'This is very important. You must ring up the police at once. The number of the police station is so and so. Ring up and tell them we are both coming there now.' It is second nature for Edna to do what she is told. She goes in, picks up the receiver and Miss Martindale comes in behind her, pulls the scarf round her neck and strangles her."

"And nobody saw this?"

Poirot shrugged his shoulders.

"They might have done, but they didn't! It was just on one o'clock. Lunch time. And what people there were in the Crescent were busy staring at 19. It was a chance boldly taken by a bold and unscrupulous woman."

Hardcastle was shaking his head doubtfully.

"Miss Martindale? I don't see how she can possibly come into it."

"No. One does not see at first. But since Miss Martindale undoubtedly killed Edna—oh, yes—only she can have killed Edna, then she *must* come into it. And I begin to suspect that in Miss Martindale we have the Lady Macbeth of this crime, a woman who is ruthless and unimaginative."

"Unimaginative?" queried Hardcastle.

"Oh, yes, quite unimaginative. But very efficient. A good planner."

"But why? Where's the motive?"

Hercule Poirot looked at me. He wagged a finger.

"So the neighbours' conversation was no use to you, eh? I found one most illuminating sentence. Do you remember that after talking of living abroad, Mrs. Bland remarked that she liked living in Crowdean *because she had a sister here. But Mrs. Bland was not supposed to have a sister*. She had inherited a large fortune a year ago from a Canadian great-uncle because she was the only surviving member of his family."

Hardcastle sat up alertly.

"So you think——"

Poirot leaned back in his chair and put his fingertips together. He half closed his eyes and spoke dreamily.

"Say you are a man, a very ordinary and not too scrupulous man, in bad financial difficulties. A letter comes one day from a firm of lawyers to say that your wife has inherited a big fortune from a great-uncle in Canada. The letter is addressed to Mrs. Bland and the only difficulty is that the Mrs. Bland who receives it is the wrong Mrs. Bland—she is the second wife—not the first one—Imagine the chagrin! The fury! And then an idea comes. Who is to know that it is the wrong Mrs. Bland? Nobody in Crowdean knows that Bland was married before. His first marriage, years ago, took place during the war when he was overseas. Presumably his first wife died soon afterwards, and he almost immediately remarried. He has the original marriage certificate, various family papers, photographs of Canadian relations now dead —It will be all plain sailing. Anyway, it is worth risking. They risk it, and it comes off. The legal formalities go through. And there the Blands are, rich and prosperous, all their financial troubles over——

"And then—a year later—something happens. What happens? I suggest that someone was coming over from Canada to this country—and that this someone had known the first Mrs. Bland well enough not to be deceived by an impersonation. He may have been an elderly member of the family attorneys, or a close friend of the family—but whoever he is, he will *know*. Perhaps they thought of ways of avoiding a meeting. Mrs. Bland could feign illness, she could go abroad—but anything of that kind would only arouse suspicion. The visitor would insist on seeing the woman he had come over to see——"

"And so—to murder?"

"Yes. And here, I fancy, Mrs. Bland's sister may have been the ruling spirit. She thought up and planned the whole thing."

"You are taking it that Miss Martindale and Mrs. Bland *are* sisters?"

"It is the only way things make sense."

"Mrs. Bland did remind me of someone when I saw her," said Hardcastle. "They're very different in manner—but it's true— there *is* a likeness. But how could they hope to get away with it? The man would be missed. Inquiries would be made——"

"If this man were travelling abroad—perhaps for pleasure, not for business, his schedule would be vague. A letter from one place—a postcard from another—it would be a little time before people wondered why they had not heard from him. By that time who would connect a man identified and buried as Harry Castleton, with a rich Canadian visitor to the country who has not even been seen in this part of the world? If I had been the murderer, I would have slipped over on a day trip to France or Belgium and discarded the dead man's passport in a train or a tram so that the inquiry would take place from another country."

I moved involuntarily, and Poirot's eyes came round to me.

"Yes?" he said.

"Bland mentioned to me that he had recently taken a day trip to Boulogne—with a blonde, I understand——"

"Which would make it quite a natural thing to do. Doubtless it is a habit of his."

"This is still conjecture," Hardcastle objected.

"But inquiries can be made," said Poirot.

He took a sheet of hotel notepaper from the rack in front of him and handed it to Hardcastle.

"If you will write to Mr. Enderby at 10, Ennismore Gardens, S.W.7 he has promised to make certain inquiries for me in Canada. He is a well-known international lawyer."

"And what about the business of the clocks?"

"Oh! The clocks. Those famous clocks!" Poirot smiled. "I think you will find that Miss Martindale was responsible for them. Since the crime, as I said, was a simple crime, it was disguised by making it a fantastic one. That Rosemary

clock that Sheila Webb took to be repaired. Did she lose it
in the Bureau of Secretarial Studies. Did Miss Martindale
take it as the foundation of her rigmarole, and was it partly
because of that clock that she chose Sheila as the person to
discover the body——"

Hardcastle burst out,

"And you say this woman is unimaginative? When she
concocted all this?"

"But she did not concoct it. That is what is so interesting.
It was all there—waiting for her. From the very first I
detected a pattern—a pattern I knew. A pattern familiar
because I had just been reading such patterns. I have been
very fortunate. As Colin here will tell you, I attended this
week a *sale of authors' manuscripts*. Among them were some
of Gerry Gregson's. I hardly dared hope. But luck was with
me. *Here*——" Like a conjurer he whipped from a drawer
in the desk two shabby exercise books "——it is all *here*!
Among the many plots of books he planned to write. He did
not live to write this one—but Miss Martindale, who was his
secretary, knew all about it. She just lifted it bodily to suit
her purpose."

"But the clocks must have meant something originally—
in Gregson's plot, I mean."

"Oh, yes. His clocks were set at one minute past five, four
minutes past five and seven minutes past five. That was the
combination number of a safe, 515457. The safe was concealed behind a reproduction of the Mona Lisa. Inside the
safe," continued Poirot, with distaste, "were the Crown jewels
of the Russian Royal family. *Un tas de bêtises*, the whole
thing! And of course there was a story of kinds—a persecuted
girl. Oh, yes, it came in very handy for la Martindale. She
just chose her local characters and adapted the story to fit in.
All these flamboyant clues would lead—where? Exactly nowhere! Ah, yes, an efficient woman. One wonders—he left
her a legacy—did he not? How and of what did he die, I
wonder?"

Hardcastle refused to be interested in past history. He
gathered up the exercise books and took the sheet of hotel
paper from my hand. For the last two minutes I had been
staring at it, fascinated. Hardcastle had scribbled down

Enderby's address without troubling to turn the sheet the right way up. The hotel address was upside down in the left-hand bottom corner.

Staring at the sheet of paper, I knew what a fool I had been.

"Well, thank you, M. Poirot," said Hardcastle. "You've certainly given us something to think about. Whether anything will come of it——"

"I am most delighted if I have been of any assistance." Poirot was playing it modestly.

"I'll have to check various things——"

"Naturally—naturally——"

Good-byes were said. Hardcastle took his departure.

Poirot turned his attention to me. His eyebrows rose.

"Eh, bien—and what, may I ask, is biting you—you look like a man who has seen an apparition."

"I've seen what a fool I've been."

"Aha. Well, that happens to many of us."

But presumably not to Hercule Poirot! I had to attack him.

"Just tell me one thing, Poirot. If, as you said, you could do all this sitting in your chair in London and could have got me and Dick Hardcastle to come to you there, why—oh, why, did you come down here at all?"

"I told you, they make the reparation in my apartment."

"They would have lent you another apartment. Or you could have gone to the Ritz, you would have been more comfortable there than in the Curlew Hotel."

"Indubitably," said Hercule Poirot. "The coffee here, *mon dieu*, the coffee!"

"Well, then, *why*?"

Hercule Poirot flew into a rage.

"*Eh bien*, since you are too stupid to guess, I will tell you. I am human, am I not? I can be the machine if it is necessary. I can lie back and think. I can solve the problem so. But I am human, I tell you. And the problems concern human beings."

"And so?"

"The explanation is as simple as the murder was simple. I came out of human curiosity," said Hercule Poirot, with an attempt at dignity.

CHAPTER 29

Once more I was in Wilbraham Crescent, proceeding in a westerly direction.

I stopped before the gate of No. 19. No one came screaming out of the house this time. It was neat and peaceful.

I went up to the front door and rang the bell.

Miss Millicent Pebmarsh opened it.

"This is Colin Lamb," I said. "May I come in and speak to you?"

"Certainly."

She preceded me into the sitting-room.

"You seem to spend a lot of time down here, Mr. Lamb. I understood that you were *not* connected with the local police——"

"You understood rightly. I think, really, you have known exactly who I am from the first day you spoke to me."

"I'm not sure quite what you mean by that."

"I've been extremely stupid, Miss Pebmarsh. I came to this place to look for you. I found you the first day I was here—and I didn't know I had found you!"

"Possibly murder distracted you."

"As you say. I was also stupid enough to look at a piece of paper the wrong way up."

"And what is the point of all this?"

"Just that the game is up, Miss Pebmarsh. I've found the headquarters where the planning is done. Such records and memoranda as are necessary are kept by you on the micro dot system in Braille. The information Larkin got at Portlebury was passed to you. From here it went to its destination be means of Ramsay. He came across when necessary from his house to yours at night by way of the garden. He dropped a Czech coin in your garden one day——"

"That was careless of him."

"We're all careless at some time or another. Your cover is very good. You're blind, you work at an institute for disabled children, you keep children's books in Braille in your house as is only natural—you are a woman of unusual intelligence and personality. I don't know what is the driving power that animates you——"

"Say if you like that I am dedicated."

"Yes. I thought it might be like that."

"And why are you telling me all this? It seems unusual."

I looked at my watch.

"You have two hours, Miss Pebmarsh. In two hours' time members of the special branch will come here and take charge——"

"I don't understand you. Why do you come here ahead of your people, to give me what seems to be a warning——"

"It *is* a warning. I have come here myself, and shall remain here until my people arrive, to see that nothing leaves this house—with one exception. That exception is you yourself. You have two hours' start if you choose to go."

"But why? *Why?*"

I said slowly,

"Because I think there is an off-chance that you might shortly become my mother-in-law . . . I may be quite wrong."

There was a silence. Millicent Pebmarsh got up and went to the window. I didn't take my eyes off her. I had no illusions about Millicent Pebmarsh. I didn't trust her an inch. She was blind but even a blind woman can catch you if you are off guard. Her blindness wouldn't handicap her if she once got her chance to jam an automatic against my spine.

She said quietly,

"I shall not tell you if you're right or wrong. What makes you think that—that it might be so?"

"Eyes."

"But we are not alike in character."

"No."

She spoke almost defiantly.

"I did the best I could for her."

"That's a matter of opinion. With you a cause came first."

"As it should do."

"I don't agree."

There was silence again. Then I asked, "Did you know who she was—that day?"

"Not until I heard her name . . . I had kept myself informed about her—always."

" You were never as inhuman as you would have liked to be."

" Don't talk nonsense."

I looked at my watch again.

" Time is going on," I said.

She came back from the window and across to the desk. " I have a photograph of her here—as a child . . ."

I was behind her as she pulled the drawer open. It wasn't an automatic. It was a small very deadly knife . . .

My hand closed over hers and took it away.

" I may be soft, but I'm not a fool," I said.

She felt for a chair and sat down. She displayed no emotion whatever.

" I am not taking advantage of your offer. What would be the use? I shall stay here until—they come. There are always opportunities—even in prison."

" Of indoctrination, you mean?"

" If you like to put it that way."

We sat there, hostile to each other, but with understanding.

" I've resigned from the Service," I told her. " I'm going back to my old job—marine biology. There's a post going at a university in Australia."

" I think you are wise. You haven't got what it takes for this job. You are like Rosemary's father. He couldn't understand Lenin's dictum: ' Away with softness '."

I thought of Hercule Poirot's words.

" I'm content," I said, " to be human . . ."

We sat there in silence, each of us convinced that the other's point of view was wrong.

Letter from Detective Inspector Hardcastle to M. Hercule Poirot.

Dear M. Poirot,

We are now in possession of certain facts, and I feel you may be interested to hear about them.

A Mr. Quentin Duguesclin of Quebec left Canada for Europe approximately four weeks ago. He has no near relatives and his plans for return were indefinite. His passport was found by the proprietor of a small restaurant in Boulogne, who handed it into the police. It has not so far been claimed.

Mr. Duguesclin was a lifelong friend of the Montresor family of Quebec. The head of that family, Mr. Henry Montresor, died eighteen months ago, leaving his very considerable fortune to his only surviving relative, his great-niece Valerie, described as the wife of Josaiah Bland of Portlebury, England. A very reputable firm of London solicitors acted for the Canadian executors. All communications between Mrs. Bland and her family in Canada ceased from the time of her marriage of which her family did not approve. Mr. Duguesclin mentioned to one of his friends that he intended to look up the Blands while he was in England, since he had always been very fond of Valerie.

The body hitherto identified as that of Henry Castleton has been positively identified as Quentin Duguesclin.

Certain boards have been found stowed away in a corner of Bland's building yard. Though hastily painted out, the words SNOWFLAKE LAUNDRY are plainly perceptible after treatment by experts.

I will not trouble you with lesser details, but the public prosecutor considers that a warrant can be granted for the arrest of Josaiah Bland. Miss Martindale and Mrs. Bland are, as you conjectured, sisters, but though I agree with your views on her participation in these crimes, satisfactory evidence will be hard to obtain. She is undoubtedly a very clever woman. I have hopes, though, of Mrs. Bland. She is the type of woman who rats.

The death of the first Mrs. Bland through enemy action in France, and his second marriage to Hilda Martindale (who was in the N.A.A.F.I.) also in France can be, I think, clearly established, though many records were, of course, destroyed at that time.

It was a great pleasure meeting you that day, and I must thank you for the very useful suggestions you made on that occasion. I hope the alterations and redecorations of your London flat have been satisfactory.

Yours sincerely,
Richard Hardcastle.

Further communication from R.H. to H.P.

Good news! The Bland woman cracked! Admitted the

whole thing ! ! ! Puts the blame entirely on her sister and her husband. She " never understood until too late what they meant to do "! Thought they were only " going to dope him so that he wouldn't recognise she was the wrong woman "! A likely story! But I'd say it's true enough that she wasn't the prime mover.

The Portobello Market people have identified Miss Martindale as the " American " lady who bought two of the clocks.

Mrs. McNaughton now says she saw Duguesclin in Bland's van being driven into Bland's garage. Did she really?

Our friend Colin has married that girl. If you ask *me*, he's mad. All the best.

Yours,

Richard Hardcastle.

Agatha Christie

The most popular and prolific writer of detective fiction ever known, her intricately plotted whodunits are enjoyed by armchair crime-solvers everywhere.

Postern of Fate

N or M?

At Bertram's Hotel

Hercule Poirot's Christmas

Elephants Can Remember

The Murder of Roger Ackroyd

Cards on the Table

The Clocks

The Labours of Hercules

Five Little Pigs

After the Funeral

Murder on the Orient Express

Endless Night

Passenger to Frankfurt

Hickory Dickory Dock

and many others

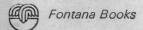 *Fontana Books*

Ross Macdonald

'Classify him how you will, he is one of the best American novelists now operating . . . all he does is keep on getting better.' *New York Times Book Review*. 'Ross Macdonald must be ranked high among American thriller-writers. His evocations of scenes and people are as sharp as those of Raymond Chandler.' *Times Literary Supplement*. 'Lew Archer is, by a long chalk, the best private eye in the business.' *Sunday Times*

Sleeping Beauty

The Way Some People Die

The Galton Case

Black Money

The Barbarous Coast

The Ivory Grin

The Doomsters

The Chill

Find a Victim

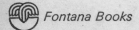 *Fontana Books*

Fontana Books

Fontana is a leading paperback publisher of fiction and non-fiction, with authors ranging from Alistair MacLean, Agatha Christie and Desmond Bagley to Solzhenitsyn and Pasternak, from Gerald Durrell and Joy Adamson to the famous Modern Masters series.

In addition to a wide-ranging collection of internationally popular writers of fiction, Fontana also has an outstanding reputation for history, natural history, military history, psychology, psychiatry, politics, economics, religion and the social sciences.